TANZEEM

An alumnus of La Martiniere College, Lucknow, the National Defence Academy, Pune, and the Indian Military Academy, Dehradun, Mukul Deva was commissioned in December 1981 into the Sikh Light Infantry of the Indian Army. He took early retirement from the army after fifteen years of service, including a decade of combat operations in India and overseas. He is now an entrepreneur, motivational speaker, leadership, business and executive coach, and consultant. He is the author of *Time After Time...It All Happened, S.T.R.I.P.T.E.A.S.E: The Art of Corporate Warfare, M.O.D.E.L.: The Return of the Employee*, and three bestselling books in the 'Lashkar' series: *Lashkar, Salim Must Die* and *Blowback*.

Praise for Mukul Deva

'The God of all things… it is tough describing Mukul Deva.'

– Business World

'Deva has a Nostradamus touch.'

– The Statesman

'India's literary storm trooper.'

– Business Standard

'Deva comes as a pleasant surprise… it is rare to find a successful, celebrated man who has enough vulnerability.'

– New Indian Express

'You can smell the gunpowder. Such is the power of the words of Mukul Deva.'

– The Hindu

'India's only military thriller writer.'

– The Week

'Here comes India's Clancy or Ludlum or Forsyth.'

– Outlook

'Deva needs to be congratulated for being part of the pioneering group in the genre of the Indian thriller novel.'

– Deccan Herald

'Mukul Deva wears the crown of India's premier military thriller writer with great skill and panache.'

– www.indepepal.com

'India finally has a writer of international caliber in the genre of military fiction.'

– First City

'[Deva's] books… represent the beginning of Indian literature's venture into fictional military thrillers.'

– Yuva (Fortnightly)

'Mukul Deva still has no rivals in the Indian political thriller field.'

– The Statesman

Praise for *Blowback*

'He's got a license to thrill... India's first military action thriller writer, Mukul Deva is back with a bang with *Blowback*.'

– The Indian Express

'His insightful writing is lucid... Deva can play political commentator and soothsayer of national defence and novelist... a heady cocktail of chill and thrill.'

– Hindustan Times

'Full of excitement and suspense... the emotive quality in Deva's writing is powerful and the logic crisply military... a surprisingly touching statement from a man who has lived by the gun.'

– Express Buzz

'The ease with which Deva combines well-known facts with popular fiction makes for a fantastic read... his writing style is top-notch... the story is tight and gripping.'

– First City

'A riveting read... unnervingly prophetic... heartbreaking... Deva's trilogy is a must read... he paints the picture of geo-politics and terrorism with fantastic clarity.'

– The Hindu

'Tightly knit, action packed and lucid.'

– The Organiser

'Simply superb... the descriptions are vivid, the plot racy and the detail very convincingly developed.'

– Mid Day

'A fun thriller, straight out of the headlines... Deva's biggest strength is the smoothness of his prose, crisp and fast moving, and you never get distracted from the story.'

– Deccan Herald

Praise for *Salim Must Die*

'Deva is back and how! Uncannily prescient. Unputdownable. *Salim Must Die* enthrones Deva as the undisputed Master of Thrills.'

– Sarthak Dasgupta, film-maker

'Taut and gripping... technical knowledge and research are remarkable, as is the plotting and the premise. Great read for the fans of Tom Clancy.'

– Delhi Times

'A ripping, edge-of-your-seat, burn-the-midnight-oil, good read. Deva sets a frenetic pace. The author's attention to detail and prodigious research skills are evident.'

– www.indepepal.com

'After his much acclaimed *Lashkar*... *Salim Must Die* continues its Tom Clancy-eqsue (run).'

– Mail Today

'Finally, an Indian thriller of quality... where neither the tautness nor the pace collapses.'

– Outlook

'Fast and furious... the action is non-stop, more sophisticated and terrifyingly real... thoroughly entertaining and extremely well-researched.'

– Business Standard

'Deva is an equal with the likes of Robert Ludlum and Sidney Sheldon...'

– Deccan Herald

'Is bound to leave an impact on you... makes you think about the dangerous world we live in.'

– Business World

'A prescient tale... racy, keeps you hooked... definitely written for the movies.'

– The Hindu

'*Salim Must Die* is as real as it gets... gut wrenching action and a deeper look into the terrorist's psyche.'

– Khabar Dilli Se

Praise for *Lashkar*

'An edge-of-the-seat-thriller.'

– Hindustan Times

'Exciting... with some action, some introspection, some retrospection... a racy read.'

– The Times of India

'For the first time, an Indian thriller set in contemporary times... a gripping tale.'

– The Pioneer

'*Lashkar* tries to make sense of the terror that surrounds our lives.'

– The Hindu

'Ludlumesque.'

– The Tribune

'A glance is enough to discover... this is a Tom Clancy on the LOC.'

– Time Out

'A real page-turner... a riveting read.'

– Business Standard

'Written with style and panache.'

– Sahara Time

'A real-life take on how the so-called jihadis are picked up from anonymous Indian streets... *Lashkar* tells many tales with great ease.'

– MetroPlus

'*Lashkar* is gripping... racy and visually captivating.'

– Indo Asian News Service

'A compelling read.'

– Govind Nihalani, film-maker

'Thrillingly Indian.'

– The Statesman

What Readers Have to Say

'The sharp zigzags of the plot kept us on edge and made for a very racy pace – each of my family members finished it at one reading!'

– Amit Kumar Bose, bose.amitkumar@gmail.com

'*Lashkar* and *Salim Must Die* will find an answering chord with many and both are bound to be made into films and have multiplexes filled with patriotic cheers.'

– Anjana Basu, anjanaorama@gmail.com

'Mukul has the knack of communicating the terrorism issue with a great degree of relevance and still make it fictional.'

– Rakesh Dalwani, rdalwani@rediffmail.com

'His in-depth knowledge of affairs military coupled with a lucid and simple style of storytelling makes the reader crave for more.'

– Brigadier Sanjeev Kanal, sanjeevkanal@rediffmail.com

'The *Lashkar* series is simply genius personified. Gripping storylines and excellent coverage and explanation of the global geo-political scenario.'

– Monish Navlani, monishn@live.com

'*Lashkar* was pacy, tight, very well knit and pleasantly vindicating. Mukul deftly blends his knowledge of military operations with his knack of thriller writing.'

– Gul Panag, gulpanag@gmail.com

'I put off everything once I started reading Mukul Deva's series and then I told all my friends. Clancy, sure, but I'm thinking the next Ken Follett.'

– Fran Lebowitz Rittman, flebowitz@yahoo.com

'People are comparing Deva's writing to the Ludlums and Clancys of the world but in my eyes he is way beyond them… somewhere close to Mathew Riley and Allen Folsom.'

– Anunay Shrivastava, anunay.shrivastava@gmail.com

TANZEEM

MUKUL DEVA

HarperCollins *Publishers* India
a joint venture with

New Delhi

First published in India in 2011 by
HarperCollins *Publishers* India
a joint venture with
The India Today Group

Copyright © Mukul Deva 2011

ISBN: 978-93-5029-033-0

2 4 6 8 10 9 7 5 3 1

Mukul Deva asserts the moral right to be identified
as the author of this book.

This is a work of fiction and all characters and incidents described in
this book are the product of the author's imagination. Any resemblance
to actual persons, living or dead, is entirely coincidental.

HarperCollins *Publishers*
A-53, Sector 57, NOIDA, Uttar Pradesh – 201301, India
77-85 Fulham Palace Road, London W6 8JB, United Kingdom
Hazelton Lanes, 55 Avenue Road, Suite 2900, Toronto, Ontario M5R 3L2
and 1995 Markham Road, Scarborough, Ontario M1B 5M8, Canada
25 Ryde Road, Pymble, Sydney, NSW 2073, Australia
31 View Road, Glenfield, Auckland 10, New Zealand
10 East 53rd Street, New York NY 10022, USA

Typeset in ClassGaramond BT 10/13
Jojy Philip, New Delhi 110 015
Printed and bound at
Thomson Press (India) Ltd.

This book is dedicated to Iqbal, the thought, not the man.

May the spirit endure!

And to that unknown, often uncared for, and mostly forgotten Indian soldier who fights on... for us.

Deg Teg Fateh!

AUTHOR'S NOTE

This book is a work of fiction, although some of the events mentioned here may have actually taken place.

All characters, countries, places and organizations described or mentioned in this book are fictitious or have been fictitiously used and any resemblance to any person, living or dead, is unintentional.

The maps given in the book are merely to facilitate a general understanding of the region where the story is based. In several cases, artistic licence has been taken with the places mentioned in the book, distances between places and the general topography.

The technical details of the various weapon systems, specifications and methodologies of bomb-making and weaponry, grid references, some geographical locations and descriptions, as well as the tactics and security procedures employed by any police, military, intelligence organization, and/or militant organization, as also all criminal, forensic and investigative procedures, have been deliberately kept slightly vague, inaccurate and/or incomplete to prevent any misuse, accidental or otherwise.

Several readers have written in or commented on this policy of mine (of not going into the specifics of military operations and terror techniques). However, I choose to retain my approach and not elaborate on these aspects any further than what I feel is required for the narrative since I believe that the possibilities of misuse are high.

There is no slur or malice intended against any religion, race, caste, creed, nation, organization or people.

PREFACE

It is with some regret that I have put pen to paper (rather, finger to keyboard) while writing this book because by now every character that has inhabited space in this four-book series has come alive in my mind. For five years, my daily routine included these characters, and a part of me is loath to put them to rest. But I also realize that I must do this since I feel that the salient aspects of terrorism and how it affects our lives today have been adequately dealt with in this series, as far as they can be in works of fiction.

I must also confess that I continue to be amazed at the sheer magnitude, intensity and variety of reader responses this series has received. Not to mention the ever increasing pressure of ensuring that not only does each successive book tell a different tale but it also lives up to the expectations of those who have adopted these books as their own.

There have been some who have accused me of being overtly hawkish about the views in this series.

To everyone who feels this way, all I can say is that I have tried to maintain a balance and let facts (which, I stress again, have been fictitiously used) speak for themselves. I have simply tried to profile the times that we (sadly) live in, without allowing any major personal biases to creep in. However, we all have our biases and some are certainly bound to emerge in one's writing.

My heartfelt thanks to each one of you who has followed this series and stood by me during this journey. It is the encouragement and, I must add, the criticism offered by you that have made these books possible.

While researching and writing this story, it became clear to me that this walk down memory lane, into the annals of history, enables us to see how easily and senselessly it all began – this scrooge of religious fundamentalism, which is tearing the world apart today. And now that we can see it, we can also understand how it could have been avoided. Of course, it is a bit late in the day for that; even so, if one were to seek a solution for it or ensure history does not repeat itself, this journey through the past few decades is imperative, for it is only in the roots of a problem that the solutions are generally found.

I end this note with the hope that you shall find *Tanzeem* a befitting end to a worthy tale.

Mukul Deva

'Hatred is the madness of the heart.'
Lord Byron

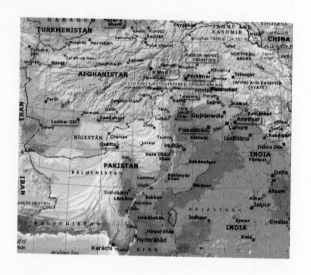

The end of birth is death;
The end of death is birth;
This is ordained!

Bhagavad Gita

'May I please be alone with Tanaz?' Iqbal's voice was flat, his gaze fixed on something in the distance. 'Please!' The last word was sharper, angrier, more a demand than a request.

Colonel Anbu nodded. As much as he wanted to help, he knew Iqbal needed to go through this alone, or there would be no closure. He gestured to Captains Mohammed Sami and Vikram Tiwathia and the three Force 22 commandos quietly made their way out of the hospital room. They were hardened combat veterans, but the events of the past few hours had left them subdued. In their hearts, they knew they had let Tanaz and Iqbal down, the young woman whose brutally tortured body now lay still on the hospital bed, and the young man whose body was alive but whose soul seemed to have been condemned to the uncertainty of hate once again.

∾

Iqbal stood at the door for a long time after the three men left the room, as though mustering up the courage to do what was expected of him. Taking a deep breath, he finally turned, squared his shoulders and walked up to the battered body on the bed.

Iqbal had neither the will nor the strength to control the tears that began to flow as he pulled away the bedsheet that covered Tanaz. She looked desolate as she lay unmoving in the middle of the bed. His beautiful Tanaz, who had looked so radiant carrying their baby the past few months, seemed to have withered and shrunk. Deep gashes crisscrossed her face, neck and upper body. He choked back a sob, fearing the sound would draw the others into the room again.

Iqbal had always regretted not having been able to bid farewell to his mother and sister and look one last time upon their dead bodies. Now he wondered if that had been a blessing in disguise.

Gently, Iqbal started washing the blood stains off Tanaz with large cotton swabs soaked in spirit. As his hands worked on her body, the flood of tears ebbed to a trickle. By the time he finished, he had become numb, as though a dark void had opened up somewhere inside him.

Mechanically, he covered Tanaz's body with a clean bedsheet. But he did not shroud her face, caressing it, instead, with one last long look that imprinted her image on his heart. It would sustain him in the days to come.

Knowing that the Force 22 officers would not leave him alone much longer, Iqbal noiselessly made his way to the French windows at the other end of the room. The second-floor windows overlooked a large, well-manicured garden. There was no one there except a couple of old people strolling at the far end. They turned and looked on curiously as Iqbal hit the ground with a soft thud. Ignoring them, he headed for the gates.

SITUATION REVIEW

From: Director RAW
To: Director NIC
Security Classification: Top Secret
Priority: Urgent
Subject: Review of internal security situation in Pakistan

American failure to capture or eliminate the Al-Qaeda and Taliban leadership has allowed them and hundreds of hardened mujahideen to acquire safe sanctuary in the Pakistani badlands of the Federal Administered Tribal Areas, a natural buffer between Afghanistan and Pakistan, occupied by 4.5 million Pashtun tribesmen.

This resettlement was facilitated by members of the Pakistan government — mostly, radicalized elements in the army and the ISI. Pakistani connivance with the Afghan Taliban is clear from the manner in which Mullah Omar has openly set up base at Quetta, acknowledged by various Pakistani political and military leaders. The Pakistan Army validates this support as a legitimate means to counter Indian influence in Afghanistan. But since the expiry of the Durand Line agreement in 1993, Pakistan needs to either be in control of the government of Afghanistan or ensure they are so embroiled in internal fighting that they have no time to worry about reclaiming the parts of NWFP and Balochistan, including the port of Gwadar, areas that were originally Afghan territory. Till date, all attempts by Pakistan to get Afghanistan to ratify the Durand Line have failed; even the Taliban refused to do so, despite being beholden to them.

Due to American insistence, General Musharraf, the then military dictator, made some cosmetic moves to hunt down Al-Qaeda. However, it must be understood that Pakistan views the Afghan Taliban and the Pakistani Taliban, along with Punjab-based terror groups like Lashkar-e-Toiba, as strategic assets and a potentially useful counter against India, both in terms of a future struggle for Kashmir and also to maintain influence in Kabul.

That is why, despite the havoc wreaked by these terror groups in their own country, Pakistan is reluctant to act against them, as shown by the ease with which the perpetrators of the 26/11 Mumbai attack have walked away scot-free.

It merits mention that Pakistan is not a 'normal' adversary for India. It came into existence only by its rejection of the idea of an Indian state. Peace with India is a serious threat to well-entrenched interests since it would change the internal power equations in Pakistan, release the military's grip on politics, reduce the relevance of Islamist groups and allow democracy to flourish.

This confrontation has helped raise Pakistan's profile (albeit artificially). Now the world tends to equate democratic, pluralist, law-abiding India with a terrorist-sponsoring failed state like Pakistan.

Other adversaries like China — which seeks to contain India — are exploiting this confrontation by buttressing Pakistan economically and militarily.

So, although stabilizing relations with Pakistan will enhance India's status, it will directly reduce Pakistan's utility to others. Thus the Indian quest for peace between these two neighbours will never stir Pakistani policy-makers and Pakistan's policies towards India will remain strategically hostile even though, from time to time, for short-term tactical reasons, it may pretend otherwise. History has repetitively provided evidence of this, ISI's Project Karachi being a prime example.

The then Pakistani leadership did not factor in the increasing radicalization of the FATA tribes or of the Pakistani Taliban when Al-Qaeda filtered into the region. Or perhaps this was foreseen and planned for by Islamized elements of the ISI and Pakistan Army and was a part of their agenda for, first, the Talibanization of Pakistan and eventually, the creation of a Greater Pakistan in accordance with the stated goals of their infamous Project M, namely the balkanization of India and establishment of Mughalstan, which is the final phase of General Zia's Operation Topac.

With Al-Qaeda now providing covert ideological, strategic, manpower and fiscal support, and with the influx of Afghan Taliban fighters into the region, the Pakistani Taliban has started taking on the Pakistani state openly. Three thousand of their fighters evicted over 12,000 Pakistani troops from the Swat Valley and forced the government into signing a peace accord which allowed the Pakistani Taliban to impose Sharia law in the Swat Valley.

In keeping with its record, the Pakistani Taliban reneged on this peace deal too and moved forward to seize control of Shangla, Dir and Buner, a mere 60 kilometres from Islamabad, the national capital.

Buffered by the rapid induction of seasoned gunmen of the Lashkar-al-Zil (the Shadow Army of Al-Qaeda), foreign fighters, Pashtun mujahideen from FATA and jihadis from other ISI-nurtured extremist groups, the Pakistani Taliban's strength increased to over 8000.

The Pakistani Taliban now systematically destroyed the Awami National Party, which had been voted in by large numbers of Pashtun just one year ago and posed a clear counter to the Talibani claim that all Pashtun are pro-jihadi extremists. It was critical for the Taliban to cow down the ANP since its version of Pashtun-wali (the tribal code of conduct) is nationalistic but moderate and favours democracy. As on date, all state institutions in the Swat Valley have been paralysed.

This has given the Taliban control over the emerald mines and timber businesses that abound in Swat and added to their already substantial drug income. There is also evidence to indicate increase in fiscal support from right-wing charity organizations based in Saudi Arabia and other Gulf countries.

Although the leadership of the Pakistani Taliban is split between several warlords, each commanding a few thousand fighters, there are increasing reports of a still-to-be-identified man known as the Ameer-ul-Momineem, who is trying to bring the groups under one operational umbrella. He is supposed to have the blessing of Al-Qaeda and Quetta Shura. Efforts are being made to identify this man based on the Identikit photograph provided by Force 22. Indications are that he may be Jalaluddin Haq, a Waziristan-based warlord who has historically enjoyed the patronage of the ISI and Mullah Omar's Quetta Shura, thus giving him credible standing with both the Pakistani and the Afghan Taliban. Known to be a sound strategist, Haq has maintained a low profile until recently. He is a ruthless hawk and will be a formidable foe should he succeed in consolidating the other groups under one banner.

With the Afghan Taliban as their role model, and possibly due to the efforts of the Ameer-ul-Momineem, several of these groups have already begun to morph into one operational entity. They have been further strengthened by strategic, tactical and operational alliances with over forty other terror groups, some of which have had no known links with either Al-Qaeda or the Taliban until now. The results of these efforts have already surpassed earlier attempts made by the Tehrik-e-Taliban Pakistan, that is, the Movement of the Pakistan Taliban, to unify the struggle against America and its allies.

As on date, there is irrefutable evidence of 157 terrorist training camps in the Swat Valley, FATA and the North Western Frontier Province. A number of these camps are training people with foreign passports for strikes against select targets in America, Europe and India.

Their increasing strength and resolve is evident from the geometric increase in attacks on the American-led ISAF in Afghanistan and on select soft and high-value targets in Pakistan, and their openly declared resolve to 'liberate' Pakistan from the clutches of 'un-Islamic' democracy and convert it to a 'pure' Islamic state where the Sharia would apply. As opposed to the ten major cross-border attacks on the ISAF in Afghanistan last year, there have already been thirty-seven such strikes this year, over seventy terror-bombing strikes into the Pakistani heartland, the attack on Mumbai, the Jakarta bombing, as well as the recent unsuccessful strike on the airliner in America by the 'underwear bomber'.

At the time of compilation of this report, almost 11 per cent of Pakistan is either directly under the control of or contested by the Taliban. Another 10 per cent of Baluchistan, in the south-west of the country, is a no-go area due to a raging insurgency by Baluch separatists. Karachi, the port city with a population of 17 million, is an ethnic tinderbox just waiting to explode and the Taliban are now penetrating Punjab, Pakistan's economic and political heartland where 60 per cent of its population resides.

Despite this, the civilian government in Islamabad and the Pakistan Army are showing no signs of taking on these groups. All their attempts have been half-hearted and show a clear lack of any comprehensive counter-insurgency strategy.

The Taliban, backed by Al-Qaeda, has taken advantage of the vacuum in governance and the failing Pakistani economy. They have had significant success in inciting fear in the populace and subverting large numbers of the unemployed, largely marginalized and ignored youth, thus enhancing their firepower, support base and area of influence.

Due to a lack of development and government control of the education sector, national literacy levels in Pakistan are abysmal. There are currently about 20 million youngsters below the age of seventeen who are not in school. Also, most of the approximately 23,000 madrassas functioning in Pakistan are firmly under the influence of the Saudi-funded Wahhabi and Salafi right-wing fundamentalists. These madrassas generate approximately 1.5 million subverted and indoctrinated jihadis every year. This massive, ever increasing support base provides the strategic depth the Al-Qaeda-Taliban combine needs to seize control of Pakistan and Afghanistan.

The Americans have finally woken up to the fact that they cannot bring the situation in Afghanistan under control unless Pakistan is tackled first. They are now also aware of the different dynamics that exist in both countries.

In Afghanistan there is only one ethnic group that opposes the American-backed government – the Pashtuns. Hence the fighting is largely restricted to southern and eastern Afghanistan. The others in the north and west are strictly anti-Taliban. In fact, even a number of Pashtuns support the constitutionally elected Afghan government. Having suffered three decades of war and the horrors of Taliban rule, the people of Afghanistan are tired and now want peace and economic development. However, they are also a fiercely independent people and do not want to see their country divided or occupied.

There is no such broad national unity or identity in Pakistan. The gap between various ethnic identities and the rich and the poor is a major divisive force. Most major ethnic groups show strong tolerance and sympathy for the Pakistani Taliban. Even in areas where they may not be popular, the Pakistani Taliban generates terror in people.

It must also be noted that over the years the Pakistani people have had to put up with conflicting versions of the state policy put forth by the army, the government, the clergy, the press and various influential sections of society. Thus they are now no longer clear as to what constitutes a threat to their security and what is required to rebuild the nation. Anti-American sentiment, subtly fostered by the state and various Islamist groups, has further clouded their minds and made the situation favourable to Taliban and other fundamentalist elements.

The Pakistani Taliban is far more ideologically radicalized than their Afghani counterpart. Fostered and funded by the all-powerful army-ISI nexus since the late eighties, they now number over 40,000 hardened fighters and have taken on the task of turning Pakistan into the cornerstone of their global jihad.

To sum up, the situation is deteriorating rapidly. The fragmentation of Pakistan – with a population of 173 million, an army larger than America's and about a hundred tactical nuclear weapons – into warlord-run fiefdoms that host Al-Qaeda and other major terror groups does not bode well for the security of India, the nearby oil-rich Persian Gulf and Central Asian countries, or for America and its allies. If the nuclear arsenal and bio-chem warfare facilities of Pakistan fall into the hands of Al-Qaeda, it will have cataclysmic consequences for the world.

The current recurring terror attacks against India must be viewed in the light of Al-Qaeda's attempts to provoke an Indo-Pak conflict which will compel Pakistan to divert forces to the Indian borders and thus reduce pressure on Al-Qaeda/Taliban in the west. The mere threat of a conflict between these two nuclear-armed countries will also detract international attention away from these terrorist organizations and provide them with the much needed breather required to regroup. The Mumbai Ghazwa (raid) of 26/11 is a prime example of this strategy, wherein the perpetrators left explicit clues to the involvement of several Pak agencies to fuel an armed Indian response.

As directed by NIC, comprehensive attempts are underway to develop quantitatively and qualitatively better human assets across the border. However, pursuant to the 1996 PMO directive to dismantle all such intelligence apparatus, this process will take more time than seems to be available, considering the speed with which events are spiralling out of control in Pakistan. Confirming the identity of the Ameer-ul-Momineem and ascertaining his plans are being treated as a top priority task.

The list of proposed actions, along with fiscal and political evaluations, is forwarded under sealed cover for perusal and approval.

The path of the righteous man is beset on all sides by the inequities of the selfish and the tyranny of evil men.

Book of Ezekiel

Walking out of the Khadki Military Hospital in Pune, the tall, athletic young man began to slice his way through the pedestrians on the street. It was a typical cantonment road: broad, tree-lined, with a clearly marked black and yellow median running down the centre, free of hawkers and vehicular traffic. The fragrance of bougainvillea hung in the air.

Impervious to everything, his eyes barely noticing the flow of life around him, Iqbal walked purposefully, without stopping. No one would have guessed he had just left behind a dead wife and a newborn child at the hospital. Only an experienced eye would have identified the large uneven patches on his dark brown trousers and pullover as bloodstains. He was vaguely aware of his heart beating. It was a dull, sporadic beat. The expression on his face was as cold and still as the emptiness within.

Iqbal was walking past a cart selling tea and samosas when a mongrel scavenging for leftovers looked up at him, smelling the blood. The dog's tail stiffened, his ears pricked up and he growled. Iqbal turned and reflexively kicked the dog, the rage in his brain bubbling over. The dog scampered away with a yelp, his tail tucked firmly between his legs. The people around the food stall stared at Iqbal and then backed away. Most of them looked disgusted. For a moment, Iqbal felt a strand of remorse. But only for a brief moment. He continued along the crowded road.

Briefly, Iqbal allowed himself to think of his infant son, whom he had left behind in the care of Colonel Anbu. It might seem to an outsider that he had deserted his child, but he knew he had done the right thing. Under the circumstances, Colonel Anbu was the best person to bring up the baby. Though Tanaz would have wanted him to raise their son himself, of that Iqbal was certain. The tiny bundle of life was all that remained of her now.

No, Tanaz would have wanted their son to be kept as far from this madness as possible. *He will be safe only so long as no one knows he is mine. Everyone who comes close to me dies.* Iqbal's mind spiralled into a bottomless, colourless kaleidoscope. Death was all that lay ahead now. He could feel it, hanging heavy all around him. He could smell it as strongly as he smelt the blood that stained his clothes. He could feel it as clearly as the cold sweat trickling down his face.

When will this killing end? Memories of his dead mother, sister and wife broke through the stillness and assailed Iqbal's mind. He staggered for a moment, before rallying again. He knew he needed to shut out all feeling if he was to survive, if he was to finish what he had set out to do.

∽

Iqbal had barely covered a mile when the shrill ring of a mobile phone broke into his thoughts. He reached for the phone cradled in his belt case and was surprised to find it silent, its screen blank. The ringing continued, unabated. There was another phone in his pocket. He pulled it out and looked at the unfamiliar handset, bewildered. Then the memory returned, hurtling him back to the small apartment that Tanaz and he had occupied during the mission to penetrate the Indian Mujahideen, to the room where the final showdown had taken place not very long ago.

In his mind's eye, Iqbal saw the knife in his hand flail out and strike Asif, the terrorist who had taken his Tanaz away from him. As the knife snarled through the breastplate and penetrated Asif's heart, he heard the man gasp and die. Tanaz lay bleeding on the floor, her tortured body struggling to keep the child in her womb safe. *I must get help!* Reaching for the mobile phone that Mujib, the second terrorist, had dropped when Tanaz shot him, Iqbal dialled Colonel Anbu's number. He realized now that he must have put the phone in his pocket after calling the colonel.

∞

The phone went silent. Then it began to ring again. Iqbal recognized the number on the screen. He had been expecting this call. A wave of anger swept through him. It was because of this man's failure that Tanaz was dead.

'Sir.' He uttered the word more out of habit than respect.

'Where are you, Iqbal?'

'Here... on the road... some distance from the hospital.'

'Where are you going, son? I understand what you are going through, but you can't just run away like this.'

Do you? Do you understand what Tanaz meant to me? Other than my family, she was the only person who loved me, who gave meaning to my life. She gave me the only home I knew since the day they sent me to Pakistan to train with the Lashkar. Can you or anyone else understand what it means to lose one's own heart, mind, body and soul?

Iqbal was overwhelmed by a sudden urge to lash out, but he did not say a word.

'Iqbal?' Colonel Anbu's voice was gentle.

'I need to be alone for some time,' he said curtly. *You promised she would be safe,* he thought bitterly.

'Okay, Iqbal, if that's what you want. But when you are done, you know where to find me.'

The compassion in Anbu's voice broke through the massive stone wall Iqbal had built around himself. He struggled to push it away, knowing it would make him feel again. And that would make him weak.

'We'll be waiting for you to return home,' said Anbu.

'I'll be back. Just give me a little time.'

'Whenever you are ready, son.' Anbu could sense the growing distance between them, and it wasn't only physical.

There was a strange expression on the colonel's face as he ended the call. It matched the bitter taste in his mouth. The taste of failure, and loss.

∞

Home. The word triggered memories of a conversation he'd had with Tanaz when he was recovering at the at the Faisalabad terrorist compound from the gunshot wounds he had sustained during the cross-border strike to take down Murad Salim.

He remembered telling Tanaz that they needed to get back to India as soon as possible, that they needed to go home.

'Home?' Tanaz had asked, her face shadowed with grief. 'I have forgotten what a home even feels like.'

'Don't worry, my love,' Iqbal had said, folding her in his arms. 'Together we shall make our very own home. You, me and one day, Inshallah, our children.'

Iqbal snapped back to reality. The woman who had set out to build and share that home with him was now dead and their child lay cradled in another man's arms. There would never again be a place that he could call home. Life had turned full circle and he was back where he had been when he returned from Pakistan to find his mother and sister killed by bombs planted by his own lashkar at Delhi's Sarojini Nagar market.

Iqbal had been so happy as he had tried to convince Tanaz that Colonel Anbu and the others in Force 22 would be glad to have them back.

'You think so?'

'I know so,' Iqbal had said.

'How can you be so sure? They are professional soldiers. For them the mission is the only thing that matters.'

'Maybe, but Colonel Anbu is special, he is different from the rest. So are Tiwathia, Sami... all of them. My heart tells me.'

Are they really different? Iqbal wondered now. *They had promised they would always watch our backs.*

Anbu's warning, that Tanaz should not participate in the mission to infiltrate the Indian Mujahideen, echoed in his head. 'You will have to do this one on your own, Iqbal. Tanaz is pregnant, I will not expose her to any danger.'

Iqbal felt a deep stab of regret. He wished he had listened to Anbu. In his heart he knew that if there was anyone he could fall back on, it was the officers of Force 22. They were as close to a family as he would ever have, especially now, with Tanaz gone. His restless mind urged him to go back and bury his wife's body, to see that she was laid to rest properly. But his heart told him it would bring him no peace, he would find closure only when those responsible for her death had paid the price. And for that he would need to find his strength again.

It was a calm, spruced-up young man who arrived at the Force 22 base in Kasauli seventeen days later. Dressed in black cords, a full-sleeve white shirt and a navy blue jacket, Iqbal looked entirely in control as he presented himself at the gate and asked for Colonel Anbu.

∽

Colonel Rajan Anbu was the first Commanding Officer of Force 22. In the four-year span in which he had held command, Anbu had set a precedent that his successors would be hard-pressed to emulate. He was a prime example of that controlled aggression which makes the Special Forces man stand apart.

Famous for leading from the front, Anbu never expected from the extraordinary men and women he commanded, anything that he was not willing to do himself. And this was no mean achievement, considering that his unit, Force 22, was one of the best Special Forces units on both sides of the Suez Canal, capable of taking on anything the world had to throw at it.

The officers of Force 22 were hand-picked from the Indian Army, Navy, Air Force and Indian Intelligence. Each one was a commissioned officer not below the rank of captain, in superb physical condition, a high achiever amongst his/her peers, trained to fight over land, sea and air, skilled in most known methods of killing, and motivated to the highest possible levels.

Like all international Special Operations units, Force 22 also had the pick of the best weapons and equipment available. Every officer was allowed to choose the weapon that best suited his or her temperament. The gadgetry they had access to enabled them to carry out previously unthinkable tasks, including the most sophisticated forms of spying, snooping, eavesdropping, detection-proof break and entry, and search-and-destroy missions. They were looped into the network of every intelligence agency in India.

Born from the bloody crucible of the three-decade long low-intensity conflict that had been thrust upon India by the singularly focused Pakistani military and intelligence establishments, Force 22 was set up by the Indian government to provide a rapid, highly professional covert response to certain situations that could not – or should not – be dealt with by more conventional forces in a more conventional manner.

This decision had been proved right and Force 22 had acquitted itself honourably when the Indian prime minister had tasked it to punish those guilty of the horrific terror bomb attacks in Delhi in October 2005. Living up to its motto of *Stealth, Speed and Surprise*, Force 22 commandos had struck deep at the heart of the Pakistani-run terror organizations.[1] The raids had taken out several key terrorists and shaken the Pakistani jihadi factory to its core. For years the Indian government had been asking Pakistan to extradite these individuals since they were wanted for terrorist activities in India, but the Pakistan government had always denied any knowledge of their deeds.

The next achievement for Force 22 had been the strike into Pakistan to cut down the terror maestro called Brigadier Murad Salim, an ISI agent who had planned and engineered a series of bold terror spectaculars in various key cities all over the globe.[2] Iqbal was not officially a part of Force 22 but he had been sent with the strike team as he was one of the few people to have seen Salim. It was during this

[1] Told in *Lashkar* (2008).
[2] Told in *Salim Must Die* (2009).

mission that Iqbal had met Tanaz, a RAW asset who had been the operational liaison in Pakistan.

After this, the Force 22-engineered infiltration of the Youth for Purity in Society (YPS) and the subsequent destruction of the IM terror cell by Iqbal had been the third major victory for Colonel Anbu's force. Not only had they managed to decimate the terror cell, they had also exterminated Mujib, the ISI agent provocateur who had set it up.[3]

Five minutes later, Iqbal was in Anbu's office. Clean and spartan, the room was furnished with a large, polished wooden table and black leather chairs, one for the colonel and three on the other side for visitors. A battery of phones and a digital radio set were placed on the left of the table. On the right stood a large Macbook hooked up to a projector that could display images on the white screen that occupied most of the wall facing Anbu's chair. A fresh cool breeze, fragrant with the smell of pines, drifted in through the open windows facing the Himalayas.

Anbu suppressed his shock when Iqbal entered. Though outwardly the same, there was no trace of the idealistic, patriotic young man who simply wanted love, and redemption. The set jaw and cold eyes revealed a barely suppressed violence

[3] Told in *Blowback* (2010)

that Anbu had seen in Iqbal only once before, at Delhi's Tihar Jail.

He remembered the expressionless eyes of the hardened inmate he had met; a man suspected of killing the two men who had bullied him when he first arrived in jail. Nothing had ever been proved but the prison grapevine knew what had happened. The men's necks had been snapped like twigs, and there were no other marks on their bodies, confirming that both murders had been cold-blooded. After that, everyone in the jail left Iqbal alone.

Yes, the man standing before Anbu was more like the killer he had first met. There was no doubt that this man could kill – and kill without remorse or pity, or even fear. Anbu felt a sadness sweep through him. This was not the path he would want a friend to tread. But he also knew that with Tanaz gone, there was no one who could rein in Iqbal.

'I am very happy to have you back, son,' he told Iqbal. 'Come, sit down.' Anbu gestured towards a chair. He was dressed in standard army issue combat fatigues, the norm for all Force 22 officers. He preferred it that way even when they weren't in the middle of an operation; it kept them mentally prepared for combat.

'How have you been?' Anbu asked awkwardly. He wasn't quite sure what to say to the aloof and seemingly controlled young man seated across the table from him. Pain is such a personal thing, after all: one can console the sufferer but one can never reduce the pain.

'I am well,' Iqbal replied curtly. 'I came to tell you that I am ready to go back to Pakistan.'

'Are you sure?'

Iqbal nodded.

'Well, I don't agree. You know it's not a good idea at all.'

'Perhaps, sir, but someone has to do it, you know that. As long as men like the Ameer-ul-Momineem are at large, there is a grave threat to India – in fact, to the whole world. Just before Tanaz gunned down Mujib, he told us that the Ameer is planning something really big – something that will ensure Mughalstan becomes a reality. I need to find out what that is and stop him.'

'We know about that, Iqbal. The ISI and, at their behest, their friends in the DGFI in Bangladesh will leave no stone unturned to try and create Mughalstan or what they refer to as Greater Pakistan. It is the final phase of their Operation Topac. We are already trying to identify the Ameer and find out what he is planning. So I am not sure what you will achieve by going back to Pakistan.'

'I will stop him.' Iqbal's chin jutted forward resolutely.

'How?' Anbu's voice radiated scepticism. 'How do you plan to do that? You don't have a clue as to who he is or where he can be found.' Iqbal did not respond. 'The Identikit picture that Tanaz helped us put together leads us to believe that the Ameer is most probably Jalaluddin Haq, one of the Waziristan-based Taliban commanders, but this has not been confirmed. Given the infighting amongst the various groups in Pakistan, there are presently many contenders for the title, especially after Mullah Omar went underground and American drones killed Beitullah Mehsud, the head of TTP. Jalaluddin may well be a red herring. The Pakis may be flagging him to hide the real Ameer. You won't even know where to start looking for him.'

'Don't worry, I'll find him and I'll recognize him when I see him.'

'Okay, let's assume you do find him,' Anbu persisted. 'Then what? How do you propose to find out what he is planning and then stop him? Do you realize that such a man is going to be heavily guarded all the time?'

'Allah will show me the way.' Iqbal shrugged. 'If He is the One and True God, then surely He will not allow this madness to continue in His name.' Iqbal's eyes had a distant look. 'My father always told us that if we want something badly enough, the entire universe conspires to deliver it to us. We just have to *know* we want it.' His voice hardened. 'And trust me, I want that bastard,' he said through clenched teeth.

'That may be so,' Anbu said patiently, 'but think about it. Be logical. You must remember we have no resources in Pakistan to support you. You are going to be on your own. Forget your chances of success, even your chances of survival would be remote.'

'But you agree that there *is* a chance, and that is good enough for me.'

'Come on, Iqbal.' The colonel leaned forward. 'We go to battle only when there is a reasonable chance of success. Operations are not launched on a wing and a prayer, especially not such a dangerous one. You should know that by now.'

'You can get me across.' Iqbal's eyes bore into Anbu's unflinchingly. 'You owe me this much.'

His words hung angrily in the silence that suddenly seized the room.

Finally, Anbu nodded. 'Okay, Iqbal, if that is what you have decided to do.' He leaned back in his chair with a sigh. 'We both know I cannot stop you. And yes, maybe I do owe it to you. Tell me how else I can help you.'

'Just get me across. I need to go back to Faisalabad.'

'I see. Well, all right.' Anbu did not bother to conceal his disapproval.

'I will also need some money,' Iqbal added. 'Not much, just a little…'

'That's not a problem either. Anything else?'

'No.'

'Are you sure?'

Iqbal nodded.

'How about I get Ankita to let you have a look at the data we have on the various people we suspect and the current situation in Pakistan. I will also tell her to set up a covert communication protocol for you,' Anbu suggested. If he couldn't stop Iqbal, at least he could try to ensure that he came back alive. 'Just in case something comes up where we can be of some help.'

'That would be good, sir, but I don't want anything to link me with any official agency here in India, in case I am taken...'

'I know what you're saying, Iqbal, but don't worry. I will have Ankita set up something appropriate. Just give me a couple of days to organize things. You stay on at the base and think this over in the meantime. I still feel the whole exercise is dangerous and futile.'

'If it's okay with you, I would like to use this time for weapon training.'

'Not a bad idea,' Anbu conceded. 'I'll tell Tiwathia to run you through a refresher.'

Iqbal got up from his chair. 'May I take your leave now?'

Anbu nodded reluctantly. He had hoped Iqbal would stay longer and keep talking so that he could try and lance the anger out of him, maybe even dissuade him from the mission he had chosen to embark upon. 'I do want you to give this some more thought, Iqbal,' he repeated. 'There is no point in throwing away your life so senselessly.'

Barely checking his stride, Iqbal gave a slight nod, unwilling to meet the colonel's eyes.

'Colonel Anbu?'

The colonel looked up to find that Iqbal had halted at the door.

'How is my son?'

'He is well.' A warm smile lit up Anbu's face. 'My wife and he are absolutely inseparable. Would you like to meet him?'

Iqbal opened his mouth to reply but no words came out. After a moment, he simply shook his head and walked out.

For one brief moment Anbu almost went after Iqbal to call him back. To talk to him. To explain that commanders often make mistakes in battle, that when mistakes are made people die, that commanders are human too, that he had tried his best. Then he sank back in his chair, knowing that in his current state of mind Iqbal was unlikely to listen to any explanations. And even if he did, it would not take away the pain. With a weary sigh, the colonel picked up the phone and began to put Iqbal's requests into action. *If it has to be done, we might as well give it our best shot.*

∽

Two days later, when they met again, just before Iqbal was to set out for the border crossing, Anbu made one final attempt to reach out to him.

'Come with me. I want to show you something.' Anbu led Iqbal across the physical training ground. There, nestled into the hillside was a tiny hut with a red tiled roof. At the entrance, guarded by an armed sentry and standing tall under a concrete umbrella, was a burning torch, its flame flickering wildly in the brisk mountain wind.

The fragrance of incense greeted the two men as they entered the hut. Barring a solitary photograph that hung on the wall facing the door, the hut was empty. The colonel stopped in front of the photograph. It was of a young Indian Air Force officer.

'This is Squadron Leader Rajesh Tiwari,' Anbu said as Iqbal came up beside him. 'He laid down his life while stopping Salim's strike on Delhi.'

Iqbal looked at the photograph of the handsome, smiling man who appeared to be in his mid-twenties. He had heard Tiwari's name before, but neither the man nor the nature of his death held any meaning for him. Anbu may as well have been talking about the weather.

'We call this the Hut of Remembrance,' Anbu explained, his voice sombre. 'Whenever we lose someone from Force 22, we honour him by placing his photograph here. We make sure his sacrifice is remembered for ever.' He paused, then added, 'Do you know Rajesh is the only one Force 22 has lost so far?'

Iqbal felt a jab of anger. He wanted to remind the colonel that Tanaz too had fallen while on a Force 22 mission.

'It is part of my job to see that no other photos are placed on this wall,' Anbu continued. 'But that's not always possible. The mission is most important, it is our raison d'être; in fact, it is sacrosanct. But so is human life.' Anbu looked at the picture on the wall. 'No commander likes to lose his men. We work to bring them back alive in addition to completing the assigned task. I met Rajesh's parents afterwards. He was their only child... he was going to be married just a few months later...'

'What good is all this to Tanaz?'

Anbu wanted to remind Iqbal that he had been totally against Tanaz's involvement in the operation. But he did not. In the end, no matter what the reasons, he *had* allowed Tanaz to go ahead. And as he was the commander, the buck stopped with him.

The two men stood in the hut for a long time. Then Anbu turned abruptly and left. He was putting on his shoes when Iqbal joined him outside. They had walked quite a distance from the hut when Anbu broke the silence. 'Are you absolutely certain you want to go across again?'

'Yes.'

'I am totally against it. I know it will be a waste of time...' Anbu broke off when he saw the look on Iqbal's face.

There was resolve there, and a strained intensity that was almost painful to behold. Iqbal was clearly fixated on the mission he had set for himself, to find the Ameer-ul-Momineem and take him out.

Anbu knew that the minute the Ameer's men had killed Tanaz, the battle had become a personal one for Iqbal. And that, as any warrior could have told him, was not the best way to go to war. Especially against a foe as formidable as the Ameer-ul-Momineem.

Understanding the source of good and evil – God is the creator of both, but people choose evil.

Deuteronomy

'The tanzeem has been constituted,' the Ameer-ul-Momineem declared in his unmistakable baritone as he put down the handset. The Ameer was a tall man with a jagged scar that ran across his right cheek. The scar was a painful reminder of a Russian bayonet and symbolized the violent times he had grown up in. He carried it with the pride of a soldier sporting a medal of honour. Had the bayonet travelled even an inch further to the left, it would have cleaved out his eye and delivered him back to his maker. But the near miss had only served to reinforce his belief that he was destined to live until he accomplished the mission for which he had been sent to earth.

It was not so long ago that this man had wrested the coveted title of Ameer-ul-Momineem from a host of brutal warlords who ruled over the tribal areas of Pakistan and large tracts of Afghanistan.

Today, he had been on the phone for hours, on six different calls, each one painstakingly routed through several domestic and overseas cutouts to mask its point of origin. 'That's it! We have all six of them now, one Ameer from each continent,' he told the frail old mullah reclining on the sofa in the middle of the room. His usually cold face was wreathed in a satisfied smile

Crossing the room in four large strides, the Ameer plonked himself on the sofa next to the mullah and threw an arm around him. The mullah had been quietly listening as the Ameer talked on the phone. Age may have whitened his hair and wizened his face, but it had done nothing to diminish the sparkle in his eyes.

Even today, Mullah Ismail Hamidi was as passionate about the jihad as he had been on that day in 1980 when he left his home near Medina and travelled those arduous miles to the rugged mountains that straddle the Pakistan-Afghanistan border. The advent of Russian forces into Afghanistan had seen him volunteer to dedicate his life to the jihad that had been launched to throw out the infidel invader. Born and bred a dedicated Wahhabi, the man was no warrior but he had the unwavering faith of a zealot and he knew he would be able to use his madrassa to breed an equally unfaltering band of jihadis. That war was over, but the jihad had continued. And it would go on until the crescent ruled the world.

As he looked at the Ameer with a sense of pride, Hamidi knew he had succeeded. His former student was on the verge of unleashing the biggest, deadliest offensive so far against the kafir. If he pulled it off, the world as it existed would completely change – nothing would stand in the way of Allah's lashkars as they swept forward and ensured the Sharia reigned supreme.

'Are you sure they are the best people for the job? We have to fill the leadership void caused by the Sheikh's and Mullah Omar's absence. Only then only can we have more 9/11s and take the jihad to higher levels,' Hamidi said, forever the sceptic and unwilling to show his excitement. 'We must be extremely careful when selecting people. The responsibilities of the tanzeem, of this group of leaders, are immense and failure would set us back by years. In fact, we may never even get the chance again.'

'I realize that.' The Ameer was used to having the mullah play the devil's advocate. It was what made the two of them such a formidable team: the old man's pessimism and experience tempered the younger man's ruthlessness and hot-blooded passion.

'Well, all six of them certainly have the right credentials to lead the jihad,' the Ameer continued. 'You want me to go over the list with you again?'

'Why not? Once we move on to the next stage, the dice will have been irrevocably cast. It will be too late to do anything then. One weak link in the chain could destroy everything we have put in place with so much effort.'

The Ameer scratched his unruly beard, his eyeballs unwittingly moving upwards as he reflected, 'The biggest bond among us is that we have all paid the price for the fight against the Russians with the blood of our families. And the fact that all of us had the honour of being taught by you at the Bajaur madrassa.' He smiled fondly at the old mullah. 'This, more than anything else, brought us together then and, thanks to you, still holds us together.'

'How can you be sure that the passage of years and their prolonged exposure to the decadent cultures has not jaded their enthusiasm for the jihad and shahadat?'

'That was easy to gauge.' The Ameer leaned forward and rested his chin on his hands. 'Did you not see the eagerness with which each one responded to our call?'

'So what? That is exactly what a traitor wanting to penetrate our organization would also have done.' The mullah was not one to relent till he had forced his disciple to re-examine all possibilities and risks. 'Every intelligence agency in the world would love to get an agent into our organization.'

'True, but in this case my gut tells me otherwise.' The Ameer sat back, patting his iron-hard stomach.

'I *know* that these six are fully aware of the threat Islam faces today and will come together to take the fight to the Crusader-Zionist-Hindu nexus that is now arrayed against us believers. Do you not have faith in what you taught us?'

Hamidi did not respond but his eyes shone with the courage of his conviction. For a moment, silence gripped the room, the comfortable silence of two men who have shared the battlefield for a long time.

'The best thing is that now, after all these years, all six of them have become firmly embedded in their societies,' the Ameer continued. 'Except for the Russian, none of them has a police record or links with any so-called subversive, terrorist or criminal organization. Just look at each of them.' He raised one finger of his right hand in the air. 'The American is a respectable family man and a reputed businessman who owns a big chain of petrol bunks across the mid-west. He has expanded the tiny business he inherited from the man who adopted him and took him away to America. In every way he represents the true-blue American success story which they pride themselves on. Who will suspect him?'

The Ameer extended another finger. 'On the same lines, the one in Australia has converted the tiny tour company he acquired from his foster parents into one of the largest, most sought after travel firms in Australia. The inbound and outbound tours he runs not only enable him to travel worldwide, they

will also allow him to facilitate movement of our
brothers-in-arms whenever the need arises. With a
wife and three kids to give him cover, he is perfect
for our cause.'

The Ameer stopped and gave the mullah a
questioning look, waiting for his response. There
was none, so he continued with number three.
'Our man in France overcame all the hardships
of life at a refugee camp. The fact that he is one
leg short, courtesy a Russian landmine, attracts
more sympathy than suspicion. Today he owns
six eateries in and around France. His kebab joints
are not huge or glitzy, but all of them are popular.
The spread of his business gives him the licence to
move around easily, and the fact that he specializes
in this particular cuisine gives him the freedom to
hire people from the NWFP. What better cover can
there be for our fighters when they need to come
over ground and mingle with society?'

'I agree.' Hamidi nodded.

'Good. Now consider the Indonesian. He, like
you, is a religious teacher, at one of the bigger
madrassas in Jakarta. This gives him the freedom to
seek capable and worthy youngsters for the cause, as
well as the moral authority to demand favours from
the faithful as and when our operations require it.
The best part is that he can function openly, totally
above ground, and yet not attract attention. In fact,
I view him as a vital asset in our plan to establish
a firm base in that country and ensure we always

have a ready supply of recruits to feed our front line. With Indonesia's nebulous political system, a huge unguarded maritime boundary and, of course, the rampant poverty, there cannot be a more apt base for us, can there?'

Hamidi nodded again, so the Ameer continued. 'Very similar to the Indonesian is the African who heads the Islamic Relief Foundation. The spread of this charity across the African continent allows him to travel freely. He can tap thousands of people festering in refugee camps all over Africa, besides offering our jihadis sanctuary in these camps. He already has a very good working relationship with AQIM, the North African Al-Qaeda leaders. They respect him and support the idea of having him as the central co-coordinating authority. That is why, in addition to supporting our strike cells, I am looking to him to provide the manpower we need to take the battle all over the world.'

'I agree with you about all of them, but what about the Russian?' the mullah asked. 'Why him? Every cop in Europe is looking for him.'

'Ah, the Russian!' The Ameer dropped his hand to his thigh. 'Yes, I know he is on every possible wanted list, but he is also on the guest list of every credible criminal organization in the world. Right from getting us the acetic anhydride to converting opium into heroin...'

'I know how important that is.' Hamidi was aware that 2.6 tons of acetic anhydride were needed to convert every 10 tons of opium into 1.3 tons of heroin. This conversion was crucial since the market value of opium was barely 45 dollars per pound as against the 1600 dollars per pound that they got for heroin. The relatively simple conversion took 900,000 dollars worth of opium to a mind-blowing 4,160,000 dollars worth of heroin and that too in a much smaller quantity, which was easier to conceal and carry. Since there were no other legal uses for this industrial chemical in Pakistan, it had to be brought in under fake labels, through a combination of threats and bribery. 'I know that if the Russian's supply of acetic anhydride stops, the poppy fields of Afghanistan become economically unviable.'

'Not only that, the Russian provides us with the carriers to get the heroin out,' the Ameer added. 'He routes the money to our offshore banks and back to us whenever we want it, and helps us procure the arms and ammunition we need to keep the war alive. *He* is the key to it all.'

'But his only motivation is money. Don't you think there is a chance that he will sell out to the highest bidder? And you know there will always be a higher bidder,' Hamidi warned. 'The stakes are just too high now. Can we take a risk with him?'

'I know we can,' the Ameer replied. 'With the Russian, I just know we can. He is a thoroughbred mercenary, but – don't ask me why – he is the one I would choose to guard my back. There was something special between us, right from the start.

You may not remember those days, but of this entire lot, it was the two of us who spent the most time together in Bajaur, and the bond we share is solid.'

The Ameer thought back to the years when the seven of them were together at the madrassa that the Wahhabis had set up in Bajaur. Their life was frugal but it was a world away from the starving, disease-ridden reality of the refugee camps that had come up like anthills all along the Durand Line in Pakistan. In Bajaur they at least got two square meals a day.

The Ameer turned to Hamidi. 'Most importantly, I know without a doubt that they are all ready to kill for the cause.'

'Any fool can kill.' The old man's voice was soft, but the gaze he levelled at the Ameer wasn't. 'Are they ready to die as easily?'

'Ah! Are they ready to die?' The Ameer laughed. 'That time alone will tell. Who can be sure how a man will respond when he comes face to face with death?' Almost as an afterthought, he added, 'But I am quite certain they are – at least I hope they are, though I would much rather they killed for the cause than died for it. After all, we know how hard it is to find such men. They are the best we could have found for the tanzeem. They are leaders, each one of them, and they will help us take the battle deep into the hearts and minds of kafir all over the world.'

Hamidi nodded, aware that none of the others whom they had considered over the months even came close to these six. He also knew that the Ameer's instincts were generally sound. 'So be it. We have formed the tanzeem. The group is in place. Now for the next step.'

'Yes, now for the next step.' The Ameer looked at the phone. He would have to pick it up again, and soon. He had to speak to the only man in Pakistan who could make it possible for the tanzeem to meet. The problem was in approaching him without letting him know that his help was required. The Pakistani general was smart; if he detected the slightest weakness he would extract his pound of flesh, especially now that things were not going so well for the jihad. Too many fronts had opened up simultaneously and too many forces were arrayed against them. With the Americans pumping more troops into Afghanistan and now the Pakistan Army also making threatening noises, the situation was becoming more and more dangerous. The Ameer knew he needed this man to stand by them, for some more time at least, until he got the tanzeem together and ensured that they hit the ground running… until the snowball ballooned into an avalanche that could no longer be stopped.

But the Ameer knew he had to make it appear as though he was doing what the general wanted him to. But how? The general was no fool.

The thought troubled the Ameer. He knew the mullah was preoccupied with the same question, they had discussed it often enough. No clear answer appeared to be forthcoming, yet. But it would come to them soon, when the time was right... Inshallah.

Blessed is He who, in the name of charity and goodwill, shepherds the weak to the valley of darkness.

For he is truly his brother's keeper and the finder of lost children.

Book of Ezekiel

Iqbal entered the mud-walled house on the edge of the nondescript village near the Indo-Pak border north-west of Amritsar, accompanied by Captain Mohammed Sami and Flight Lieutenant Ankita Bhatnagar. He immediately recognized the dark-haired, stocky man waiting for them inside.

As on the two previous occasions, he was dressed in the typical attire of a farmer out to work in his fields. Anything else would make him stand out like a sore thumb. If caught during a border-crossing, the only possible way out would be to pretend he was a local farmer who had lost his way and wandered across. It would be his only chance of avoiding some hellhole of a jail in Pakistan where he would die forgotten.

It was from this village that Force 22 had begun its infiltration into Pakistan to hunt down Murad Salim. And this man had taken the strike team across the border. He had also brought Tanaz and Iqbal back to India when they had finally fled the Faisalabad terrorist compound.

'Rehmat?' Iqbal said. 'Isn't that the name?'

'It's as good a name as any,' the guide replied, giving Iqbal an indifferent smile. A native of one of the many villages on the Indo-Pak border which had been split in two by the Partition, Rehmat was a veteran cross-border traveller. For many years now, he had put his unusual skill to good use on behalf of RAW, by taking people in and out of Pakistan, people without any legitimate business there. 'You again?'

'Yes, me again.' Iqbal returned the smile but his eyes remained cold and watchful.

'Has something happened? You're different.'

'Am I?' Iqbal held his gaze.

'Yes, you have changed and...' Rehmat stopped in mid-sentence. 'You are either very brave or very stupid,' he said.

'Why do you say that?' Iqbal asked, bemused.

'In all these years I have taken only five people across the second time.' Rehmat paused. 'And only one of them ever came back.'

'He will be the second,' Captain Mohammed Sami cut in smoothly, stepping forward.

Although still a year short of thirty, Sami was the seniormost officer after Anbu and, therefore, the second-in-command of Force 22. He was a practical, no-nonsense man like his boss and had personally led both Force 22 missions into Pakistan.

'Come on, Rehmat, let's go over the route once more.' Sami led the guide out of the room so Ankita could give Iqbal the final briefing.

Ankita Bhatnagar, an attractive young flight lieutenant from the Indian Air Force, was a crack shot, adept at martial arts, and boasted a sharp, analytical mind that had made her a logical choice for the intelligence team. Along with Captain Manoj Khare, her Force 22 associate and now mutually designated life partner, Ankita had succeeded in cracking open Salim's nefarious plot to execute a series of terror attacks all over the globe.

'Iqbal, let's go over the communications plan,' she said. 'It's pretty basic but it's the best we could do, considering the terms of reference I've been given.' She switched on her laptop and waited for the data card to connect to the network. 'Do you remember your mobile number?'

'I do.' Iqbal repeated the number of the phone he had used during the YPS penetration. 'But I am not carrying it with me on this trip.'

'That's fine, you don't need to carry it with you,' Ankita replied. 'For this particular website, we just need an operational Indian mobile number. So this number is going to be kept alive as long as you are out there. Whenever you wish to get in touch with us, this is what you need to do.' She quickly tapped some keys as the browser opened up. 'Log into this website: www.indirocker.com.' She paused, allowing Iqbal to register the name. 'It is a social networking website. Your profile has already been created and Manoj, Vikram and I have been added as your friends. To get in touch, all you need to do is send us a private message.'

'What if I need to get in touch urgently or need an immediate reply?'

'Then simply click on the "Send sms" option, add our telephone numbers to the recipients' list, and send it.' Her fingers flew over the keyboard as she spoke and, almost instantly, her phone beeped. 'See, I just sent myself a text message from your profile. Whenever you do that, one of us will immediately log in and reply to your message. I am basically your designated first point of contact but if I am not around, either Manoj or Vikram will deliver the appropriate response to you.'

Iqbal nodded as he memorized the name of the website, his username and password.

'No, that's not good enough,' Ankita interjected. 'I want you to try it out and make sure you are familiar with the procedure.' She stood up and watched as Iqbal went through the process. He certainly lacked the ease and familiarity that Ankita had displayed, but he completed the process without hesitation or error. Once again her phone beeped as the message sent by him chimed in.

'Good.' Ankita dug into her satchel and pulled out a mobile phone, a bundle of Pakistani currency notes and a Type 77 pistol – a fairly simple pocket-sized weapon with a seven-shot capacity that fires a 7.65mm Type 64 cartridge. 'Here is a phone with a local Pakistani SIM card, and some cash. The pistol is of Chinese make so you will be okay even if the jihadis find it on you – there are dozens of these floating about in the area.'

Iqbal stuffed the phone and money into his pocket. Expertly ejecting the magazine, he checked the load, cocked the weapon, slipped on the safety and then pushed the gun into his waistband, against the small of his back, where it would be accessible if the need arose.

'Avoid using that phone except in an emergency and whenever you do, please keep in mind that all overseas calls, especially those to India, are almost certainly monitored by the ISI.'

'Where I am going, I doubt the phone will be of much use. I don't know if I even want to carry it.'

'Well, if it's not, it's not.' Ankita shrugged. 'We can only try and cover the options. In fact, when you decide you definitely don't need it, destroy the phone. On the other hand, if you have to use it, then assume they are listening to you; that will ensure you always err on the side of caution.'

'Right. Anything else?'

'Well, if you want, I can give you a couple of GPS locator chips which will help us keep track of you, but –'

'I don't think that would be very smart,' Iqbal completed the sentence with a smile.

'That's it then, Iqbal.' Ankita grinned back at him gamely. 'Sorry, but given the mandate, this is the best we –'

'It's enough,' Iqbal cut her off, he was in a hurry to get moving. 'Right then.' His handshake was unusually formal. 'Thanks for everything.'

'All the best. Travel safe and get back in one piece, and soon.' Ankita tried to sound optimistic as she shook Iqbal's hand.

Iqbal turned and walked out of the house to where Sami and Rehmat were waiting. For a long moment Sami and Iqbal just looked at each other, then Sami reached out to embrace him. Pulling away, Iqbal extended his hand. Sami masked his hurt as they shook hands. Iqbal quickly headed for the jeep where Rehmat was already waiting in the driver's seat.

'Come back soon, Iqbal,' Sami called out as Iqbal got into the jeep beside Rehmat. 'We will be waiting for you.'

'Inshallah,' Iqbal muttered as the jeep pulled away. He did not want to tell Sami that at this point he did not care whether or not he came back; all he wanted was to get far away from everyone who

was associated with Tanaz's death. He just wanted
to find the Ameer-ul-Momineem. And kill him.

Deep down, Iqbal knew that Sami, like the other
officers at Force 22, only meant well and cared for
him the way he cared for his other comrades-in-
arms. But at this moment all he could feel was hatred
and anger, and yet, it was all he could let himself
feel if he was to retain his sanity, otherwise the grief
festering within would tear him apart.

Iqbal forced himself to focus on the journey
ahead. They drove without a word, the silence
broken only by the purr of the engine as they
threaded their way through the inky night. At least
an hour's drive lay ahead before they dumped the
jeep and completed the border-crossing on foot.

∞

Daybreak was still a few hours away when Iqbal
and Rehmat left the jeep hidden between a cluster
of haystacks in a field and started walking. The first
hour passed without incident. Then Rehmat slowed
down and began to inch forward stealthily. They
had hit the border.

Except for the faint whisper of undergrowth
brushing against their legs and the pounding of their
hearts, the night lay silent around them. Suddenly
Rehmat slipped. There was a loud crack as the
torch in his hand hit the ground and shattered. The
sound echoed in the darkness, bringing them to an
instant halt. The two men hit the ground and lay

still, waiting for a reaction; the sound could not have gone unnoticed.

It did not. Night turned to day as a para-illuminating round burst high overhead. It gained brightness as it slowly parachuted down towards them.

'Don't move!' Rehmat hissed.

Iqbal did not reply. He knew that only movement could give them away right now. That, or the misfortune of a patrol stumbling right on them because this area was in the blind zone of the Pakistani battlefield surveillance radars.

Just then, he heard the rustle of men moving through the undergrowth. It sounded like a section-size patrol. They were close. Iqbal swallowed hard. The pounding in his heart escalated as the patrol drew closer. He drew his pistol, even though he knew it would be useless against a group of armed men. The feel of the cold metal in his hands lent him no comfort.

The flare had begun to flicker as it lazily glided earthwards. Before it died out, a second one exploded high above it, and the entire area sparkled with light again. The sound of the men grew louder. The patrol was very close now, coming directly towards them from the north-west. Moving an inch at a time, Iqbal brought the pistol closer to his head. *I will not be taken alive.* Dying was better than rotting in jail again, he thought to himself, especially one where he was certain to be tortured.

Rehmat saw the pistol in Iqbal's hand. He shifted closer and clutched his shoulder hard. 'No,' he whispered in Iqbal's ear. It was more a plea than a command. Iqbal heeded it.

When the patrol was barely metres away, the second flare began to splutter. Suddenly a radio set hissed; it was silenced immediately, replaced by a faint murmur. The second flare slowly spiralled down as it died away. Then a command was given; it was not loud but Iqbal felt Rehmat start. The light went out completely, returning blinding darkness to the night. Iqbal knew it would be a while before his vision returned to normal. He closed his eyes and remained still, breathing as quietly as possible.

The patrol seemed to have pulled back, and the men were meandering now. Eventually, there was quiet. But Iqbal and Rehmat stayed put. They knew this could just be a ploy on the part of the patrol leader to lull them into a sense of security and have them move again. Both knew that if anything moved, it could be seen. If it could be seen, it could be hit. Neither was in a hurry to die.

By the time Iqbal felt his heart slow to a regular beat, the chill of the night had started gnawing at his bones. Rehmat nudged him when he finally deemed it safe to move again. Standing up, they resumed their silent journey, though Iqbal was unable to shrug away the fear that suddenly a hail of bullets would rip the night apart.

∾

Dawn had just breached the horizon when they reached a lone hut at the end of the field, on the Pakistani side of the International Border. Both men were breathing hard by now. Despite the bitter January cold swirling around them, they were drenched in sweat and their muscles were corded with tension. They were still shaken by their close escape from the patrol. This, after all, was one of the most volatile borders in the world. On either side were swarms of soldiers, fingers dangerously close to the triggers of their weapons. It was only Rehmat's familiarity with the terrain and deployment of troops that had allowed them to navigate safely through it.

Across the embankment, Iqbal could see a tiny track snaking through the fields. It led to the main road. This was where the red and white station wagon had been parked the last time they crossed this border. Iqbal remembered Tanaz standing by it, draped in a black burqa.

'You know the way ahead from here?' Rehmat asked.

'Not really...'

'Faisalabad is that way,' Rehmat said, gesturing. 'You just keep going down that track till you hit a tri-junction; from there you turn right on the metalled road and then follow the signposting. Try to get hold of a bus or a truck. Avoid private cars and government vehicles. They always ask too many questions. If you stop the wrong one, you may well end up dead or, even worse, alive and left to rot in some prison.'

Rehmat's words reminded Iqbal of the terrorist camp at Hari in Kashmir and the Lashkar sentry who had briefed Omar and him on how to reach Srinagar from the Line of Control.

Same shit, different day.

'Seems simple enough,' Iqbal replied.

'It isn't,' Rehmat said sharply. 'At all costs, avoid the army and Ranger patrols. And if they stop you, don't try to run. No one hesitates to shoot these days. In fact, I suggest you stick to the fields on either side of the track till you hit the tri-junction.'

Iqbal nodded. The first strands of doubt flailed him, making him wonder what he was doing here. He pushed the doubt away firmly, it was too late to turn back now.

'Hope to see you coming back,' said Rehmat with a wave, unaware of the conflict raging within Iqbal. 'When you are ready, just let them know.' He jerked a thumb back at the border, implying Force 22. 'And I will be here to take you back. Inshallah.'

Returning the wave, Iqbal began to walk at an easy lope, ensuring the track was always in sight. When he turned around after a few minutes, Rehmat had vanished. He was absolutely alone.

∞

It took Iqbal all day to reach the tri-junction and find a bus to take him to Faisalabad. He made his way through the town and headed for the compound where the Ameer's men had taken Tanaz and him after their near-fatal encounter with the Pakistani soldiers.

Darkness had already set in by the time Iqbal spotted the lights of the terrorist compound. Deciding it would be better to enter during the day, he halted when he was about two miles away. The biting cold was not something he relished, but getting shot at in the dark by a nervous, ill-trained sentry was certainly a less desirable alternative.

The sleepless night, laden with painful memories, passed slowly. Iqbal got up and walked about every fifteen minutes to stay warm and keep his blood circulating. He was almost sick with relief when the night finally began to fade away.

Fighting the urge to move on quickly, Iqbal waited till the sun was up and had begun to dispel the night chill before he started again towards the compound. The fields had ended and he was now passing through a patch without any trees, totally devoid of undergrowth and hence offering no cover. Iqbal knew that if a sentry had been posted here, he would have spotted Iqbal by now. So he moved steadily and confidently, making no effort to conceal his approach.

Iqbal came up to the compound from the west, the same direction in which Tanaz and he had fled all those months ago. The place bore no scars of the sudden Pakistan Army raid that had driven them out.

In fact, the colony of mud-walled huts still had the same ill-maintained, almost dilapidated appearance which Iqbal remembered all too well. The mud walls encircling the compound seamlessly blended with the surrounding terrain.

Even from a distance, Iqbal could identify the tiny hut that Tanaz and he had occupied while he recuperated. In the centre of the compound was the slightly larger brick-walled hospital hut in which the Ameer's doctor had operated upon him and removed the bullets from his body. Instinctively, Iqbal speeded up.

He was about thirty metres from the parapet when two men with rifles rose from behind it.

'Where do you think you're going?' They cocked their rifles with grating metallic snicks. They were young beardless sentries, barely out of their teens. Precisely the kind who are stupid enough to shoot first and ask questions later.

The one who had spoken seemed to be the younger of the two; his tone was gruff and reeked of the arrogance of a man wielding a newly-acquired weapon. Iqbal noticed that their rifles were as dirty and badly maintained as their clothes, indicating their poor level of training. But both rifles were aimed at Iqbal, bringing him to a halt. Dirty or clean, the bullets they fired would be lethal and at this range even an idiot could not miss.

'I need to see the doctor... Pervez,' Iqbal replied confidently, switching to the local dialect he had mastered during his previous stay here. He also made sure he kept his hands in plain sight the entire time.

'Why? Who are you?' the older sentry asked, eager to assert his authority.

'Just call the doctor. He knows me well.' *I hope the bugger is still alive*. Iqbal knew from experience that it was best to stonewall them. In this part of the world no one gave away too many details about himself, not unless there was a gun held to his head or a knife to his balls. In any case, these two sentries looked like they had no idea what they were supposed to be doing. Iqbal guessed they had been posted to keep out the occasional errant villager or provide early warning of approaching security forces.

The guards, meanwhile, taking note of the fact that Iqbal was apparently unarmed, exchanged uncertain glances, shrugged and then, at a nod from the older one, the younger sentry went off to fetch the doctor. The other perched himself on the parapet and kept watch on Iqbal. His rifle was still pointed at him, but his demeanour was casual now. If he wanted to, Iqbal could have taken him down before the guard could even think of bringing his rifle into action. And he would not even have to use the pistol concealed in his waistband.

'Oh! It's you!' Iqbal heard the reedy, once familiar voice and looked up to see Pervez striding towards him. He was dressed as shoddily as before and the unpleasant smell of disinfectant hung about him. The smell grew stronger as he came closer.

'What are you doing here?' Pervez asked. 'I thought you had gone back...'

'I had.' Iqbal hailed him with a wave, forcing a smile. 'Then they sent me across for another mission.' He gestured over his shoulder towards India. 'Now I am on my way back.'

'Then why did you not go straight to Muridke? Wouldn't that have been much closer for you?'

'Not from where I am coming.' Iqbal had anticipated this question. After all, the Lashkar-e-Toiba campus, sited on 77 acres donated by the Pakistan government and built with money from the same Saudi groups that financed Al-Qaeda, was the logical destination for any LeT operative returning from a mission in India. Ankita's intelligence reports had provided him with the right answer. 'In any case, Muridke is totally out of bounds for me.'

'I know!' Pervez broke into a sharp, nasal laugh. 'Almost everyone is staying clear of it these days, ever since the Mumbai operation. We really fucked their happiness with that one.' He gleefully rubbed his hands together, then suddenly stopped and looked around. 'Where is that woman of yours?'

'She didn't make it,' Iqbal replied flatly.

'Oh.' For a moment Pervez seemed unsure of what to say. 'Tough luck, miyan. We are losing a lot of people these days. But the jihad calls for many sacrifices.' He spoke with the glib assurance of one who had never faced a gun and never would; such men are always more willing to sacrifice human life.

An uncomfortable pause followed as Iqbal fought the urge to draw his weapon and pump all its bullets into the man's head.

Unnerved by the cold look in Iqbal's eyes, Pervez hurriedly broke the silence. 'Come, let's get you something hot to drink,' he offered. 'You are planning to stay long?'

'No, I will rest for the day and then move on.'

'To Muzaffarabad?' Pervez automatically assumed Iqbal would proceed to one of the other LeT bases.

'No, I don't think so. I need to find the Ameer.'

'The Ameer?' Pervez swivelled to look at Iqbal, his eyebrows arched in surprise. 'The Ameer-ul-Momineem?' He guffawed when Iqbal nodded. 'You must be joking. Just because he picked you off the streets once...'

'The mission I was on for the past few months was run by one of his key people.'

'Who? Where is he?'

'You wouldn't know him. And in any case, he didn't make it either.' Iqbal controlled his irritation. He needed to get Pervez to talk freely; this was his best chance to get information. 'That is why I know the Ameer will want to meet me.'

'Yeah, sure.' The doctor gave a sarcastic laugh. 'Anyway, don't you know?'

'Know what?'

'Nobody finds or meets the Ameer. Not unless the Ameer wants them to. In fact, *only* if he wants them to.'

'Or if it is Allah's will,' Iqbal shrugged.

'That is so, of course.'

They had reached a smaller hut adjacent to the hospital. Pulling a kettle off the fire, Pervez poured tea into two old, unclean mugs. He handed one to Iqbal, then threw himself on one of the charpoys that lay askew outside the hut and motioned Iqbal towards the second one. 'There are biscuits in that tin, if you want some.'

'I am fine.' Iqbal shook his head, taking a sip of the tea. It was awful, overbrewed and terribly sweet, but he drank it. His body needed the sugar. 'Do you have any idea where the Ameer might be?' he asked Pervez.

'Me? How would small fry like me know?' Pervez cackled. 'He could be anywhere.'

'But if one has to look for him, where should one start?'

'Head for the north, where else? Everything seems to be happening there these days.' The doctor mused awhile. 'Not a very healthy place to be in, though.' He saw the query in Iqbal's eyes and continued, 'Maulana Fazlullah's forces have overrun the Swat Valley and are in complete control of it. So it is possible that the Ameer is there. They say many of the senior commanders have moved there since it is out of range of those fucking missiles the Americans keep throwing down from the skies every now and then.'

'So I heard,' said Iqbal. 'But is it really true about the Swat Valley? You mean the government has just…'

'…rolled over and died,' Pervez finished with a smirk. 'Oh, they go around making the usual noises about restoring the government's writ, blah blah…' He mimed a flapping mouth with the fingers of his right hand. 'Now we hear they are gathering troops to retake the Valley, but the simple fact is that today the Sharia is supreme in Swat.'

Iqbal was speechless.

'And further down in Waziristan, the security forces are already on the run. So the Ameer may well have returned there to take charge. Who knows? It is all very confusing.' Pervez pondered for a moment. 'That's why, if I were you, I would try Waziristan. It is his home base after all. Head for the Manba Ulom madrassa. They all say it is his headquarter.'

There was silence as both men mulled this over.

'We hear that even Peshawar may fall any day now,' Pervez said.

'Peshawar! But the army is very strong there.'

'So what? You know as well as I do that the Pakistan Army does not have the heart to take us on. Actually, more and more Pakistanis are starting to see things the way we want them to.' Pervez looked heavenwards reverently. 'I don't think it is going to be long before the NWFP, FATA and FANA are completely in our control.'

'Inshallah,' Iqbal murmured dutifully, concealing his surprise.

'There is some talk that the army might launch an offensive to regain control of the Swat Valley, but they will get a real jolt if they try. From all over the country, our boys are rallying to defend the Swat. From what we have heard, it is just a matter of time before the heartland also falls into our control.'

'Fantastic! That is really encouraging.' Iqbal forced a smile. *So Colonel Anbu was right. If everything this guy is saying is true, the Talibanization of Pakistan is just a matter of time, and not too much time at that.*

'That is why I am telling you to be careful when you reach. With the Americans, the Pakistan Army and our own people all mucking about there, not to mention some of the local lashkars, it is a real bugger's muddle. No one knows who is shooting at whom and why. See what I mean?'

'I do, I do,' Iqbal nodded. 'I'll be careful.'

Pervez slurped his tea. 'Another bit of friendly advice: be careful whom you speak to about the Ameer. Out there, they don't care much for people who go around asking too many questions, especially about him. You start shooting your mouth off and you may well end up losing your head.'

'I'll keep that in mind.'

'I suggest you head back to Muridke or Muzaffarabad and ask your bosses what you should do. They will know where the Ameer is. There is a lot of talk going on these days, of all the groups coming together and functioning in tandem.' Pervez got up and poured them some more tea.

'Is that really happening?'

'Well, I have not seen it myself but I believe they have already started sharing training camps and administrative bases.'

Iqbal gave a low whistle. 'That is awesome.'

'Yes, I even heard they are planning to start sourcing weapons jointly and target allocation will also be coordinated centrally.'

'By whom?'

'All that I am not sure of. The Ameer himself, I suppose,' Pervez shrugged. 'I'm just telling you what I've heard from those who pass through.'

'You seem to hear an awful lot,' Iqbal said with a laugh, trying to keep the man talking.

'Well, you know what it is like,' Pervez chuckled. 'People love to chat with the doctor, the barber and the whore.'

Iqbal feigned amusement, then said, 'I like your idea of going back to Muzaffarabad, though.'

'That would be your best bet, certainly the safest. Though if you do wish to go north, you can leave with the group heading for Swat tomorrow.'

'Oh, really?' Iqbal was not sure of the consequences of doing so. On the one hand, going with others would aid his anonymity and be a lot safer. On the other, it would leave him open to questioning by his travel companions, thus increasing the chances of his cover being blown.

'Look, there's Yasin.' Pervez suddenly sat up and pointed at a man who was walking across the compound. 'He is the leader of the group leaving tomorrow. Here, let me introduce the two of you.' Before Iqbal could react, Pervez got up and waved at the stranger. 'Oye, Yasin! Yasin miyan.'

'Come, come, Yasin bhai,' he said when the man walked up. 'I want you to meet someone. This is Iqbal.' Pervez thumped Iqbal on the shoulder. The hearty introduction worked well for Iqbal since it seemed to allay any doubt that Yasin may have had; he only appeared curious at the moment.

Dressed in the Pathani suit commonly worn in the area, Yasin was a bulky man of medium height, his round face half covered by a heavy beard. He greeted Iqbal with a nod, neither hostile nor suspicious, but not too friendly either.

'I thought the two of you should meet since he is also heading your way,' Pervez continued helpfully, pouring another cup of tea and handing it to Yasin. 'So I suggested he go with you.'

'Are you going to join the defence there?' Yasin asked Iqbal, ignoring Pervez. That did not go down very well with the doctor who enjoyed being at centre stage, like most men on the fringes of fighting.

'No, Yasin miyan, he has just come back from

a mission and is on his way to rejoin his group in Waziristan,' Pervez answered before Iqbal could.

'Where are you headed?' Iqbal spoke quickly, stalling further questions from Yasin or comment from Pervez.

'We are going to join up the defence there.' Yasin saw the query on Iqbal's face and added, 'Haven't you heard? The Pakistan Army is planning to start an operation against our brothers in the Swat Valley. We... all of us,' Yasin looked at both of them pointedly, 'need to ensure they do not succeed.'

'How could he have heard?' Pervez came to Iqbal's rescue. 'He has just returned from there,' Pervez gestured towards India and dramatically lowered his voice, 'from a very important mission.'

'Well, whatever.' Yasin shrugged. He had obviously had enough of the doctor's company and lost interest in Iqbal as soon as he learnt that Iqbal would not be joining forces with them. 'We can drop you more than halfway to Waziristan if you wish to go with us.'

'That would be fine.' Iqbal decided the trip was worth the risk. He would simply have to be careful not to get into too much conversation with his fellow passengers.

'Be ready by five then. Meet me at that hut.' Yasin pointed across the camp. Then he put down his cup and hurried away.

'There! That takes care of more than half your

problems.' Pervez bestowed a satisfied smile on Iqbal, who thanked him.

By now Iqbal had realized there was nothing more he could get out of Pervez, so he made very visible efforts to stop yawning.

'Tired?' Pervez asked. 'Why don't you eat something and then get some sleep?'

'Thanks, I will.' Iqbal was not hungry, but he knew his body needed food. Pervez doled out some dal, vegetables and roti on a plate. Like the tea, the food was indifferently cooked and overly spicy, but it was hot. Iqbal's stomach, starved of food the whole day, initially rebelled at the sudden gluttony. But he ate till he knew he had enough inside him to last till morning. Then he put the plate away and asked Pervez where he could sleep.

'You can use the hut you stayed in earlier,' Pervez said. 'It is vacant today. In fact, it has been lying unused for quite a while. I will tell the sentry to wake you up in the morning.'

Iqbal approached the hut with mixed feelings, not sure if he wanted to rekindle any memories, yet desperate to reach out and hold onto anything that brought Tanaz closer to him, even momentarily. When he finally pushed open the door, his heart was racing and his hands trembled. Beads of sweat lined his brow. Every fibre of his mind and body felt painfully, acutely alive.

The unmistakable mustiness of a room closed for too long greeted him. Small puffs of dust blew wherever his feet landed. He immediately noticed that everything inside had changed in the months gone by; despite that, a strong sense of familiarity and loss seeped through him. He felt achingly alone.

∾

When Iqbal reached Yasin's hut the next morning, there were five men with Yasin. No one asked him any questions. Like Yasin, they were all in their mid-twenties and were similarly attired. No weapons were visible. From what Iqbal had gathered during his conversation with Pervez, it was not safe to travel with weapons any more. The jihadis no longer had the carte blanche that the Pakistan Army had allowed them all these years.

Iqbal had already dropped the mobile phone Ankita had given him into the field latrine outside the compound. It would be of no use where he was headed. And if discovered on him, it could be the cause of his death.

It was still short of daybreak when the men threw in their rucksacks, squeezed themselves into the rickety van and started off with Yasin at the wheel.

The first question came when they were about a mile away from the camp. 'I heard you just returned from across,' the man sitting beside Iqbal said to him. 'How are things there?'

Iqbal looked at him. His thick accent indicated he had not had much schooling. He appeared to be the typical canon-fodder variety which most jihadi groups recruited in large numbers. Men who would satisfy the ever-hungry guns of the security forces. Men who were too dumb or too hungry for the few rupees thrown at them by the terror maestros to question why they should be so ready to die.

'Not very good, especially after Mumbai,' Iqbal replied, keeping his tone formal. The mention of Mumbai elicited satisfied smiles from the others. 'The Indians are really riled up and are coming down hard on anyone and anything they suspect.'

'Well, it's not much better here these days,' the man seated across from Iqbal said irritably. 'Those treacherous government and army bastards have decided they are going to fight America's war.'

'It's the same story everywhere,' Iqbal muttered. Hoping to ward off further conversation, he leaned back and closed his eyes.

The van became quiet again. Soon the others dozed off as well. Two of the men were squashed into the front seat beside Yasin and the other three were huddled together in the rear with Iqbal and all the rucksacks. It was a tight fit. Each time the van hit a pothole – and there were plenty of them – the knees of the men in the back knocked together. The journey had barely begun and already the stale smell of unwashed bodies and dirty clothes was settling down upon them like a stifling cloak. Dust and the bone-chilling January cold poured in through the open windows, adding to the discomfort.

∽

It was the sudden lack of motion that jolted Iqbal awake. Yasin had pulled up off the narrow road. He was craning his neck to look at something down the road, as were the two other men in the front seat. Iqbal stooped to get a clearer look himself.

In the distance, through the dirty windscreen and the dust slowly settling around them, Iqbal could see two army jeeps parked on either side of the road. Soldiers milled around, stopping every vehicle and searching it. Right now their attention was focused on the state transport bus they had halted.

'We have to turn back, Yasin bhai,' the man seated beside Yasin said. 'There is no way we can take a chance with them.'

'Does anyone know of any other way to get to Mianwali?' Yasin asked.

'Not from here,' replied the man next to Iqbal, 'but if we turn back towards Hadali, I can take us through Chinji to Talaganj.'

'There will definitely be a security checkpoint on that road too,' Yasin countered.

'Yes, but I know that area well. We can stay off the road and go on the kuchcha track through the fields,' the man said with the confidence of someone talking about his home turf.

'Will we be able to drive on it?' Yasin asked, tapping the steering wheel.

'Well, it will not be very comfortable but we should be able to get past.'

And get past they did. The drive was bumpy; in fact, at some places the track winding through the muddled fields was so narrow that they barely managed to squeeze through. But eventually they made it, without encountering a single man in uniform.

∽

There was something familiar about the building the van pulled up outside after twelve gruelling hours on the dirt track. As Iqbal dusted his clothes like all the others and stamped his feet to get his blood circulating again, it occurred to him that this was the same place they had halted at when they had driven down from Karachi to the training camp at Muzaffarabad after the Lashkar had recruited him in Delhi and sent him to Pakistan for training.

The Talaganj madrassa, Iqbal recalled. A glance at the dusty signboard confirmed it. *Nothing seems to have changed. The jihadi mill continues to operate just as it did then.*

Iqbal followed the others inside. There were two men in the front room, which seemed to be some kind of office. One of them recognized Yasin and greeted him with a bear hug. He showed the men to a dormitory and allowed them to freshen up before cornering Yasin again.

'It is not going well, bhai,' one of the men said when Yasin had told them about the roadblock they had encountered. 'From now on you will meet police patrols all the way. The slightest doubt and they will take you in. I suppose they are aware that our men are moving to Swat from all over. They must be trying their best to ensure reinforcements do not get in before they start their operation. Two of the last three batches that left from here have been apprehended.'

'So what do you suggest we do?' Yasin asked. 'We need to get to Swat, no matter what it takes.'

'That is true, but you will have to stay off the main roads. Perhaps the best thing would be to get you to one of the camps and then...'

'What camps?' Yasin interrupted.

'The refugee camps, miyan,' the other man replied. 'They are now all over the place and each one is bursting to the seams with people who have fled from the Swat Valley.'

'How will that help us?'

'It will. Several of the camps are being run by the Jamaat-ud-Dawa.'

'I thought the Jamaat had been banned.'

'It has, but that is no big deal,' the man snickered. 'Only the name had to be changed. Now we call it the Falah-e-Insaniat Foundation and everything is back to business as usual. In fact, now we are even working with the United Nations to provide relief to the refugees from Swat. It gives us easy access to the area and it's also a good opportunity to recruit more people. Many of them are really angry with the government for allowing them to be driven out of their homes.'

They all laughed. Watching them from across the room, Iqbal felt a pulse of anger spike through him. *Nothing is sacrosanct for these bastards. It makes no difference to them that hundreds of thousands of people are being rendered homeless.*

'So, from the camp you guys will be taken across in our aid vehicles most of the way and you can do the rest on foot,' the man resumed. 'Once you get to Buner you will be safe. Don't worry,' he reassured Yasin as he saw the doubtful expression on his face.

'I hope so. We have not come all this way to rot in some prison cell.'

'Don't worry, miyan, you won't.'

'Inshallah!' Yasin turned towards Iqbal. 'What about you? Do you want to come with us or will you find your own way from here?'

'Where is he going?' the man asked before Iqbal could answer.

'He needs to get to Waziristan and report back to his group.'

'In that case, he can go with us up to Kohat or Peshawar and head to Waziristan from there.'

'That is what I'll do then,' Iqbal agreed at once,

anxious to get them off the topic before they could ask any more questions. That settled the matter and the conversation turned to other things.

∾

After another day of bumpily inching along pot-holed dirt tracks, the group finally reached the first refugee camp a few miles before Kohat. When Yasin brought the van to a halt, a wave of relief ran through Iqbal and his five travel companions. They quickly got out, aching to stretch their stiff, frozen limbs.

Then Iqbal's eyes took in the sight in front of him and he felt as though someone had punched him in the stomach.

As far as he could see, a massive sea of plastic lay like a ghastly shroud over the huge camp. No attempt had been made to put a boundary wall or fence around it, as though the organizers knew they would soon need space for more tents. Swarming with people, this place was beyond anything Iqbal could have imagined in his wildest dreams. The stench of excreta from the open latrines that had been dug on one side of the camp was a mark of the inhuman conditions that prevailed. The cries of unfed children could be heard among the mass of men and women, most of whom looked thoroughly beaten and defeated. Desperation, disease and death loomed over the camp like an insidious pall. Iqbal did not know it then, but over the coming months, just as it had happened in Afghanistan, over 3 million people would be displaced by the Pakistan Army action and end up in camps like this.

Yasin and his group were led by their guide through the unending rows of tents towards the centre of the camp. They had gone about a hundred metres when they came across a man addressing several youngsters gathered around him.

'Have you ever asked yourselves why you are living like animals in these camps?' The man's voice rose angrily as he spoke. 'Because these corrupt politicians and army generals have been paid off by the fucking Americans, that's why! Why else do you think they are ready to take up arms against their own countrymen? Against the men who have given up everything for the sake of the jihad, for the glory of Islam. Now the army dogs are calling these brave lionhearts terrorists and are ready to kill them just because the gora bastards want them to do it.'

'What do you want us to do?' Iqbal heard someone ask.

'What else is there to do?' the speaker retorted. 'Join us and fight these traitors. Do you see anyone but us helping you people? Who is giving you food, shelter, medicine and clothing? Who is getting doctors here to treat you? Who is supporting you when everyone else is stabbing you in the back? But remember, we can do all this only if you stand by us...'

His vehement voice faded away as Iqbal followed the others deeper into the desolate camp, his mind in turmoil. Much as he wanted to, he knew it would be suicidal to go back and tell those people the truth, to warn them of the senseless death and destruction that lay ahead on the path they were being conned into. Instead, Iqbal closed his mind and focused on the task ahead. He knew that these low-level leaders did not matter in the long run. It was men like the Ameer who had to be taken down if the war against terror was to be won; they were the ones who posed a real threat to peace. Only when the ones at the top were cut down would the body begin to atrophy.

Iqbal returned to reality with a jolt as the man in front suddenly stopped walking. They were in front of another plastic-sheeted tent. It was much the same as the others except that an unarmed man stood guard at its entrance, though not so obviously as to draw attention.

'This is where you will be staying,' the guide told Yasin. 'Rest today. Tomorrow we will get you out with the relief convoy that leaves for Buner.'

'What about weapons?' Yasin asked softly.

'No weapons, miyan. Sometimes the army searches the convoys. But don't worry, you will find enough at Buner. We have adequate stocks there.' He turned to leave and then stopped. 'I suggest you don't mingle with anyone here. The fewer people who know about you, the better. These days, you never know who is an informer.' With this warning, the guide left.

Yasin went inside and the others followed him in, one by one. Iqbal was acutely aware of the pistol tucked into his belt. He would be in trouble if the others spotted it, but he did not want to give it up yet. There was no knowing when he would be able to get his hands on another weapon.

The tent was as pathetic inside as it was from the outside. The plastic covering ensured it was stifling despite the cold. It promised to be a long, uncomfortable night. The constant wailing of sick, hungry children and the high-pitched grumbling of men and women continued unabated. It was as though the camp never slept.

Where is the Pakistan government? Why isn't it doing something to help these people? Does it not understand how many of them will soon find themselves with guns in their hands and the killing heat in their hearts? Where is all the aid from America going? Iqbal's head reeled with questions. *Does no one here realize that Pakistan is facing the consequences of breeding and fostering terrorists all these years?*

Iqbal found himself feeling almost triumphant that the Pakistanis were finally suffering what they had inflicted on the world for over three decades. He knew the feeling was not right, but each time that guilt nagged at him, he heard the voice of the

Lashkar handlers talking to the ten men who had attacked Mumbai the previous year.

'Line them up against the wall, brother, and shoot them in the back of their heads... don't worry, brother, jannat is waiting for you... Inshallah.' The echoes of the conversations between the two terrorists who had seized the Jewish-owned Nariman House in Mumbai and their LeT handlers in Pakistan, which had been recorded by various intelligence agencies and played on television channels all over the world, reverberated in Iqbal's head.

The suffering around them seemed to have no effect on the others. This was evident from the snores that resonated through the tent. Somehow, Iqbal was not surprised.

After all, how much compassion can a man retain once he has learnt to kill so easily and thoughtlessly?

≫

Iqbal was glad to finally be on board the convoy that left the camp early the next day. The group was split in ones and twos in the five-truck convoy. Loaded with an assortment of clothing, blankets and food items, the old decrepit trucks thunderously belched smoke into the cold morning air as they headed north.

An hour later, when they halted after crossing Kohat, Iqbal hopped off and bid farewell to Yasin. As he was talking to him, two jeeps roared down the road and stopped next to the truck. A man waved at Yasin from the first jeep.

Yasin swung out of the truck and went up to him. They greeted each other warmly. 'I cannot tell you how happy I am to see you, Shahbaz. I was going crazy with all this.'

'So you finally got here,' Shahbaz said. 'Good. We need every man we can get. Come on, get your men out and hop in. We are not going through Peshawar; too many checkpoints on that route.'

Yasin hollered to the others to leave the relief convoy.

They were moving their bags to the jeeps when Shahbaz noticed Iqbal standing to one side. 'Are you with Yasin? Why aren't you coming with us?'

Before Iqbal could reply, Yasin murmured something to Shahbaz, who raised his eyebrows and then gestured to Iqbal to come forward.

'Is it true what Yasin bhai is saying?'

'I don't know what he said to you.'

'Have you just returned from a mission for the Ameer?' Shahbaz asked in a low voice. Iqbal nodded. 'You are going back to him now?' Another nod from Iqbal. 'Well, his messenger was here a few hours ago. Had you reached here just a little while earlier, you could have gone back with him.'

'Really?' Iqbal controlled the flush of excitement that ran through him. *This is just the lead I need. Allah is certainly on my side.* 'Where is the messenger now?'

'He left for Jalakhel about three hours ago. If you hurry, you might catch up with him.'

'Is that where the Ameer is?'

'I have no idea where the Ameer is.' Shahbaz shrugged. 'That is where the messenger came from and I know that is where he is going only because he mentioned it.'

'Right. I'll try and catch up with him then.' Iqbal shouldered his rucksack and began to stride away.

'Cut across that way and hit the road,' Shahbaz called out. 'You will get there faster.'

Iqbal turned to see him pointing to the right and changed direction. 'Shukriya. Khuda hafiz,' he said with a wave.

'Allah hafiz,' Shahbaz emphasized, reminding Iqbal to make sure he got the greeting right from now on. Such slip-ups could be fatal in the long run.

Behind him Iqbal heard the engines rev up as the men drove off in their jeeps. He picked up his pace.

As he walked, he began to thread together the information that Captain Manoj Khare had given him about FATA, during the final intelligence briefing at the Force 22 base in Kasauli.

∞

In addition to the four provinces of Pakistan, located along the Afghan-Pak border are the Federally Administered Tribal Areas, spread over nearly 27,000 square kilometres of some of the most brutal and rugged terrain in the world, with Afghanistan lying to the north-west, NWFP to the east and Baluchistan to the south.

A creation of the illogically drawn Durand Line, which split the Pashtun people in two different countries, the FATA comprises seven tribal agencies, namely, Khyber, Khurram, Bajaur, Mohmand, Orakzai, North and South Waziristan besides the six frontier regions of Peshawar, Kohat, Tank, Bannu, Lakki and Dera Ismail Khan.

FATA's location, terrain and largely Pashtun population with strong links in Afghanistan are mainly responsible for the Islamization of this region. By virtue of its location along the Af-Pak border, during the years of Russian occupation of Afghanistan it was the ideal launchpad for operations against the Soviet troops, thereby becoming a hub for intense mujahideen activity.

The rapid induction of Saudi petro-dollars and the compelling Wahhabi need to wrest control over the hearts and minds of the people saw the emergence of hundreds of madrassas and mujahideen training camps all over the FATA.

In cahoots with the CIA, the ISI pumped in thousands of young, illiterate Muslim youth from all corners of the world into these seminaries. All of them eventually emerged as singularly focused, rabidly fundamentalist killing machines who followed whatever convoluted brand of Islam was fed to them by the right-wing, subversive, mostly self-appointed mullahs who ran these madrassas.

The nature of the inhabitants of the FATA and their determination not to accept any governance except their own once led Lord Curzon to comment: 'No patchwork scheme will settle the Waziristan problem. Not until the military steamroller has passed over the country from end to end will there be peace.'

Fortunately, Curzon never had to do so, but it was now clear that if America wanted to solve the Afghanistan problem, the steamroller would have to enter the FATA, especially the severely rugged Waziristan area, and eliminate all traces of Al-Qaeda and the Taliban from there.

Looking at the prevalent situation, it would have been impossible to tell that this very same region had once been a bastion of Gandhian non-violence. It was in the Pashtun area of Pakistan (Pashtunkhwa) that, in the first half of the twentieth century, Abdul Ghaffar Khan, the Frontier Gandhi, raised a non-violent army of 1,00,000 volunteers known as the Khudai Khidmatgars. These volunteers played a vital role in freeing the Indian subcontinent from British rule.

To counter the KK, the British played the religious card, not allowing political parties a free hand while simultaneously giving carte blanche to the religious groups. This process was continued by the Pakistan government and led to the emergence and strengthening of mullahs who had been, at best, marginal political players in Pashtun society until then. The lack of political activity, the continual weakening of the tribal power structure by the state, and their replacement with clerical fiat allowed the transformation of the FATA into Taliban Central.

For several years, the no man's land of the FATA remained a key area for the high stakes double game played by Pakistan. While General Musharraf allegedly cooperated with the US-led war on terror, he gave free reign to the terrorists in this area.

～

On the day Iqbal set out towards the FATA he had only a vague idea of the turmoil prevalent there. As the Pakistan Army marshalled its forces to seize control of the Swat Valley, hundreds of fighters from different jihadi groups were flocking towards Swat to defend it. Simultaneously, several Taliban leaders were quietly slipping out and filtering into the much safer FATA.

This oft-threatened invasion by the Pakistan Army added to the tension already simmering in the region. Suspicion stalked the streets, breaking loose with deadly force at the slightest provocation. In all jihadi camps frantic preparations were underway to counter the army. Iqbal saw repeated evidence of this from his precarious perch on top of the lorry that had given him a ride. The cold wind made it a miserable ride, but the hope that he would be able to catch up with the Ameer's messenger kept him going.

Night was setting in by the time the driver dropped Iqbal off near Jalakhel. Iqbal had not caught up with the messenger yet. He swung his rucksack over his shoulder and walked into the gathering gloom, down the winding track the driver had indicated.

∾

Iqbal crested a slope and reached the periphery of Jalakhel. He was almost at the village when a strange whooshing sound erupted out of the darkness. He stopped at once. Although physically exhausted, his senses were alert and working overtime. His ears perked up as he tried to decipher the strange sound, which was increasing with startling speed. Then realization struck like a shockwave.

Iqbal turned and began to run for his life.

He had barely started moving when the first wave of Hellfire missiles from the unseen, unheard UAV circling overhead erupted out of the darkness like glowing pinpricks of light and vanished into the village.

For a fleeting moment, the fiery-tailed missiles simply melted into the darkened cluster of houses. Then a series of massive, blinding explosions ripped the village apart. A hurricane of debris, human and material, ballooned out. The second set of missiles struck seconds later, adding to the carnage.

Then the screams began.

A chunk of a wall of the hut nearest to Iqbal leapt into the air with an explosive snort, driving him into the ground. His hands instinctively fanned out to break the fall as he hit the ground hard. Dust and debris flew everywhere. It seeped into his lungs, making him cough. Throwing off the brick and mortar, his head ringing with the noise, Iqbal fought his way up. That was when he heard the dreaded whir of chopper blades cleaving through the still night air.

Special Forces! Bloody hell!

The rapidly escalating sound made it clear they

were closing in fast. Iqbal estimated that it would take a minute at the most for the choppers to reach, another minute or two for the shock troopers to hit the ground. And they would come in with their guns blazing.

These guys don't mess about. They are here to kill.

Iqbal wondered who they were after. He knew it had to be a really big fish and the intelligence had to be rock-solid, otherwise no commander would risk sending in a Spec Ops unit.

Iqbal knew he had to get out of the area if he wanted to stay alive. But he had barely taken a few steps when something rammed into him, once again knocking him down.

This time it was a huge man, partially undressed. He had come out from the now decimated hut in front of Iqbal. The entire left side of his body was covered with blood. The smell of charred flesh and burnt hair emanated from him.

Working on blind instinct, Iqbal regained his footing, threw his arm around the blood-soaked hulk's waist and began to guide him away from the village towards which a host of armed men were headed. He could hear the commotion as helicopters began to circle the target area.

Ideal for night-time low-level insertion and extraction of Special Force teams, the two American MH-47E choppers had 7.62 mm miniguns mounted on both the side doors. The M60D 7.62 mm machine gun on the rear cargo ramp of each chopper put down a lethal blanket of suppressive fire, ensuring the other two birds could offload the strike teams without interference from anyone on the ground.

Iqbal was unable see any of this from his position but, having witnessed Force 22 teams practise search-and-destroy missions several times, he could visualize how dangerous it was for anyone caught in the line of fire. He knew he had to get as far away from the doomed village as possible. He also knew he couldn't abandon the injured man because he would draw the troops into the area. He shuffled away as fast as he could, dragging the man along.

He managed to get about 50 metres away from Jalakhel as the continuous roar of covering fire from the choppers died away and the shocktroopers hit the ground. Almost at once, short, sharp bursts of small arms-fire erupted behind him.

Fuck! They have landed! He hurried towards the narrow ravine along which he had come up to the village. He had barely made it to the edge when he heard the sound of gunmen rampaging through the darkness, accompanied by the hiss of radio sets and the ammunition-conserving, two or three round bursts that Special Forces are trained to fire.

They couldn't be more than 50 feet away. Iqbal knew the time had come to go to ground; after all, movement is always a sure giveaway. Lowering the injured man against a rock, he drew the pistol from his waistband and cautiously raised himself up, trying to peer over the lip of the ravine at the village.

A man suddenly emerged in front of Iqbal, barely ten feet away. Even through the layer of camouflage paint, the expression on his face, in the sporadic light of the several fires that had seized Jalakhel by now, showed that he was equally surprised. The fact that the commando was Caucasian added to Iqbal's shock.

For a second, both men froze. Then training reasserted itself with blinding speed and the weapons in both hands exploded to life almost simultaneously.

Although a solid reliable weapon in most circumstances, Iqbal's 7.65 mm, Type 77 Chinese-make pistol was no match for the 5.56 mm calibre M-4A1 Special-Operations Peculiar-Modified carbine that the American SOF soldier wielded.

A shortened variant of the M-16A2 rifle, the light weight, gas-operated, air-cooled M-4A1 SOPMOD carbine with a collapsible stock was designed to provide the American SOF soldier with the capability to tailor the configuration of his weapon in accordance with the mission and operational environment. It was a formidable weapon with an array of accessories that increased operator survivability with enhanced weapon performance, target acquisition, signature suppression and fire control.

The Laser Aiming Module fitted on it imparted

an eerie Star Wars quality to the M-4A1. It was pointed directly at Iqbal. He could not see it, of course, but his mind could almost feel the tiny red dot thrown out by the LAM. It seemed to be burning a hole between his eyes. Iqbal aligned his weapon at the shock trooper racing towards him and fired.

In the time it took Iqbal to unleash his first bullet, the SOF operative had triggered off two short bursts. The only thing that saved Iqbal was the fact that he was still woozy from the onslaught of the debris. When he raised his pistol to fire, the sudden movement made his foot slip on the loose shale beneath. As he stumbled, Iqbal dropped below the mouth of the ravine and both bursts from the M-4 whined away metallically in the darkness above his head. The terrifying buzz and strong smell of cordite froze him into inaction.

Fortune, they say, favours the brave. Sometimes dumb luck also has a say. This was one of those moments.

When Iqbal lost his balance, his hand hit the edge of the ravine. The bullet that should have caught the commando somewhere in the safe confines of the Kevlar jacket protecting his body, instead took on a higher trajectory when Iqbal's pistol hit the ground and jerked the barrel up. It shot past the SOF operator's body armour and found its way just above his upper lip. The tiny piece of lead ploughed through his frontal faceplate and came to rest in his head. He died instantly, his body landing with a dust-billowing thud, inches from Iqbal's face. Iqbal was unable to tear his eyes away from the man's unflinching gaze.

It seemed like a very long time before Iqbal began to breathe again. He knew the others would come looking for the guy he had just shot. Forcing himself into action, Iqbal hauled up his injured comrade and began to move down the slope. They were almost at the base when Iqbal heard voices overhead. He pressed his companion and himself into the face of the mountain, ensuring they were invisible from above. Soon he heard the men moving away.

Iqbal knew the commandos would be in a tearing hurry to get out of there before a coherent ground response to the raid could develop. And rightly so, since the success and survival of Special Forces depended purely on speedy infiltration and a speedier getaway.

The gunfire, the hiss of radio transmissions and the sound of men moving around faded away. It was replaced with the rumble of chopper blades and a renewed roar of gunfire that covered the retreat of the helicopters till they were out of range of the small arms fire.

Finally, the noise died down. With shocking suddenness, barring sporadic screams of pain and grief, silence returned to the night.

Still feeling unsafe and shaken by his near encounter with death, Iqbal huddled against the rock face. He stirred only when he heard voices floating through the darkness. The Pashtun accent was hard to miss, making it clear that the search for survivors had begun.

'Here!' Iqbal called out. 'There are two of us here.'

'Come on up,' someone from the search party yelled back.

'I need help. This guy with me is badly hurt.'

'Hang on then. We are coming down.'

Iqbal heard several footsteps begin the descent down the ravine. Small stones and debris slithered down the slope like a continual advance guard. Iqbal found the sound strangely comforting. Five minutes later, a group of men encircled them, the yellow light of their torches dancing on Iqbal and the wounded man.

'Allah be praised,' one of them exclaimed excitedly. 'It is him!'

This triggered an immediate reaction from the others. The light increased as several more torches came alive and more men could be heard rushing down the ravine. Iqbal was wondering what the fuss was all about when his gaze fell on the long, angular scar on the cheek of the injured man. Recognition was instant.

The Ameer-ul-Momineem.

∞

Iqbal could not believe his luck. At the same time he cursed himself for not recognizing the Ameer earlier. *I could have easily left him to die, or even cut him down myself.*

'Who the hell are you?' The man questioning Iqbal seemed more puzzled than alarmed. 'I have not seen you before.'

'That is because I just got here.'

'From where? Who are you?'

'Oye! Enough of that for now,' another man interrupted. 'Let us get the Ameer up first. We need to take care of him, he is bleeding heavily.'

'You guys take him.' The interrogator was persistent. 'I am going to search this man. For all you know, he could be the one who directed those firangi bastards here.' The others nodded and rough hands began to search Iqbal.

'Then why would I have dragged him here to safety?' Iqbal retorted, knowing that offence was the best possible defence right now. But he did not fight the search, knowing they would find nothing suspicious on him.

'He is clean.' The searcher stood back and surveyed Iqbal.

'Come on, we don't have time,' one of the men called out. 'Get moving and bring him along.'

Keeping a close watch on Iqbal, the men followed the stretcher on which the Ameer was being carted.

They were soon moving away from the village.

'I thought the village is that way,' Iqbal pointed.

'It is,' the man next to him replied, 'but there is

no way we are going back there now. They might send in more of their bloody missiles. It is obvious that someone has squealed and those gora shaitans knew the Ameer was here. They must have known, otherwise there is no way in hell they would have sent their commandos into Pakistan. Drones and missiles, yes, but men – no way! The Americans have never done that before.' He jerked his head angrily. 'Someone has betrayed us. The bastard... wait till we find him.' An echo of curses sounded from the others.

There were three vans waiting when they finally reached level ground. The engines were already running and they sped away into the darkness as soon as the group was on board. Iqbal was pushed into the rear of the last vehicle.

The headlights were off but even in the faint light of the running lamps, the drivers navigated the narrow mountain terrain with practised ease. To avoid further questioning, Iqbal hunched forward and pretended to doze off. He need not have worried; every man in the vehicle was only talking about the Ameer's injuries and whether he would survive. For a moment the traitor, whoever he was, seemed to have faded from their minds. Of course, the man who had saved the Ameer featured in the conversation more frequently than Iqbal would have liked, both during the drive and later at the village where they halted. Everyone came to gawk at him, some came to talk to him. In no time at all,

they had even given him a name. 'Al Hindustani!'
The Indian.

∾

'Indian! The Ameer wants you. Now!' The battle-
scarred mujahideen was dressed in the trademark
black attire that the Ameer's close-proximity
protection detail wore. In the four days that he had
been here, Iqbal had seen them hovering around the
hut in which the Ameer was recovering. Hauling
himself up, he wordlessly followed the messenger
through the village.

Huddled deep in the South Waziristan tribal area,
the Zangari village lay encircled by a ring of rugged
mountains. At the moment, it was buzzing with
intense activity and a large number of the people
seemed to be foreigners. Iqbal was not sure who they
were, but from their dialects and accents it was clear
they were neither Pakistani nor Afghan. Iqbal primed
himself for his meeting with the Ameer. He was not
sure why, but he knew his life depended on it.

The room he entered was done up far more
lavishly than anything Iqbal had seen since he had
entered Pakistan. In fact, by the standards of jihadi
life, it was opulent.

On the large bed at the far end of the room,
propped up against a pile of pillows, looking much
better though still obviously weak, was the man who
had faced down the American and Pakistani security
forces for so many months, the man who was firmly

riding the crest of the wave that threatened to seize control of Pakistan. Standing behind him was a vaguely familiar, heavily-bearded man wearing horn-rimmed glasses.

Isn't he the one who tended to me in Faisalabad... Iqbal wondered. It was hard to be certain since he had been largely unconscious during the two or three days this man had stayed at the Faisalabad compound.

'So, you are the one who saved me.' The Ameer's voice brought Iqbal back to the present. Despite being severely injured, he sounded authoritative.

'Salaam waleikum, janab.' Iqbal bowed his head. 'Allah sent me in time to return the favour you did me once.'

'What favour?'

'You saved my life.' Iqbal recounted the incident of the shoot-out near the Indo-Pak border and how the Ameer's convoy had picked up Tanaz and himself. His two-man audience heard him out, their unblinking stares acutely disconcerting. As Iqbal proceeded with his story, he could see the gleam of recollection in the eyes of the man who stood behind the Ameer.

'And who are you?' the Ameer asked.

'My name is Iqbal. I am from India and I have come to meet you.'

'Why?'

'To serve with you, Ameer.'

'Why me? Why not with your own group?'

'My group has been destroyed and I have nowhere to go. In India I am a wanted man. In fact, that is why our leader told me about you just before he died.'

'This leader of yours, who was he?'

'We called him Mujib but I do not know if that was his real name.'

'Describe him.'

Iqbal did. The hateful image of the man who had been responsible for the death of Tanaz was so firmly engraved in his head that the picture he painted was vivid. As he spoke, he could see the light of recognition on their faces; it was obvious they knew Mujib well.

Finally the Ameer asked, 'How did Mujib die?'

'We had been carrying out bomb blasts in several Indian cities as per Mujib's plan, but then things started to go wrong.' Iqbal paused. 'Perhaps there was a traitor amongst us, perhaps we got unlucky... I am not sure, but we lost several people in a shoot-out with the police in Delhi last month and the very next day, the rest of us were pinned down by the police in Pune.'

Iqbal narrated the story that Ankita and he had decided on, about the final showdown in Pune in which the police had killed Mujib, Asif and Tanaz, while Iqbal had managed to flee under cover of darkness. The account was carefully hinged on real events and plausible facts to ensure it stood up to sustained questioning, if it came to that.

'So now you are the only one from the group who is alive?' the Ameer asked.

'No, two of the others, Imtiaz and Khalid, are also alive. They were captured by the Delhi police during our last strike.' Iqbal pretended to hesitate. 'At least, that's what we saw on television, but Mujib was not sure if they were captured by the police or if one of them was the informer who gave us away.'

'And then you crossed over and came looking for me?'

Iqbal nodded, aware that he was treading dangerous waters. The Ameer's scepticism was obvious.

'You seem to be very lucky. How did you get across the border so easily?'

'I used the same route we took while going to India.'

'Which is?'

Iqbal described his journey. There was a long silence when he finished.

'That is an incredible story,' the Ameer said finally. 'Rather too good to be true.'

'It is true, Ameer. Why else would I be here?'

'Why else indeed?' he said quietly, his eyes bore into Iqbal's. A few minutes passed before he spoke again. 'And you reached just when the gora bastards did? Is it not strange the way death follows you around, especially the deaths of our brothers, of the faithful?'

Iqbal did not say anything. He simply shrugged as

he forced himself to meet the Ameer's eyes without flinching.

'So who are you really? Deep down… here.' The Ameer tapped his chest. 'Friend or foe, a victim of circumstances or a traitor to the cause?'

'I am Allah's soldier, Ameer, a loyal soldier.'

'Really? The first time I met you there were a handful of dead Pakistani soldiers all around you.' The Ameer narrowed his eyes. 'Now you tell me that your entire group has either been killed or captured by the Indian police. And on the very day that you arrived here, the kafir missiles paid a visit. Even more surprisingly, the Americans sent in their commandos – something they have never done before and would only do if they had confirmed intelligence about someone they are really desperate to get their hands on.' He raised his eyebrows. 'How did they know I was in Jalakhel?'

'Ameer, I do not know the answer to that. Even I did not know you were there. If I had any intention other than to serve with you, why would I have rescued you?'

The Ameer's stance did not soften. 'Do you know what we do with traitors around here? We do not allow them to die till they have suffered more pain than you can even begin to imagine. And then, just before they die, we cut off their balls and stuff them down their throat.'

'I know who I am, Ameer.' Iqbal realized his enemy was bordering on a decision, one that would mean life or an excruciatingly painful death for him. He could feel the blood pounding along his temple. Under his clothes a thick layer of sweat stuck like oil over his body. But he retained his cool, ignored the final question and the implicit threat, and pleaded, 'Just give me a chance to prove myself.'

'That I will. I certainly will, though I do not believe in coincidences. But you did save my life and maybe you are not lying.' He gave a sly smile. 'Let Allah be your judge.'

'Thank you, Ameer.' Iqbal forced himself to show the required reverence, concealing his relief. 'He will not find me lacking.'

'So be it. Go now.' The Ameer turned towards the quiet man by his bedside. 'Hand him over to Karamat,' he said with a smile. 'That will give us enough opportunity to gauge his true worth – and his loyalty.'

There was something about his words and smile that made Iqbal uncomfortable. But he knew it was naïve to hope that he would be accepted so easily in these troubled times.

'Shukriya, Ameer. Allah hafiz.' Iqbal nodded his gratitude and walked away.

∽

There was a long silence when Iqbal left the room.

'What do you think?' the Ameer asked the Egyptian doctor standing behind him. 'Is he a traitor, or just the unlucky one who comes along when death is near?'

'I do not believe in coincidences either,' the doctor replied gruffly. 'He is a stranger and death rides too closely in his wake. Why take a chance?' He shrugged. 'Kill him.'

'But he did save my life so let's give him one chance. If he makes it out alive from Special Tasks then it is Allah's will that he lives.'

The doctor did not reply, but his silence conveyed his displeasure at the decision.

'How is the old man now?' the Ameer asked, turning to face him.

'Not so good.' The doctor hesitated. 'In fact, he is slipping away fast. We have tried everything but there has been too much internal damage. Maybe I could have done something if I had the facilities of a full-fledged hospital available to me. Right now, here...'

'I want to see him.'

'Now?'

'Now.'

The doctor carefully helped the Ameer to his feet and began to walk him outside. Halting at the door, the Ameer shrugged off the doctor's support, straightened his back and stepped out, unaided. He was enough of a leader to know that in this part of the world any sign of weakness was unacceptable. Weakness was a clear invitation for the enemy to close in for the kill, and Allah knew that a man like the Ameer had enough enemies. He commanded his body to ignore the pain and followed the doctor to the hut across the alley.

Moans of pain greeted him at the door. The smell of spirit and blood assaulted his senses as soon as he entered. There were two men hovering around the frail old mullah lying on the bed. More than half of Hamidi's upper body was drenched in blood. He seemed to be just about holding onto life. Miraculously, his face had been left untouched by the American missiles.

At a glance from the Ameer, everyone left the room except the doctor, who maintained a careful vigil at the door.

'How is it going, old man?' There was affection in the Ameer's voice as he settled down on the bed beside Hamidi and took one of his hands in both his own.

'Not so good.' Hamidi's whisper was almost drowned out by his wheezing.

The Ameer had to lean forward to hear him. 'We will soon have you up and about,' he said, trying to sound encouraging.

'No, you will not.' The mullah gave a weak smile. Another bout of coughing seized him. Flecks of blood spotted his lips and beard. Picking up a wad of cotton from the bedside table, the Ameer gently wiped his mouth clean. It was an uncharacteristically gentle gesture for the cruel warlord.

Hamidi acknowledged it with a grateful smile.

'But there are no regrets, my son. We have had a long and eventful journey, haven't we?'

'Yes, we have and, by the grace of Allah, it has been a glorious one.'

'Do you remember how it all began?'

'Of course I do. Can I ever forget?'

'Don't ever let go of the past. Remember that we are what we are because of what lies behind us.' Another bout of coughing interrupted Hamidi. Then he drew a deep breath and added, 'You will remember what Allah wants from you? You will not stray from the path, will you, Jalal?'

'Of course not.' The Ameer's fingers pressed down reassuringly on Hamidi's fragile hand.

'Promise me.'

'I promise.'

'Good. Do not let these treacherous army bastards get away with this betrayal. Remember that Pakistan was established so that the Sharia and the rule of Allah the Magnificent could be implemented.'

The Ameer's face shone with anger. 'If they think they can play with us they are mistaken. Don't worry, I am going to make the traitors pay.'

'You must, but be very careful. Remember, there is much at stake. Everything we have worked for is now almost within our grasp.' Hamidi wanted to say more but he was tiring fast. He started coughing again. More drops of blood sprayed out from his mouth this time, the internal hemorrhaging had intensified. His hand, clasped between the Ameer's, betrayed the pain that wracked through his body.

'Can I ask you a favour?' the mullah murmured. 'One final favour for an old friend?'

'Of course,' he replied sadly.

Hamidi smiled. 'You know me well, my son.'

'How could I not? You have been like a father to me, the only father I have ever known.' There was great affection in the look they exchanged. 'Are you sure?'

'Yes, I am sure.' Hamidi's voice was laced with pain. 'There is no point in delaying the inevitable and prolonging the agony, my son. Let me go now.'

The Ameer looked at the doctor, desperately seeking some hope, but saw none. He turned back to the mullah and nodded reluctantly. There was gratitude in the smile he got in return. He leaned forward and gently raised the old man in his arms and held him close. 'Sleep well. I shall miss your guidance and support, especially now, when the end is almost within reach.' His grip on Hamidi tightened briefly before he freed his right hand, reached for the pistol stuck in his waistband, and placed it against the dying man's heart.

Mullah Ismail Hamidi looked into his former student Jalaluddin's eyes, meeting death as he had lived his life: head-on, without flinching.

The doctor manning the door winced as the pistol shot reverberated through the room.

Hamidi's body jerked and then went limp in the Ameer's arms. Tiny pungent wisps of cordite floated up in the air, momentarily overpowering the smell of blood. They slowly dissipated and the bloody aura of death returned.

The man who had pulled the trigger did not seem to notice any of this. He was watching his teacher's sightless eyes with his own unseeing ones.

He lowered the body back onto the bed. He gently closed the eyes and with the bedsheet he covered the hole the bullet had made in Hamidi's chest.

Finally, the Ameer got up and headed for the door. His pace strengthened with every passing step and the pain in his eyes receded. By the time he left the hut, there was no trace of emotion on his face.

Only when he reached his room did the Ameer allow himself to slump down on the bed and let his feelings surface. That night, long after the silence of uneasy sleep had settled over the village, the Ameer lay awake, his gaze fixed on the darkness outside the window. His mind went back to the bloody, treacherous road the mullah and he had travelled together. It was a road he did not like to walk on, but that night he journeyed down it again.

Born because of the karma of their past mistakes, they make more mistakes and fall into more mistakes.

Sri Guru Granth Sahib

The Manba Ulom madrassa lay on the outskirts of Danda Darpa Khel, not far from Miramshah in North Waziristan. About 3 kilometres to the east of the madrassa was a nondescript cluster of mud-walled huts.

A little Pashtun boy named Jalaluddin played in the dusty open area behind his house. Although still a month away from his eighth birthday, the boy was taller than most of the ten-year-olds in his village. Other than that, he was just like the other boys.

Like most men in the village, Jalaluddin's father, Rehman Haq, made ends meet through a combination of agriculture and the drug trade.

Straightforward, fun-loving, god-fearing but not rabidly so, these people lived by the Pashtun code of conduct. At the end of the day, life was simple if not easy, satisfying if not gratifying and, above all, free from external interference of any kind, which was the one thing the proud, fiercely independent Pashtun could not tolerate.

'Jalal! Jalal!' The boy looked up when he heard his mother's excited call. He left his playmates and ran inside the house. 'Your father says we are going to meet the rest of the family.'

This did not make much sense to Jalal; as far as he was concerned, the family comprised his parents, infant brother and himself. Seeing the bewilderment on his face, his mother explained, 'Your father has an older brother who lives near Lashkar Gah in Afghanistan. He was just telling me that both your birthdays, which are just a week apart, will be a good time for all of us to meet.'

'Is it far?' Jalal asked.

'I am sure it is.' Like Jalal, his mother had not travelled a lot, though she had been to Miramshah several times.

That got Jalal excited. The more they talked about it, the more thrilling it all sounded. By the time he sprinted out to share the news with his friends, he was swelling with pride. He did not know many boys who had gone further than a few villages away. It had never even occurred to him that there was a world beyond the periphery of the village.

∽

Several hundred miles away, in Moscow, a handful of men were getting together to discuss an issue that had been troubling the corridors of power in several countries for several centuries.

The late afternoon sun bathed the car park outside the Kremlin conference hall where the meeting was scheduled to take place.

The hall was one of several rooms where members of the Politburo of the Soviet Communist Party's central committee met. However, an official meeting of the Politburo hadn't been scheduled that day. Instead, converging in the conference hall was a smaller group of men, oligarchs who held the real power in Soviet Russia. They were the ones who ran the state, making secret decisions and arriving at resolutions by consensus, avoiding any individual responsibility.

Mikhail Suslov, the chief party ideologue, was the first to arrive. Right after him was the Russian defence minister Dmitri Feodorovich Ustinov. The remaining three, general secretary Leonoid Brezhnev, KGB chairman Yuri Andropov and foreign minister Andrei Gromyko, arrived a few minutes later. Their cars swept into the heavily guarded car park in a tight cavalcade. A host of aides rushed forward to relieve the cars of their occupants.

Supported by his assistants, Brezhnev, a bloated, bushy-browed bear of a man, was flanked by Andropov and Gromyko when he entered the conference room. The meeting was immediately called to order. The quorum was complete, though it is said that the Russian prime minister Alexei Kosygin arrived a few minutes later and was present when the momentous decision was taken. This, however, was never confirmed. The decision certainly was.

It was 12 December 1979. And the burning issue for these five (or six) gentlemen was Afghanistan.

While many guesses have been hazarded and many theories put forward, there are no existing records of that meeting and the decisions taken. The only publicly available record of the meeting is a cryptic handwritten note by Konstantin Ustinovich Chernenko (who would go on to become the general secretary of the Communist Party of the Soviet Union). The note says nothing about military action. In fact, it highlights nothing except that Andropov, Ustinov and Gromyko were authorized to undertake certain measures to address the situation in 'A', which was how they referred to Afghanistan. The note was signed by Brezhnev and seconded by members of the Politburo.

The stance each man took is now largely a matter for conjecture. Suslov and Ustinov probably favoured military intervention. It is likely that Andropov was initially against military action but was convinced by his hawkish deputy, Vladimir Kryuchkov, to support it. Gromyko apparently tilted towards it once Taraki, Afghanistan's first communist president, was assassinated.

It is also possible that Brezhnev's emotional attachment to Taraki was an important consideration that led these men to order the elimination of Amin and his replacement by the far more malleable Babrak Karmal.

Afghanistan's proximity to the Soviet Central Asian Muslim population and the Russian fear of US intervention, maybe even invasion of Afghanistan, were compelling reasons for what happened next. Compounding their fear was the fact that Ayatollah Khomeini had recently toppled the Shah of Iran and established the wilayat al-faqih (by which a Muslim cleric becomes the supreme leader) and called for an Islamic revolution. The situation was made worse by the takeover of the Grand Mosque in Mecca, Islam's holiest site, by a group of Saudi and Egyptian extremists who claimed that the Mahdi, the Guided One, had come to restore righteousness and redeem the world by forming a just Islamic society. All these factors came together to force a decision that would soon impact the security of many nations.

∾

Jalaluddin's family were preparing for their journey to Afghanistan when the tragic sequence of events, initiated by that momentous meeting in Moscow, was set in motion.

On 13 December 1979 Hafizullah Amin, the fourth president of Afghanistan during the period of the Communist Democratic Republic of Afghanistan, was served a poisoned Coke. The attempt to kill him failed when the Coca Cola bubbles blunted the effect of the poison. Much to Russian chagrin, Amin survived.

∾

Having made the run across the brutally rugged border areas several times as a mule for the drug trade, Rehman Haq was well aware of the dangers involved, especially since this time he was crossing it with his wife and young children. The family traversed across the Durand Line, mostly during the dark, due to the illegal nature of the journey. They climbed up narrow mountain tracks, where a false step meant certain death. However, to Jalal this trek did not seem any different from the short family jaunts he had gone on with his parents.

Jalal, of course, had no way of knowing that this journey into Afghanistan to meet his relatives on the other side of the border had been rendered illegal by a gentleman named Sir Mortimer Durand who, over a hundred years ago, had been the foreign secretary of faraway India. For reasons best known to himself and other foreign office mandarins in the British Raj, Durand had drawn a line that split the Pashtun people into two different nations: Afghanistan and what is now Pakistan.

It may have created two different countries but the Durand Line did little to separate the Pashtun people or weaken their ties.

The Pashtun, an eastern Iranian ethno-linguistic group, is the world's largest patriarchal tribalized society, numbering about 45 million. It makes up approximately 42 per cent of the population in Afghanistan and 16 per cent in Pakistan.

Since 1893, when the line was drawn, the Pashtun regarded it with total disdain. Most were unaware of its existence. Those who were, crossed it without compunction as they went about their daily lives.

When Jalal's family started out from Waziristan, the little boy had no idea that the journey across the Durand Line would throw his life into a bloody upheaval from which he would never recover. Or that it was a journey he was destined to repeat many times during his life.

∽

Amin's survival did not sit well with the Soviet high command. Unwilling to concede to failure, it immediately came up with new ploys to deliver Amin to his grave. The result was Operation Storm-333, launched by the Russians on 27 December 1979.

For reasons that have been charred by the incinerator of history, this assassination attempt snowballed into a full-blown invasion of Afghanistan and two weeks later, the first Soviet troops arrived in Kabul.

Equally bewildering is the ease with which the

Russians forgot the lessons of history and the fates of the empires that ventured into Afghanistan.

∞

The fate of Afghanistan has been decided more by its position on the globe than by anything else. From time immemorial it has been a strategically important crossroad. Whether it was Cyrus the Great in sixth century BC or Alexander the Great who came along 300 years later, followed by the British, the Russians and the Americans, all were afflicted by the same insane urge to venture into the graveyard of empires.

The wave of invasions achieved little for the invaders themselves, but it began a culture of warfare between the disparate tribes and ethnic groups that inhabit Afghanistan: from the Uzbeks, Tajiks and Turkmen in the north to the Hazaras in central Afghanistan, the Nuristanis in the north-east and, the most powerful of the lot, the Pashtun majority in the south.

Historically, these groups have continually fought among themselves except when united by the common goal of expelling the latest intruder. Other than this strong resentment for invaders, the only thing Afghans have in common is Islam, with 80 per cent of them being Sunnis and the remainder (the Hazaras and the Ismailis) being Shias.

It was this constantly simmering, seething cauldron that the Russians stepped into.

∞

The midday sun was high in the sky, desperately seeking to dispel the winter chill, when Jalal and his family arrived at the tiny village of Saret Koleh in Afghanistan's Helmand province, from where they had sprung forth decades ago.

Located barely 20 kilometres from the Af-Pak border, trapped in a mire of mountains and the river Helmand, Saret Koleh is a scattered line of mud houses. Like most villages in this area, it plays a vital role in the drug trade. Not surprising, considering Helmand is the world's largest opium-producing region, accounting for 42 per cent of the global production.

Rehman's brother and other family members, who had gathered for the reunion, greeted the family with great joy. The aroma of sweetmeats and other delicacies wafted through the tiny house that buzzed with a host of relatives who had flocked in from all over.

∞

Not too far away, at the presidential palace, Amin and some of his key officials were attending a special luncheon held in honour of Ghulam Dastagir Panjsheri, a central committee member who had just returned from the Soviet Union.

Two Russian girls working as waitresses in the palace, possibly secret agents, mixed a light poison with the soup and *ashak* which they were serving.

Since Panjsheri was the only one who did not consume the poisoned food, his role in the matter is automatically suspect.

The luncheon was in progress when a number of Afghan leaders and army officers were arrested at a Soviet-hosted reception held at the Intercontinental Hotel in Kabul. They were being escorted out under guard when an explosion ripped through Kabul's general communications system. This marked the onset of the Russian invasion of Afghanistan. Approximately 5000 Soviet soldiers (four motor-rifle divisions, two airborne divisions, paratroopers, *Spetsnaz* special forces and the KGB secret police) who had been landing at Kabul International Airport over the past three days rolled out.

In a few hours, all strategic centres of Kabul were under Soviet control. The Soviets had taken every precaution to occupy the nerve centres of the city while the Afghans were still unaware that they were being invaded. Russian advisers on attachment to Afghan army units repeated simple tricks they had used during the 1968 invasion of Czechoslovakia; Afghan soldiers were told to turn in all live ammunition and substitute them with blank rounds for a 'training exercise', batteries were removed from army vehicles for winterization due to an alleged fuel shortage, diesel from the older tanks was siphoned off for the replacement armour scheduled to come in. Soviet advisers even persuaded key personnel of the Kabul air base to go on vacation and hand over their duties to the Soviet experts who had just arrived.

While it is said that he was poisoned and later shot, there is much controversy over how exactly President Hafizullah Amin died. Later, his bullet-riddled body was displayed to the half-jubilant, half-petrified leaders of the new Soviet client state of Afghanistan.

The dawn of 28 December 1979 saw Babrak Karmal firmly installed in the hot seat and Soviet forces in command of all key installations in the capital.

By end January 1980, there were 50,000 Soviet troops in Afghanistan, and their number increased to 80,000 by the end of the summer.

∽

Blissfully unaware of the escalating catastrophe, Jalal was playing with his newfound cousins with the enthusiasm of any eight year old. He was looking forward to wearing the new clothes that he had got for his birthday and savouring the delicacies that he knew would be served.

For the next two weeks Jalal's innocent life remained untouched. He felt the impact only when Russian armour rolled through and met with the still random and disorganized resistance that had begun to spring up in the Afghan countryside. The Afghans do not take kindly to intruders.

Jalal felt a thrill the first time he heard the dull, resonating boom of Russian armour in the fading sunlight. Fascinated by all things military, like most young boys, he was very excited with the metallic monsters trundling past the village.

It did not take long for his excitement to turn to fear as he realized that the Soviet tanks meant death to all that lay in their path.

≫∽

The third Russian T-62 tank had just passed by Saret Koleh and the fourth one was coming level with it when four men darted out of the darkness. Running in pairs, they attacked either side of the advancing armoured column. They were armed with Molotov cocktails.

First used by General Franco's Spanish Nationalists against the Spanish Republicans, the Molotov cocktail attained prominence when the Finns used it against the Russians during the Winter War in 1939. This simple weapon is basically a glass bottle filled with petrol fuels or wood alcohol and turpentine, ignited by an alcohol or paraffin soaked cloth. The Finns so named it to mock the Soviet Commissar for foreign affairs, Vyacheslav Molotov, who often claimed in radio broadcasts that the Soviet Union was delivering food to the starving Finns when in reality they were dropping bombs.

The weapon became exceedingly popular and was mass-produced by the Alko Corporation at its

Rajamäki distillery. Production totalled 450,000 bombs during the Winter War. The original design of the Molotov cocktail was a mixture of ethanol, tar and gasoline in a 750-millilitre bottle fitted with two long pyrotechnic storm matches.

The bombs used by the Afghans that evening were basically a petrol and diesel mix ignited by alcohol-soaked fuses. They proved more than adequate.

The newly inducted Russians, not yet subjected to the hammer blows of retaliation, were so complacent that all the tank commanders had their hatches open and were casually surveying the countryside, behaving more like tourists than soldiers in a combat zone.

Both pairs of attackers dropped their lethal Molotov cocktails into the open hatches of the tanks, then spun around and escaped.

The bottle bombs exploded even as the attackers leapt clear of the tank. Within minutes, flames consumed both tanks. As the screaming crew jumped out, a crackle of rifle fire greeted them. The rifles were ancient, bolt action ones, but the bullets they threw out were lethal, and the men wielding them were anything but novices.

By the time the Soviet patrol got its act together there was nothing to hit back at. The attackers had melted into the darkness. This was the pattern of most such attacks in the years of Russian occupation that followed. It took a while for the Russians to understand this and even longer for them to develop an adequate tactical response to combat it.

The reaction to this opening strike was as predictable as it was regrettable. The Russians were clear that the attack could not go unpunished. An example had to be set. So the Soviet column turned its wrath on the only identifiable thing around: the village they had just crossed.

∾

The staccato commands yelled out in Russian meant little to the villagers who stood gawking at the Russian foot patrol that entered Saret Koleh. A couple of tanks were on either side of the patrol, their guns sweeping across the area menacingly.

Some of the villagers were pulled out of the crowd and taken to the centre of the village. Jalal's father and uncle were among them.

The twelve men were lined up along the wall of one of the huts and an equal number of Russian soldiers formed up, facing them. The other villagers watched in disbelief as a sharp command was snapped out and the rifles in the hands of the soldiers came level. At a second command, the Russian rifles fired in ragged unison.

It was hard to tell what impacted the minds of the villagers first – the crash of gunfire or the sight of their men thrown backwards, hitting the wall behind with a thump and then slumping to the ground, leaving uneven blotches of red on the mud wall.

'Each Russian life will cost you two of your own,' the patrol leader shouted at the stunned villagers.

The first to react was Jalal's mother. Screaming, she ran towards her husband's body.

When the Russian infantryman saw a hysterical woman rushing towards the firing squad he acted on blind instinct – the way armed men respond when confronted with the uncertain or the threatening – he opened fire, emptying his magazine into her.

Jalal watched as the brute force of the bullets picked up his mother and smashed her against the wall of the same hut where his father had been shot.

Jalal did not cry. Not that day. Nor the next, when the last rites were performed. In fact, no one would see Jalal shed tears ever again.

He became very quiet. From that moment on he did not speak to anyone except when he was asked a direct question, to which he replied in monosyllables.

The only family he had left now was his aunt who, in one fleeting moment, had not just become a widow, but had also been left with five children to take care of. She was too devastated to notice the ominous quiet that had enveloped her young nephew.

∞

A few days later, Jalal's aunt did what she thought was the best thing to do: she took her three children,

Jalal and his brother, and fled for what she assumed was the safety of the Pakistan border. Since the invasion was still in its early stages, the flood of humanity that would eventually surge towards this nebulous sanctuary had not yet begun in earnest; yet with every passing day, the crowd heading there was gaining strength.

It was a brutal journey, especially for a lone woman travelling on foot in the bitter cold with five children.

She lost her youngest boy to the fever he picked up on the first night. The second child, another victim to the unforgiving Afghan winter, succumbed two days later. She herself barely made it to the border with the three surviving children.

∾

They were within touching reach of the border when the Soviet helicopter gunships found them.

The gunships would have left them alone had it not been for two men in the mass of people heading for the border. The only excuse for their foolishness was the fact that both had lost their entire families in the week gone by and were seething with rage. The gunships sweeping past provided a focal point for their anger. Futile though the act was, the men impulsively raised their rifles and opened fire. Their bullets clanged off the armoured underbelly of the gunships. But they certainly drew the attention of the crew. Both gunships swung around in a wide loop and aligned themselves with the crowd below as they swooped in.

The Mi24 helicopter (called *Krokodil* by the Russians) was the first version of the Hind gunships. It was armed only with a 12.7 mm machine-gun, AT-2 Swatter Anti-Tank Guided Missiles and simple rockets or bombs. Despite its relative inefficiency (compared to modern equipment), it was more than adequate to mete out quick death to the confused civilians below.

By the time the screaming crowd of refugees could take shelter, Jalal's aunt and his infant brother, whom she had been carrying in her arms, both lay dead.

∾

'Kismat.' The elderly, white-bearded Afghan shrugged as he came across Jalal and his cousin Hassan huddled in the bloody swarm of bodies, long after the choppers had departed and the survivors had started sifting through the dead for signs of life. 'Who can fight what has been written? I suppose this was Allah's will.'

His philosophical words fell on deaf ears. Already struck by the relentless blows fate had dealt them in the past two weeks, the assault by the gunships had delivered the final assault on their young, impressionable minds. By now both boys had lost all sense of reason. It is doubtful whether they would have survived if the old man had not taken them under his wing.

∽

It did not take long for the Good Samaritan to display his true colours. On the second night, he took Jalal and Hassan away from the other refugees. Driven to the very edge of reason by grief, hunger and fear, they lacked the strength or maturity to understand when the exploitation began. When the kind-looking man who had saved them took out his penis and asked them to take turns in rubbing it, they did. When he asked them to suck it, they did. When he made them turn around and sodomized them, it hurt beyond belief, but they silently complied.

Having satisfied the demons that possessed him, two weeks later their Samaritan finally dumped them at the gates of a refugee camp on the outskirts of Bajaur in Pakistan.

∽

The refugee camp – if one could call it that – was a massive, unruly cluster of tents that had sprung up in the middle of nowhere. The tents were grossly inadequate to keep out the bitter cold, and the food available was barely enough for a child to survive. Even so, as it became clear that the war was not going to end any time soon, the camp started to acquire a more permanent appearance. With the passage of time, it was engulfed by the endless deluge of people fleeing the destruction of Afghanistan.

It is estimated that by the time the dust finally settled, approximately 3 to 5 million Afghans had fled from the advancing Russian juggernaut. Although many fled to other countries, a large number ended up in refugee camps in Pakistan. Lost in this sea of people were Jalal and Hassan.

The two cousins would not have survived had it not been for the arrival of Abdullah Al Azzam, a key player in the Jordanian branch of the Muslim Brotherhood, who would soon acquire the dubious status of being the intellectual architect of the jihad against the Russians. With him came Mullah Ismail Hamidi and a host of like-minded zealots and self-proclaimed mullahs.

Hamidi picked Jalal and Hassan, along with numerous other orphans, and took them to the newly established madrassa a couple of miles away from the Bajaur refugee camp. As soon as they reached the madrassa they were given food. They gulped down every morsel. They were then lined up and asked to introduce themselves one by one.

'Just tell us your name, age and whatever else you want to about yourself,' Hamidi gently told the children.

'Jalaluddin,' said the young Pashtun boy when it was his turn. 'Jalaluddin Haq.' And then he went quiet. Unlike the other children, he spoke neither of his village nor his family. Jalal's mind was a clean slate.

∞

For most children in the madrassa, the memory of their parents had become hazy amid the successive shocks that life delivered to them. It did not take long for the firm but kindly Hamidi to assume a god-like position in their guileless heads. Soon, every thing he said was their gospel.

When he told them there was no god but the One God, they believed him. When he said they were suffering because the kafir wanted to decimate Islam, they did not question him. When he told them they must dedicate their lives to the defence of Islam, they did so unflinchingly.

A few years later, when he told them they should go across the Af-Pak border and fight the Russian infidel who was raping their country, they willingly took up arms and followed him.

And when he told them Allah would open the doors of jannat to them if they were to die in His cause, they believed him. And thus the ultimate jihadi killing machine was born.

∞

Perhaps, viewed in isolation, the Russian invasion of Afghanistan would not have been as cataclysmic an event as it eventually became. In the last 5,600 years of recorded history, approximately 14,600 wars have been fought, about three wars per year. Like so many others, this war too would have faded into time had it not been for the games that nations and governments play; thoughtless, vicious games in the name of diplomacy, economy, projection of power, influence, personal glory and, of course, religion.

It came as no surprise to anyone when America, eager to gift a Vietnam to its traditional enemy, decided to back the rebel movement that had erupted in Afghanistan against the Russians.

'Ladies and gentlemen,' said the CIA officer, briefing the officials and agents who had been assembled to handle the situation, 'we will fight the Russians to the last Afghan.' And that was precisely what they went on to do.

Thus began Operation Cyclone, the longest-running and one of the most expensive covert operations ever conducted by the CIA. Decreed under President Jimmy Carter's signature on 3 July 1979, the sole purpose of Op Cyclone was to arm and equip the Afghan mujahideen against the Russians.

Starting with a relatively paltry 20 to 30 million dollars in 1980, the sum eventually rose to 630 million dollars per annum by 1987. This money poured into Afghanistan in the form of automatic weapons, explosives, Stinger missiles, land mines and other death-dealing munitions that would eventually claim more Afghan lives than Russian.

Having no direct access into Afghanistan, the Americans turned to their traditional, if generally unreliable ally, Pakistan, to act as the conduit through which money, arms and ammunition could flow to the mujahideen.

The then Pakistani dictator General Muhammad Zia-ul-Haq accepted the offer with alacrity. He had recently executed Zulfikar Ali Bhutto, the legally elected Pakistani premier whom he had deposed after a bloody coup d'état, and launched a secret nuclear weapons programme, so he was desperate to get back into the good books of the Americans.

However, veteran schemer that he was, Zia rejected the 400 million dollars that Carter offered him in 1980. The gamble paid off because the very next year, Ronald Reagan, the newly elected American president, upped the amount to 3.2 billion dollars.

Zia, out to to take full advantage of the situation, accepted Reagan's offer only after the Americans confirmed that Pakistan would have complete control over the materials that went into Afghanistan and that American contact with the mujahideen would only be through the Pakistani ISI. This suited the Americans because it allowed them to deny any involvement with the sordid mess that Afghanistan was rapidly degenerating into.

Consequently, Pakistan had a free hand with the money that could be diverted either to the Swiss bank accounts of the generals in power or to the terror groups that had been set up to harass the Indians in Kashmir. They determined how much actually reached the mujahideen in Afghanistan. They were the ones who reinforced certain mujahideen groups and ignored the ones who did not toe the line.

Given the fundamentalist mindset of Zia and his ISI chief, General Akhtar Abdur Rehman Khan, Pakistan dominated the infamous Peshawar Seven, an umbrella organization that formed the core of mujahideen resistance to the Soviets. They ensured that four of the seven parties – the Khalis faction (set up by Khalis), Hezb-i-Islami (Hekmatyar), the Islamic Union for Liberation for Afghanistan (Sayyaf) and the Jamiat-i-Islami (Rabbani) – were hardcore political Islamists and outweighed the three traditionalist parties: National Islamic Front for Afghanistan (Gailani), Afghanistan National Liberation Front (Mojaddedi) and the Revolutionary Islamic Movement (Mohammadi). Not surprisingly, all but one of the Peshawar Seven – Rabbani's Jamiat-i-Islami – were Pashtun.

It was during these years that Zia established and consolidated the links between the terror groups, which had been declared strategic state assets by Pakistan, and the Islamic fundamentalists in the Pakistan government. Zia also completed the Islamization of the Pakistani armed forces and the ISI.

Soon, the lines between the ISI, the Pakistan Army and the mujahideen groups blurred and, from being a secular state, Pakistan turned into a country where the Islamists yielded tremendous power.

Perhaps they did not know that one day, not far in the future, this legacy would rear its ugly head and tear apart the fabric of Pakistan, or perhaps that had always been their plan.

∞

Not to be left out of the rat race, China, perpetually jockeying for power with Russia and India, also began to pump munitions into Afghanistan. So did Egypt and a host of other countries. To conceal this aid, most of the donor countries funnelled Soviet-origin arms – which were far cheaper than American weaponry – into Afghanistan.

However, none of this would have had a resonating effect on the future had it not been for the entry of Saudi Arabia on the scene. Looking to restore its image as the Defender of the Faith, which had been delivered a severe blow when Mecca was held hostage by a group of extremists, the Saudi regime was keen to strengthen its ties with the conservative Wahhabis.

Despite the fact that the Saudi agenda was deeply rooted in history and should have been known to one and all, the CIA displayed a remarkable level of shortsightedness and acquiesced to Saudi's nefarious plans.

In concord with the alliance struck between the House of Saud and the purist Muhammad Ibn Abd al Wahhab in the eighteenth century to eliminate all deviations from the practice of Islam, Saudi Arabia agreed to double the amount given by America. Afghanistan was a predominantly Muslim country with low literacy and high poverty levels – a perfect mix for the Saudis to spread the Wahhabi doctrine and unleash a jihad against the kafir, at almost negligible cost.

Madrassas mushroomed all along the Durand Line; it was not long before they outstripped the number of refugee camps. And all of them had a singular objective: to further the cause that had been espoused almost two hundred years ago by Muhammad Ibn Abd al Wahhab.

≈

The refugee camps that came up in Pakistan soon transformed into open breeding grounds for the mujahideen. Pakistan encouraged the Islamists to open offices in the camps and also set up their own refugee camps, making it mandatory for all refugees to become members of the party that ran the camp.

It did not take long for the camps to develop into full-fledged operational bases from which attacks on Afghanistan could be organized. In fact, Osama bin Laden, the man who would one day be held accountable for the 9/11 attacks on America, set up the first mujahideen training camp as early as 1986.

To add to the mayhem, a multitude of mujahideen recruits, mostly criminals and convicts, were sent in from Egypt, Jordan and Saudi Arabia. Then there were the Uzbeks, Tajiks and Kyrgyz, who were members of the Islamic Movement of Uzbekistan or Islamist members of the opposition during the Tajik civil war. Fighting shoulder to shoulder with them were regular and commando units of the Pakistan Army, ensuring that the Islamization and radicalization spread with equal fervour among the Pakistani armed forces.

It was in this violent, tumultuous cesspool that Jalal, Hassan and thousands of other ill-fated orphans grew up.

∾

Jalaluddin Haq was thrilled beyond words on the day Mullah Hamidi finally told the young men that they were now fully-trained mujahideen, ready to take up arms for Allah. Jalal did not show it, of course, as he seldom expressed his emotions, but deep down he felt something stir. He was unable to put his finger on it but he knew there was something festering inside him, yearning for release. The cold metal of the gun in his hand felt comforting and reassuring. It gave him a sense of power, of being complete, of knowing that he would never again be exploited and violated. That he would never again have to stand by and watch his loved ones die. That he could and *would* make a difference.

The hankering within grew when he fired at a human target for the first time. The sight of the Russian soldier falling to the ground, screaming with pain as a large bloody hole erupted where his stomach had been, gave him a rush of energy he had never before experienced. It made him feel alive. Like an addict craving his next fix, Jalaluddin began to seek it again. And again.

≈

The group of youngsters crossed the Af-Pak border with Hamidi. The mullah, being no warrior himself, handed them over to the man who met them at a designated rendezvous. This tall, bearded man who took charge of the young warriors was dressed in black, in the attire that would soon be known as the Taliban dress code.

Jalaluddin did not know it then, but this was the second person who would have a huge impact on the path his life would take. If Hamidi was the initiator, it was this man, Omar, who provided Jalaluddin with the focus and direction he needed.

When they first met, Omar was one of the senior commanders of Hisb-e-Islami (Khalis). The group had been started in 1979 when Younis Khan, one of the tribal leaders from Pakhtia province, opted out of the original Hisb-e-Islami to blaze his own trail.

Omar took Hamidi's brood of fledglings under his command. Fresh out of the training camp, the men were raring to go. They did not have to wait long.

≈

Cautious after seeing what happened to those who were not, the Russian patrol comprising several BTR-70 armoured personnel carriers (*Bronetransportyor* in Russian, literally 'armoured transporter') and a troop of T-62 tanks was sweeping past when the young mujahideen attacked.

They were full of zest, but they lost control and panicked when the 115 mm tank guns began to boom and the 14.5 mm machine guns on the BTRs hummed into action. Without realizing that the Russians were firing blindly, hoping to keep the attackers at bay by laying down sheets of suppressive fire all around, most of the mujahideen broke ranks and fled from the ambush site.

Jalaluddin, however, held firm. Pumped up by the sight of the Russian he had recently gunned down, Jalaluddin was by Omar's side when his rocket launcher took out the Russian BTR closest to them. He stayed with Omar when the tanks returned fire and one of the tank shells exploded right in front of them.

A deadly shower of shrapnel sprayed forth, blanketing the area around. One of the burning pieces of metal embedded itself in Omar's face, cleaving out his right eye. A jet of blood spurted out, but Omar lost neither control nor consciousness.

Even as he retched at the ghastly sight of the eyeball hanging from its socket, Jalaluddin grabbed Omar and began to drag him backwards, away from the ambush site which had suddenly turned into a death trap. He knew they had very little time, he could hear the Russian infantry preparing to counterattack the ambush.

They had barely fallen back a few yards when two Russian soldiers exploded over the embankment they had gone behind. Reacting in a flash, Jalaluddin unleashed a long burst from his rifle, emptying the magazine. The Russian soldier leading the charge was picked up by the burst and blown away. The second soldier had closed in by then. Unable to shoot back since his compatriot was in the line of fire, the terrified Russian lashed out wildly with his rifle. The gleaming, razor-sharp bayonet fixed on its muzzle arced through the air and sliced open Jalaluddin's right cheek. Shock ploughed through his mind, pulverizing his body into inaction. That was when Jalaluddin knew he was going to die.

Jalaluddin heard a gunshot next to him. Still knocked out by the pain and unaware who had fired, he waited for the Russian bullet to punch holes into him. But after a moment, when nothing happened, he turned to see a smoking pistol in Omar's hand and the second soldier lying dead.

Another salvo of tank shells exploded around them, blasting into oblivion the embankment they had been positioned behind moments ago. The two wounded men began to crawl away. They could hear the Russian soldiers on the other side. Sporadic bursts of fire fractured the rapidly deepening darkness.

Jalaluddin and Omar did not exchange a word till they were back in the safe confines of the caves high up in the mountains from where they operated. Omar was whisked away to the inner cave as others took charge of Jalaluddin.

It did not take long for the hastily strung bandage to stop the blood flowing from Jalaluddin's cheek. The wound would take much longer to heal. The scar of course would never go. Every day of his life he would see it, feel it and remember that Allah had saved him so he could deliver the jihad its rightful victory.

∞

'What is your name?' Omar asked the mujahideen who had stood by his side when all the others had fled.

'Jalaluddin Haq.'

'You are a brave young man.'

For the first time in years, there was some trace of emotion on Jalal's face. It was pride. He was happy not just to have been acknowledged but because his commander had called him a man, not a boy.

'I owe my life to you, Jalaluddin Haq. Inshallah, one day I shall repay the favour you did me today. I shall wait for that day,' Omar promised.

That night, Jalaluddin slept as he had not slept in years, not since that evening when he had seen his parents fall to Russian rifles. He saw a glimmer of his life ahead, still remote, but the seeds had been sown. He put his past behind him that night and began to look to the future.

In the months that followed, Jalaluddin fought alongside Omar on several occasions. And each time, his respect for the man increased. Omar may have lost an eye, but it neither eroded his ardour nor impaired his aim.

If Allah had permitted it, Jalaluddin would have fought under the man's banner for ever, so content was he doing so. Unfortunately, that was not to be.

∞

The Soviets soon realized their grand offensive was going nowhere and they began to seek an honourable way out of Afghanistan. That was when they realized that it is far easier to begin a war than to end it.

None of the countries that had staked a claim in this senseless conflict wanted it to end, not unless the end was in its best interest; the fate of Afghanistan and its people was the last thing that influenced their decisions.

Realizing that the crippling war was causing untold damage to their traditional enemy, the Americans flatly refused to work with the Russians in setting up a tenable government in Afghanistan. On the contrary, they did all they could to ensure that Russia remained embroiled in the mess as long as possible.

The Pakistanis were clear that the war could

only cease if they were allowed to retain control of Afghanistan. They needed a pliable government in Afghanistan, one that would ratify the Durand Line. Furthermore, the end of the war would put a stop to the billions of unaudited dollars flowing into their coffers.

Saudi Arabia, forever striving to restore Islam to its pristine glory, did not want to see the end of the innumerable madrassas that were churning out the singularly focused, fundamentalist mujahideen.

Adding to the confused mess, in 1984 Osama bin Laden arrived. He brought not only his personal funds but also Abdullah Al Azzam and Umar Abd al Rahman, spiritual leaders of the radical Egyptian Islamist group Al Jihad, who set up a network of recruiting and fund-raising offices all over the Arab world, Europe and America. This network, known as Maktab-al-Khidmat (service office) or Al-Khifah, morphed into Al-Qaeda in 1988.

By the time the last Russian soldier stepped off Afghan soil on 15 February 1989, 1.25 million Afghans (approximately 9 per cent of the 17 million national population) and 15,000 Soviet soldiers (75,000, if one takes the more accurate unofficial estimate) had lost their lives. Another million people, Afghan and Russian alike, had been wounded. And a few million Afghans had been displaced and condemned to life in refugee camps.

So devastating was the drain on Soviet economic and military might that it eventually brought the

superpower to its knees, leaving the world at the
fickle mercy and uncertain wisdom of America.

The Soviet withdrawal and subsequent American
loss of interest in the region left behind a ruptured
Afghanistan. But this largely illiterate nation with
a devastated infrastructure now had in its hands a
stockpile of arms and ammunition big enough to
fight several wars for several decades.

≈

The Taliban, a new group that was fast gaining
prominence in southern Afghanistan, grew out
of the void left by the violent anarchy that seized
Afghanistan after the Russian withdrawal. Mainly a
product of this uprooted war-torn society, adherents
of the Taliban latched on to the messianic Islam
preached by fundamentalist mullahs who had honed
their skills in the refugee camps and madrassas that
had flourished along the Durand Line.

The Taliban were trained by Pakistan to take
on the less amenable mujahideen commanders
and funded by Saudi Arabia to spread the tenets of
the rigidly intolerant Wahhabism. And they were
welcomed by the locals who, weary from decades
of war, sought peace and stability. It was not long
before they had overrun most of Afghanistan.

The era of the Taliban was now set to begin. And
the flame was ignited by one tiny spark.

≈

The eleven-member family was travelling from Kandahar to Herat to attend a wedding. Two of the men, the oldest woman and the youngest child, an infant, were riding inside the truck. Three women, two older children and two men were in the open rear.

The women caught the eye of the commander of the so-called 'security checkpost' on the outskirts of town. High on opium, he climbed somewhat unsteadily into the truck and pawed one of the women.

This drew an immediate response from the men, which in turn infuriated the strongman. The men and the two older children were beaten senseless before the three women were carried off to the nearby huts. Their screams pierced the sky as one by one the mujahideen manning the security post took turns in raping them before throwing them back in the truck. After that, they set fire to the truck. The exploding fuel tank quickly put an end to the terrified screams of the burning family.

In the melee none of them noticed the oldest woman slip away with the infant in her arms.

Cowering behind a hut some distance away, the woman watched in silence as her sons, daughters-in-law and grandchildren were engulfed by the flames. Finally, she wandered off in a daze, clutching her grandchild in her arms. Sometime later she found herself at the schoolhouse in Dand, where a few days earlier, a group of madrassee Taliban had set up camp.

A few minutes later, she found herself in the presence of the commander of the Taliban detachment, a tall, heavily bearded, one-eyed man dressed in a black Pathani kameez and ankle-high salwar. The stony expression on his face did not change as he listened to her story.

An hour later, a group of jeeps with heavily armed Taliban swept up to the checkpost and surrounded it.

The four men relaxing against the wooden barrier had no time to react to the weapons pointed at them.

A crash of gunfire brought the others rushing out of the huts on either side of the barrier. All of them were in various stages of undress but had their weapons ready. It was not long before the weapons had joined the bodies of their four comrades on the dusty road.

'Who is your commander?' Omar growled as he jumped out of the jeep, his boots clicking on the hard ground.

'He is.' Totally unnerved, the nearest man pointed at the burly figure who tottered out of the hut, trying to pull up his pants.

'Who the fuck are you people?' The Kandahari strongman was no coward. 'Don't you know this is my area?'

Omar flicked his fingers and two of his men

converged on the blustering strongman and frog-marched him to Omar. By now there was fear in his eyes.

'Are you the commander?' Omar leaned forward till his face was almost touching the captive.

'Yes.' The man cringed involuntarily.

'Do these men obey you? They do what you tell them?'

'Of course.' The Kandahari attempted an arrogant laugh. It came out a whimper. 'They'd better.'

Omar gestured at the charred remains of the truck. 'So, they did that under your orders?'

The strongman did not reply this time. Omar stepped back, raising his voice as he spoke again, this time addressing the hapless mujahideen hovering around nervously, 'Such things will not be tolerated. Not now. Not ever. Do you understand?' His solitary eye gleamed as it swept over them. 'I want everyone to understand that.' Gesturing at the men holding the strongman, Omar commanded, 'Take off his clothes and hold him down.'

Before the strongman could even struggle, a rifle butt had clubbed him down, driving him to the ground. Rough hands seized him and in moments his clothes had been torn off.

'He who steals shall have his hand cut off. He who kills shall forfeit his life.' Omar stepped forward, drawing a long knife from the scabbard at his waist. His voice was now a high, eerie chant. 'He who rapes...' Omar bent down and seized the naked man's penis and sliced it off with the knife.

For a moment there was silence as blood spurted out of the man's body. Then his mind registered the pain and he let out a high-pitched scream. Omar allowed the scream to reach crescendo before he dropped his knife and stuffed the dismembered penis into the man's open mouth. The scream died into a gurgle.

Raising himself to his full height, Omar said, his solitary eye blazing, 'All this will not be tolerated any more. Not as long as we are alive.' Then, abruptly, he stooped, scooped up his knife from the ground and walked away. 'Kill them.' The last two words were delivered in a flat command as he returned to his jeep.

Gunfire thundered out, felling the mujahideen who had raped and murdered the family.

By the time Omar reached his jeep, they were all dead. Omar asked the old woman who had accompanied them, 'Are you satisfied now?'

There was a stunned expression in her eyes. She seemed unable to tear her gaze away from the Kandahari strongman who lay dead a few feet away, his bloody penis poking grotesquely out of his mouth. Finally, she nodded.

'So be it.'

Twenty minutes later, when the jeeps pulled away from the now abandoned checkpost, each of the men involved with the rapes and murders had been beheaded and their bodies strung from the wooden barrier across the road.

In the days that followed, before nature and wild animals rendered the bodies into a mangled mass, every man, woman and child who crossed that checkpost in Kandahar would take note of them. The sight would strike terror in every heart. And the story of Taliban justice would be embellished each time it was told.

The Kandahar incident set the trend for others to approach Mullah Mohammed Omar. It was not long before he was firmly positioned as an idealistic, pious fighter for justice.

The rise of the Taliban continued unchecked until all of Afghanistan was under its control.

∾

Jalal would always remember that day in April 1996. People had flocked to Kandahar from all corners of the nation. A current of passion and high drama pulsated through the city that morning. Jalaluddin Haq was standing on the podium along with those favoured by Omar.

When Mullah Mohammed Omar finally emerged from the wings and came onto the stage, bursts of salutary gunfire accompanied the welcoming roar of the people. Suddenly, there was a hushed silence. Jalaluddin broke his gaze away from the crowd to see what they were staring at. All at once his mouth fell open too.

Omar was dressed the way he always did, but today there was a camel fur cloak around his shoulders.

Is this really the same one?

Jalaluddin had heard rumours that Omar had taken the cloak from the Mosque of the Cloak of Prophet Mohammed in Kandahar. While some said the Amir of Bukhara had given the cloak to Ahmad Shah Durrani in 1768, others believed it was the Prophet's cloak which Durrani had brought back from Bukhara.

'Could it really be the same one?' A whisper ran through the crowd.

'But why would a man like Omar deceive anyone?' Jalaluddin reminded himself. 'It must be true.'

'Simply by standing in the holy cloak's presence, the mute have walked out speaking, the blind seeing,' the Taliban leader standing next to Jalal said. 'In the past hundred years, the holy cloak has left the shrine only twice; once in 1929, when King Amanullah took it out to save Afghanistan, and again in 1935, to stop the cholera epidemic.'

Jalaluddin fought the urge to run forward and touch the hem of the holy cloak.

'The Prophet's cloak can be removed only by a true leader of the faithful,' someone else added in a hushed voice. 'Mullah Omar has the right touch, that is why Allah unlocked the chest for him to wear the very cloak worn by Prophet Mohammed and be proclaimed commander of the faithful.'

'Ameer-ul-Momineem! Ameer-ul-Momineem!'

The chant rose till it reached the faraway hills and ricocheted back. The crowd stopped only when Omar raised his hands and sought silence. His speech was short.

'The Taliban will ensure that the pious and the devout suffer no more indignity and violence. The Sharia will reign supreme. Justice will be prompt. People will sleep peacefully in their homes from now on.'

The crowd roared its approval.

The euphoria would last for all of two weeks.

∞

Things began to change within days. And the change was anything but subtle. One morning, the people of Afghanistan woke up to find posters plastered on the walls of all major cities and towns.

'Our beloved Muslim brothers, shaving off one's beard is a great sin,' the posters said.

To begin with, the posters evoked much mirth among the Afghans. But the amusement was as short-lived as the recent euphoria.

Whatever doubts anyone may have had about the severity with which the Taliban leadership viewed disobedience were soon put to rest when beard patrols rampaged through towns and the offenders were caned. The caning mutated into more severe forms of punishment over time. It was not long before the Taliban was using the head found without a beard like a football.

The next set of posters was not taken lightly by anyone. These were lists of people considered troublemakers, collaborators or those who did not respect Islam as per the Taliban's version of the Sharia. The wording was unequivocal: they were to be hunted down and killed by the Taliban regime.

Things became worse when several girls' schools were bombed and jihadis rampaged into boys' schools, demanding the right to lecture the students, to select and recruit those they deemed fit for the jihad. Music stores were burnt, barber shops were forced to shut down, girls' schools ceased to exist entirely, and morality patrols began to scour the streets. Women were stoned to death for stepping out of their homes without a male family member accompanying them, women on their way to work vanished without a trace. The slightest un-Islamic act drew immediate punishment.

Slowly but surely, the exodus, which had slowed to a trickle when the Russians left, gathered force. Yet again, hundreds began to flee. Doctors, teachers, scientists, students, whoever could escape from the country did. Whatever little hope Afghanistan may have had of finding some semblance of peace and normalcy, evaporated swiftly as the Taliban crescent grew from strength to strength.

∾

In May 1996, having been expelled from Sudan due to American and Egyptian pressure, Osama bin Laden returned to Afghanistan. This time, he came bearing untold wealth and massive jihadi networking influence, both of which had become synonymous with Al-Qaeda. His arrival gave the Taliban the required impetus. Four months later, Kabul fell into their hands. Now, barring scattered pockets of resistance, they had taken control of all of Afghanistan.

The stage was set for the war against the Crusader-Zionist-Hindu nexus to be taken to the next level.

The camps and madrassas that had shown signs of inactivity after the Soviets left slowly began to buzz with life. But now the target was the elusive gora shaitan sitting in safety, surrounded by oceans; the bastard Jew who had rendered so many Muslim brothers homeless; the Hindu kafir reigning over Kashmir – they would all pay.

And at the forefront of the attacks stood the figure of Mullah Mohammed Omar.

∾

The next time it was not kismat that brought Jalaluddin face to face with Omar; the mullah sent for him.

'How are you, Jalaluddin Haq?' Omar asked, embracing him warmly.

'I am well, Ameer.'

'The time has finally come for me to repay you for saving my life. Not that my life is worth anything beyond what it achieves for Allah.' Omar held him at arm's length. 'Tell me what I can do for you now.'

'Tell me how I may serve the cause as diligently and unwaveringly as you.' Jalaluddin's speech may have sounded rehearsed and politically correct but, looking into his eyes, Omar knew the man standing before him meant every word he said.

'Why did I know you would say that, Jalaluddin Haq?' Omar's face broke into a smile.

'Because what other meaning could life possibly have? I am merely a mirfaqa, a tool. Tell me what I need to do and I will do it... or die trying.'

Omar surveyed him for a moment before he spoke again and when he did his low monologue continued for a long time.

'How can I take on your mantle, Ameer?' Jalaluddin protested when Omar finished. 'It belongs to you and you alone.'

'I know what I am doing, Jalaluddin. Great events are in the offing. The tide will turn many times before things begin to move in the direction we want them to. Not long from now, I too will fade into the shadows.'

'You, Ameer?' Jalaluddin was incredulous.

'Yes, I must,' Omar replied softly. 'For so it has been written.'

'But who will lead us then?'

'I cannot tell you any more than that right now, but I have seen it in my dreams. It will happen.' Omar gazed at Jalaluddin, his solitary eye glinting with purpose. 'You will just have to trust me.'

'I do trust you.'

'Then do as I command.' Omar laid a firm hand on his shoulder. 'Do you think you can do that, Jalaluddin Haq?'

'No, Ameer, I *know* I can do that. And I am honoured that you would entrust me with this task. I will die before I allow your trust to be broken.'

'You have always proven worthy of trust, Jalaluddin. So are we agreed?'

'Yes, we are. You have my word.' The two men clasped hands.

'Very well then. Return to Waziristan and no matter what you see or hear, keep a low profile,' Omar ordered. 'The produce from Helmand will continue to reach you regularly. You know how to get it out. Hassan leaves for Russia to set up the conduits. Between the two of you, pump it into America, Europe... wherever you can. Let the white powder eat away the innards of those kafir bastards. Convert the profits into arms and ammunition and store them safely, for the right time.'

Jalaluddin nodded.

'And keep him by your side.' Omar gestured at Hamidi, who was standing near them. 'He is a good advisor to have beside you.'

'That he is,' Jalaluddin agreed.

'And remember, no matter what happens or what the others do, *keep your head down*,' Omar emphasized. 'Not far into the future a day will come when those who are too visible will become dispensable and will have to pay the price for it.'

'Yes, Ameer.'

'Good. Wait for my summons. That is the day you will surface and take charge.'

They embraced and parted.

Jalaluddin had walked a few steps when Omar's voice stopped him.

'And always bear in mind that though they support us today, the Pakistani intelligence and army must not be trusted. Confide in them and use them only as long as it suits our purpose. They are fickle bastards, more interested in lining their pockets than in anything else. You never know when they will turn against you.'

'I will keep that in mind, Ameer.'

Then he left, with Mullah Hamidi in tow. After that day, the relationship between the teacher and student altered and became a more equal one.

∾

A week later, Jalaluddin Haq was back in Waziristan, not far from the village where he was born. After another week, he began the task the Ameer-ul-Momineem had given him. He took all possible precautions to ensure that neither his name nor his face featured anywhere in the list of people driving the jihad forward. He made sure the precious opium delivered to him from Helmand was moved out. He used the carefully constructed chain set up by Mullah Omar and Sheikh Osama to move the money back. A lot of it was expended in the historic small arms bazaar of Dara Adam Khel near Peshawar. The arms and equipment acquired in turn moved to countless, strategically located, well-concealed caches all over the frontier region, on both sides, well away from prying eyes. Guarded by trusted minions, most of them clansmen and blood relatives, they lay in wait for the day they would be used.

And Jalaluddin patiently waited for the summons that he had been told would reach him one day.

∞

Jalaluddin watched in silence as the brouhaha in Afghanistan died down and the Pakistanis turned the mujahideen machine against the Indians in Kashmir. He sat silently when the Al-Qaeda strike teams brought the twin towers in New York crashing down. Within hours the world had changed permanently.

Within weeks, the Americans were back in Afghanistan. But this time they were back as invaders. Their arrival was met with the same anger and resentment as the Russians' had been years ago. But this time the weapons fielded by both sides were capable of much worse.

Yet again the sound of guns shattered the silence. And once more, blood began to bathe the mountains and valleys of Afghanistan.

The American forces hounded the Taliban out of huge tracts of Afghanistan. Omar fled to the safety of Quetta and Sheikh Osama to the mountains of Chitral.

Jalaluddin did not react even when Abdul Rashid Dostum, one of the brutal warlords who rose against Omar's rule, locked up 2000 Taliban fighters in shipping containers and left them to die. He wanted to use the weapons he had so carefully hoarded and the scores of fighters he had nurtured and trained, and deliver Dostum to the most hideous death possible. But he trusted his mentor and sat still.

True to Mullah Omar's prophecy, the Pakistanis turned traitors and trained their guns on the Taliban in the Swat Valley. And they threatened to do the same in Waziristan.

And through all this, Jalaluddin held his peace and continued to do as Omar had bid, using the drug money to silence the generals, to stockpile arms, ammunition, supplies and train his men.

༄

The weeks turned into months and the months into years, but Jalaluddin did not lose heart. And his patience paid off, for one day the summons finally arrived.

The messenger was a short, slightly-built man who strode out of the night, exuding an electric energy.

'I have a message for Jalaluddin Haq,' he told the sentries who accosted him at the perimeter defence.

'From whom?'

'Just tell him I come from Quetta. He will understand.'

The messenger was subjected to a thorough body search. Except for a piece of cloth that had been carefully folded and wrapped in plastic, he carried nothing. A few minutes later, he was brought before Jalaluddin.

'The Ameer told me to give you this.' He held out the cloth.

Puzzled, Jalaluddin unwrapped the packet. It contained an old camel fur cloak. As his fingers caressed the cape, his hands began to tremble. His mind went back to when Omar took on the mantle of Ameer-ul-Momineem in Kandahar. 'Could this really be...'

'It is not the one,' the messenger replied. 'The real one is safe in Kandahar. I was asked to tell you that you would understand the symbolism.'

'What else did he say?' Jalaluddin asked when he finally found his voice.

'That you are now responsible for ensuring that the symbol is honoured. He said you would understand.' He paused. 'He also said I was to stay with you.'

'What for?'

'He said you would need me to take care of things... things that others will baulk at.' He smiled. 'My name is Karamat. I was trained by the Sheikh himself and used to take care of jobs for him, special jobs.'

Jalaluddin examined the man before him. Apart from the vibrant energy he radiated, there was nothing about his appearance that backed what he said. But Jalaluddin knew Mullah Omar would have sent him for a reason.

'Tell me about yourself,' he said finally.

Karamat spoke in a low, even tone. He did not take long, he did not need to. Whatever he said, coupled with the unshakeable faith Jalaluddin had in the man who had sent him, was enough.

'You shall stay, Karamat. We need men like you.'

That was the beginning of a relationship that would end only with the death of one of them.

∾

His hands were not steady as Jalaluddin carefully, reverently, donned the cape; real or not, the cloak was a powerful symbol. It felt heavy with the weight of the tremendous responsibility that had been passed on to him. But Jalaluddin Haq was ready. He had been ready since the day Omar had told him to be prepared to take on this role.

When he finally took the cloak off, there was a gleam in his eyes. 'If Allah wills it, maybe one day it will be my destiny to wear the real one.'

For now, Jalaluddin understood what Omar had ordered him to do. He knew the moment he had been waiting for all these years had finally come.

∼

Jalaluddin did not waste any time. He moved swiftly and ruthlessly, with the confidence that comes from years of planning and preparation. He reached out to shady generals, corrupt politicians, mullahs in Islamabad and warlords on both sides of the Durand Line. He struck alliances that only money could buy. Those who did not concede were paid surprise visits by suicide bombers who blew them into oblivion. Those who tried to betray them were greeted by the assassin. Others found American missiles seeking them out.

Yet again, the terror began to escalate.

Once again, the madrassa-generated jihadi death factories began to spread, not just along the Durand Line, but deep in the heartlands of Pakistan, churning out a wave of religious fundamentalism.

∼

The Ameer's past unfolded in his mind as his eyes stared at the darkness outside. Finally, fatigue pulled him into the folds of restless sleep. For the first time in many years, the morrow he faced would be without the comfort of Mullah Hamidi, his friend and his guide. He felt somewhat incomplete.

Of course, this did not weaken his resolve to take

the jihad to every doorstep in every kafir country in the world. No matter what life threw at him, the Ameer knew the fight would go on.

Till the Caliphate once again reigned supreme.

But if you do not listen to me and do not keep my commandments…
I will scatter you amongst the nations and keep the sword drawn against you.

Leviticus

The ferret-like intelligence on his face matched Jahangir Karamat's infectious energy. But it did not diminish the hard edge beneath his quick, easy smile. Iqbal instinctively knew this was not a man to be taken lightly.

'So you are the one who saved the Ameer?' Karamat asked.

Iqbal simply nodded.

'Allah will surely bless you then,' he said. 'Do you know what they call us?'

Iqbal shook his head.

'We are the Special Tasks unit. You know what we do?'

'Special tasks?'

That seemed to amuse Karamat.

'Smart! Very smart! Not a smartass, I hope. Those don't last long here.' Another smile flashed across Karamat's face. 'But I like people with a sense of humour. Allah knows there are too few of them. Tell me,' he changed tack, 'are you familiar with weapons?'

'I can manage.' Iqbal's cool demeanour communicated that he could do a lot more.

'Bombs?'

'Not really.' Iqbal shrugged. 'I never got a chance to work with bombs.'

'What about communication equipment?'

'Only what they taught us in Muzaffarabad.'

'That is basic stuff but good enough for now. In any case, we do not use the radio much. Or even satellite phones, for that matter.' Karamat saw Iqbal's quizzical expression and elaborated. 'The Americans monitor everything that goes out there,' he gestured with a sweep of his hand. 'One transmission is enough to have them send in the missiles.' He looked at Iqbal. 'Physically, you seem to be in good shape. Any injuries or problems I should know about?'

'Nothing current or relevant,' Iqbal replied, unwilling to explain the two bullet wounds he carried on his body.

'Perfect. Go with Altaf and get a weapon from the armoury. Pick what you are most comfortable with and try it out on the range. Just make sure you don't shoot any of the villagers. As it is, we are having a tough time keeping them on our side.'

'I will be careful,' Iqbal assured him before he turned to follow Altaf, the young man who had been standing behind Karamat.

They had taken barely two steps when Karamat called out, 'Be ready to move out tomorrow night.'

'Where are we headed, janab?'

'You will know when we reach.' Karamat gave an enigmatic smile. 'But rest assured that it will be an eventful trip... lots of kafir to kill.' He chuckled. 'Eat well, sleep well and, of course, pray hard. Remember, we Special Tasks men are like Roman gladiators.' His words were at stark variance with the rural dialect he spoke. It was impossible to tell that he was not a native of the area.

'Already dead, huh,' said Iqbal.

'Ah! Well read too.' Karamat nodded approvingly. 'Now let us see how good you are when the bullets begin to fly.'

∞

Including Karamat, a total of fifty-three men left from Zangari the following night. All of them wore identical sneakers, web gear, Pathani kameez and Al-Qaeda-height salwars – regular trousers but ankle high, the way Wahhabi and Salafi jihadis wore them, since they followed the hadith that clothes which touch the ground are a sign of pride and vanity. That, in fact, was the way almost all the men Iqbal had encountered around the Ameer were dressed. He had quickly acquired shorter ones for himself; it was always better to blend in with the crowd. Here, particularly, it was a prerequisite for survival.

Hearing Karamat call him Indian, one of the men asked Iqbal, 'Are you also from the Lashkar?'

His obviously Kashmiri accent took Iqbal by surprise. Recovering quickly, he shook his head. 'You?'

'Yes, the twelve of us are.' He gestured towards the knot of men around him.

Iqbal examined the raiding party closely. It was divided into four teams of twelve men each, with the remaining four grouped directly under Karamat Each twelve-man section comprised men from a particular region. From the differences in their behaviour and with the LeT jihadi's admission, Iqbal realized that people from several different groups had been put together for this mission; some spoke Arabic, some Urdu, others Pashto or Dari. The rest spoke languages that Iqbal was not yet able to identify.

He was mulling this over when the team leaders began inspecting their men, in exactly the way Iqbal and his fellow trainees had been checked by their trainers before they moved out from the Chakoti Post to infiltrate into India after their training at the Lashkar camp in Muzaffarabad.

I hope we do not meet the same fate our party

encountered that night, Iqbal thought. Funnily enough, the memory of machine guns scything through the night and the screaming, dying men all around no longer had any impact on him. Death no longer seemed the same to Iqbal ever since he had seen Tanaz die. It had lost its sting.

'Make bloody sure there is nothing on you that makes any noise or shines in the dark.'

One by one the team leaders checked their men and reported back to Karamat.

'Weapon loads?' he enquired.

'All okay.' Knowing that ammunition was what kept one alive on the battlefield, every man was carrying as much as he could; dry fruits and water constituted the balance of the load. Every rucksack was bulging to the brim, making the men hunch forward.

The vehicles left at irregular intervals of ten to fifteen minutes. All of them ran without lights, though they knew this did not afford safety from the heat-seeking equipment fitted on most American aircraft and drones. They were well aware that the eyes in the skies were technologically so powerful that they could see every detail miles below. The best they could do was have each vehicle travel alone, so that it did not draw the attention a convoy would, and even if it did and was taken out, the losses would be relatively minimal.

∞

The journey was uncomfortable and painfully slow. But Iqbal noticed that none of the men seemed very anxious.

It was only when they halted that signs of tension began to emerge. It was obvious that the Durand Line had been crossed and they were now in the combat zone.

'From here we go on foot,' one of the old-timers murmured to Iqbal, who was studying the bleak terrain around them.

At a signal from Karamat, they set off at a brisk pace. The cold seeped in through the layers of clothing and cut straight to the bone. Even standing still for a few moments was enough to chill the body.

A few hours later, lights began to twinkle in the distance. It was probably the Afghan city of Jalalabad.

The lights were still far away when they halted. Karamat gathered together the leaders of the four strike teams. He unfurled a map and began briefing them under the faint glow of a shaded torch. It was a military grade map and had been annotated with blue and red markings.

Iqbal noticed that the men had taken up all-round defensive positions as soon as they had stopped, similar to an army unit. Unlike the badly-trained jihadis Iqbal had met in Muzaffarabad and Faisalabad, there was no slackness in this lot. He now understood how they had kept the Pakistan Army at

bay all these years and how a mere 3,000 of them
had been able to send over 12,000 Pakistani troops
slinking out of the Swat Valley the previous year.

The hushed briefing lasted only a few minutes.
The section commanders returned to take charge of
their men. Another round of whispered instructions
followed and they set off.

They were all moving in the same general direction,
but following different routes. Five minutes later,
Iqbal lost track of the other sections.

The pace now picked up. The thin mountain
air and the heavy load ensured that the going was
rough.

They halted so suddenly that Iqbal crashed into
the man in front of him. The section commander
hissed and everyone hit the ground. Iqbal suddenly
realized that the section commander had melted
away into the darkness. So had the two men
immediately behind him.

Twenty minutes later, one of them returned.
There was another hurried conference and he
vanished into the night, taking two more men with
him.

Moments later, one of them returned to signal
the rest. 'Come on, this way.' They followed him
up the steep slope as fast as possible.

The section commander and two of the men
were standing near a shallow trench on top of the
mountain. The fourth man lay dead a few feet away,
a bayonet sticking out of his chest. In the trench

lay three more bodies. The smell of freshly drawn blood hung in the air.

'That is our target... the gun post.' The section commander raised a commando knife and pointed up the slope. Dirty red blood glowed on the blade. Iqbal could faintly see some men moving around a camouflaged gun pit about 900 metres away. They did not seem particularly alert. He could hear the sound of their voices even from this distance.

'The second outpost should be on the other slope,' the section commander pointed again. 'You four,' he gestured at Iqbal and the last three men, 'follow that ledge and get there. Take them out silently... No guns, okay? If something goes wrong, only you will fire.' He pointed the knife at the man wielding a silenced carbine. 'You have a ten-minute head start. Then we go for the main gun post, okay?'

Weapons at the ready, the four of them moved along the edge of the mountain, hunching down to ensure they were not skylighted.

The second machine gun was also manned by three men. None of the three was as alert as he should have been. One of them was even asleep. He did not wake up as his comrades fell to the knives of the assaulting quartet. By the time he stirred, Iqbal's knife had torn into his heart and put him to sleep again. This time more permanently.

Iqbal felt a surge of satisfaction as he wiped the blade clean on the dead man's clothes.

The last man was gasping his way to death when a commotion broke out at the gun post. They seemed to have spotted the main assault team. Not that it did them any good. A series of muted spits punctured the night as the section commander's silenced carbine spat lead. A minute later, the muted light of a torch flashed at them from the direction of the gun post. Once. Twice. Thrice.

The man with the carbine turned to Iqbal. 'Indian, get to the gun post now.'

As he was walking away, Iqbal saw them throw the dead bodies out of the trench and swing around the machine gun till it faced the Kabul–Jalalabad–Peshawar road; earlier it had been guarding the slope leading up to the main gun post.

As he walked up to the main gun post, Iqbal could see the section commander kneeling on the ground. Lying in front of him was another Afghan. The whimpering man had a large bloody hole where his left eye had been.

'Give me the password.' The section commander prodded the man's wound with his knife. The captive screamed. It was not long before he began to talk.

'Are you sure you are not lying to me?'

'Allah is my witness, I am not lying,' the man said frantically, desperate to show he was cooperating.

The section commander seemed convinced because he drew his knife smoothly across the man's throat.

Iqbal could not keep his eyes off the body as he heard the section commander give the call sign and code words to the first rocket launcher team.

'Are you familiar with this?' he asked Iqbal as he swivelled the huge twin-barrelled ZU-23 2 mm gun around; now it too was facing the Kabul–Jalalabad–Peshawar road ahead.

Iqbal shook his head; he had never even seen the weapon system before.

Another reminder of the Russian invasion, the ZU-23 2 is a short-range air defence canon. The ZU or Zenitnaya Ustanovka is an anti-aircraft mount. The 2A14 23 mm auto canons of the weapon have a practical rate of fire of 400 rounds per minute. The weapon is aimed and fired manually with the help of a ZAP-23 optical-mechanical sight that provides automatic aiming with the help of manually entered data. It also has a straight tube telescope for use against ground targets. Depending on the target and role, the ZU-23 2 can fire the BZT Armour Piercing Incendiary-Tracer (API-T) rounds or the OFZ High Explosive Incendiary-Tracer (HEI-T) rounds.

'Damn! Yusuf was.' The section commander was referring to the man they had lost while taking the first machine gun trench. 'Okay, come here. See… this is all you have to do.' He showed Iqbal how to reload the weapon, making him practise it a few times.

By the time he got the two rocket launcher teams deployed, one on either side of the ZU, the first rays of sunlight had begun to appear. They went to ground and began to wait.

Unknown to Iqbal, the second section which had gone with Karamat's HQ team had also carried out a similar operation and taken up position on the mountain across the narrow defile in front. The road wound through the defile before vanishing round the bend. Between the two teams, they now dominated the road.

The third and fourth sections had looped around and taken position on either side of the selected ambush site, just off the road. They would seal off the road at both ends as soon as the ambush was sprung, thus ensuring no one was able to get away from the killing ground.

The wait lasted six hours.

Their quarry came up the road a little short of noon. Three Stryker Infantry Carrier Vehicles led the convoy and two brought up the rear.

Named in honour of Pfc. Stuart S. Stryker, who received the award for his actions during World War II and Spc. 4 Robert F. Stryker, who received the Medal of Honour for his actions during the Vietnam War, the Stryker ICV is only the second American Army vehicle named after enlisted personnel. Armed with the .50 calibre Browning machine gun and capable of carrying nine soldiers, in addition to a two-man crew, the Stryker is often referred to as the Kevlar Coffin, due to its vulnerability to large IEDs.

The Strykers were escorting a dozen ISAF supply trucks. The tactical markings made it clear that they were American, which is possibly why this particular convoy had been selected for special treatment. After all, they had to pay for the blood their Reaper and Predator drones had drawn.

As the first vehicle approached the heart of the killing area, the adrenaline began to flow again in the frozen limbs.

'Easy! Easy now!' the section commander manning the ZU breathed as the vehicles droned closer. 'Hold fire till we get the signal.'

Iqbal barely heard him, he was so keyed up.

The convoy was moving cautiously, perhaps aware that the defile was a natural ambush ground.

Suddenly the radio crackled to life. It startled all of them, even though the call was expected. Iqbal was too far away to hear what was said, but he could see the expression on the operator's face as he spoke. The relief on the man's face mirrored the section commander's as the code word was given and accepted.

Banking on their Afghan allies who had been deployed on both shoulders of the defile, the convoy speeded up as soon as they heard the correct words delivered on the correct frequency. No one in the convoy expected trouble now.

Iqbal watched the convoy roll into the kill zone. Unconciously, his fingers began to caress the ammunition that he had to reload into the ZU.

There was a dull bang from across the defile as
the leading Stryker crossed the centre of the killing
ground. An anti-tank rocket vroomed forward.
Iqbal saw the fiery-tailed warhead hammer into
the Stryker.

Almost immediately, the RPGs on either side
of Iqbal fired, aiming for the ICV that brought up
the rear.

The first rocket slammed down on top of the
ICV and exploded with a roar. Within seconds,
the escort vehicle buckled and burst into flames.
The sound was relatively muted, but the effect was
spectacular.

The unfortunate vehicle was flung up into the air,
before it crashed back on the ground. The driver
leapt out of the burning vehicle and began to run.
A few more men crawled out and staggered away
from the charred mess. They had hardly taken a few
steps when machine guns on either side of the defile
opened up and hammered into them, throwing their
bodies on the ground.

The Stryker ICV bringing up the rear met with
the same fate. Now, with burning vehicles blocking
the road at either end, the rest of the convoy was
trapped in the killing ground. The duck shoot
began.

The ZU thundered to life with a roar, making
Iqbal start. A stream of hot lead beamed out from
it, instantly pulping the soft-skinned cargo carriers
into nothingness. One moment there was a vehicle

moving along the road, the next it had been rendered into a battered, burning hull.

By now, there was total panic. Barring a few sporadic bursts of retaliatory fire from the surviving Strykers, there was no response to the ambush. There was not much they could do, given the massive quantum of firepower that had been unleashed on the kill zone.

Another barrage of rockets snaked forward from both sides, converging on and smashing the Strykers like fiery bolts of lightning. Men ran screaming from the burning vehicles, only to be mowed down by the constantly stuttering machine guns and the hail of bullets from the ZU.

Iqbal watched in fascination as his hands loaded and reloaded the gun. By now the ZU barrels were flaming red. The heat reached out and singed the hair on his arms as he frantically reloaded, again and yet again. He was not sure how long it lasted; from one level it looked as though the killing had been going on forever, from another it seemed as though only seconds had elapsed.

Silence returned to the killing ground with suddenness. The section commander jumped out from behind the ZU with a yell and, grabbing his carbine, hurtled down the mountainside. Iqbal snatched up his rifle and followed. From both sides of the defile, men converged on the burning vehicles.

There were hardly any survivors by the time

they reached the convoy. Those that still lived were finished off with mechanical efficiency.

'This one is not wounded,' Iqbal heard someone call out.

'Take the bastard along,' Karamat replied. 'Let's go now. If they managed to radio out, their air force will be here pretty soon.'

They moved fast, the need for stealth no longer an imperative. It was far more important to get as far away from the ambush site as possible.

The American soldier who had been taken alive was carried on a pole, trussed up like a goat, his hands tied at one end and legs at the other. Iqbal could hear him moaning, more with fear than pain.

They halted about seven miles and one mountain ridge later. By now every man was breathing hard and was layered in sweat despite the cold. The killing heat which had possessed them earlier had been replaced by the physical strain of their rapid exit from the ambush area and the growing fear of aerial interference from the ISAF.

As they halted in the lee of a cliff, they roughly threw down the American soldier. He screamed as he hit the ground hard.

'Not so brave now, are you?' one of the two men who had been carrying him chuckled, kicking him in the ribs. 'You fuckers are only good at attacking people from the air. You need to know how real men fight.'

'Don't worry.' A kick from the second man followed. 'We will give you a taste of real battle.'

'Hey you, Indian! And you,' Karamat called out to Iqbal and another man. 'Tie the American bastard to that tree.'

Everyone started grinning. This was obviously something they had done before.

The American began to struggle as they carried him to a tree. Suddenly irritated, Iqbal slammed the butt of his rifle on his head; not hard enough to crack it open, but hard enough to almost knock him out. He held him up as another man tied him to the tree.

Iqbal was walking away from their captive when a battle cry rang out. He turned to see several mujahideen lined up, facing the tree. One of them was running forward with his rifle held in assault position, the bayonet fixed on it pointing straight ahead. Iqbal felt a strange sensation engulf him as he saw the bayonet disappear into the American's belly. Iqbal knew he should be revolted. Instead, he felt a strange curiosity.

The man screamed in pain, and the unmistakable stench of shit and piss rose in the air as his bowels and bladder voided themselves. The ambush party broke into jeering laughter.

Iqbal was unable to take his eyes off the soldier. A sweet, metallic taste swirled in his mouth as yet another bayonet sliced into the captured American. His scream, more a ragged shriek now, rang out again.

'Oye, you stupid fucker!' someone yelled. 'Stay away from his chest. Aim for the belly or his arms and legs. We want to see how long that sissy cunt lasts.'

The screams continued as the bayonets thumped periodically into the man; loud cheers accompanied each strike.

'Hey, Indian,' Karamat called out. 'What's happened to you, my brave mujahideen? Don't you have the balls for a little blood? Come on, show us your mettle.' Karamat strode up to Iqbal and pushed him to the head of the line. 'Go on, take a poke.'

The men began to cheer as Iqbal fixed the bayonet on his rifle and began to close in on the American.

The rifle felt alien in Iqbal's hand. His mind was devoid of thought as the distance between the bayonet and the half-dead victim narrowed. There was no change in his expression as the bayonet slid into the American's belly. The captive did not even whimper.

Iqbal watched in fascination. He was so engrossed that he forgot to pull out the bayonet; the thrust-in and pull-out need to be accomplished in one swift motion else the body begins to grip the intruder. When he finally tried to do so, the bayonet refused to budge, as though the American's body was reluctant to let it go. Iqbal tugged again but to no avail. Finally, he planted his boot on the victim's body and jerked the bayonet out with all his might. The others cheered as Iqbal's bayonet emerged, leaving a fountain of blood in its wake.

Iqbal felt nothing as he walked away from the soldier. Thought, feelings, anger, hate, rage, pity, remorse; nothing touched him. *What would Tanaz say?* The thought was bludgeoned aside by the animal that had been unleashed.

The bayonet practice resumed, but now that the American was no longer conscious, the men lost interest. Karamat finally slit his throat with one short slash. His torment finally over, the American slumped forward with a tired gasp, his head lolling weirdly to one side. He seemed to be smiling.

A couple of minutes later, they were off again.

'Where are we going now?' Iqbal asked the man walking beside him. 'Back?'

'Back? Why? The fun is just beginning.' Coming up from behind, Karamat laughed as he thumped Iqbal's shoulders. 'Now, my young mujahideen, you will know why they call us Lashkar-al-Zil – the shadow army. In the coming days we shall strike again, right at the heart of the kafir. The Americans will soon realize they are not the only ones who can deliver shock and awe.'

Karamat appeared to be in a good mood, buoyed by the success of the ambush. Or was it in anticipation of what lay ahead?

∞

That night, they halted at a series of caves sunk into the face of the mountain they had spent all afternoon climbing. Every now and then they were forced to take cover as American gunships soared overhead, searching for the men who had ambushed the ISAF convoy. Every jihadi knew his chances of survival were bleak if the AH-64 Apache gunships, with their 30 mm M230 chain gun and the mix of AGM-114 Hellfire missiles and Hydra 70 rocket pods found him. Even deadlier were the AC-130 Spectre gunships which, with their two 30 mm mini guns, two 40 mm canons and a 105 mm Howitzer, had more firepower than a US Navy destroyer. Every time the gunships failed to spot them, the men would make crude gestures and jeer, as much in relief as anything else.

Darkness and the bitter cold that came with it had already set in when they reached the caves. Iqbal was amazed at how deep the cluster of caves ran and the degree to which it had been developed. The caves in front were the living accommodation; to one side there was a designated cook house and a well-equipped sick bay. The other side was used to store arms and ammunition. Iqbal followed the others to collect food from the cookhouse and replenish the ammunition he had expended. In addition to bandoliers of small arms and ammunition, there were piles of rocket launchers and mortar shells stacked against the walls. Right at the back he spotted a few crates of Stinger missiles. The whole set-up had obviously been created over a long time and with sustained effort.

By now they had been on the move for over twenty-four hours and every man in the assault team was showing signs of fatigue. Barring the two sentries at the entrance to the caves, most of the men were asleep within minutes. The cave was damp, the cold seeping in from all sides, and the men huddled close to stay warm.

As Iqbal prepared to get some much-needed rest, he noticed Karamat huddled to one side with his section commanders. Sitting next to him was a young Chechen who seldom strayed far from Karamat. They were bent over a map, holding an animated but quiet discussion. He would have loved to hear what they were talking about, but Iqbal was so exhausted that he could not focus any more. He soon drifted into tormented sleep.

His dreams were filled with the screams of the American soldier. The man's eyes followed him everywhere, staring at him in accusation.

Iqbal woke up with a start, confused and disoriented, not realizing he had screamed. Then he saw Karamat and the men in the far corner of the cave staring at him. After a while, Karamat got up and came across to him.

'What happened, Indian?' he asked, kneeling next to Iqbal and placing a hand on his shoulder.

Iqbal was trembling.

'Are the faces of dead men calling to you?'

Karamat's eyes searched Iqbal's face. His tone was surprisingly gentle. 'Don't worry. It happens to the best and the bravest of us. Soon the faces will begin to fade and one day they will no longer come back to torment you, for we ride on the path shown to us by Allah. Remember, always remember, that we are truly blessed.'

Iqbal did not know how close he was to death at that moment. He did not know that if Karamat decided the man in front of him was weak, he would put an end to his life, without pity, without remorse. There was no place for the faint-hearted in the ranks of Lashkar-al-Zil.

Karamat patted his shoulder. 'Don't worry about it and don't think so much. You did well today. Sleep now.' He returned to his conference.

Disgusted that he had almost given himself away, Iqbal crawled deeper into his lumpy sleeping bag. A few minutes later he was asleep.

When he felt someone shaking him awake, it seemed to Iqbal he had barely slept for a few minutes, though the entire day had fled past. His tired body felt like one massive bruise, throbbing all over with pain.

He got dressed quickly and wolfed down some cold dry bread, leathery meat and a handful of dry fruits. He was ravenous. He remembered what they had drilled into his head during his training at Force 22: 'Sleep, water and food – these are your ultimate weapons. Never say no to them.'

Half an hour later, they were off again. Daylight had just begun to turn into shades of grey when they began their descend down the other side of the mountain. Then followed another trudge through the dark night, through treacherous shale and narrow winding paths. As usual, Iqbal brought up the rear along with the ever watchful Altaf, who seemed to have been designated as his mentor, perhaps even his minder.

Once they left the rugged mountain trail and headed across the valley, the endless march seemed easier. However, the danger of enemy patrols and detection had mounted; the strike force was now moving with greater caution and the distance between each man increased considerably.

Just as Iqbal started getting used to the walk, they halted yet again. He joined the others in the all-round defensive posture they always adopted. Iqbal listened as Karamat briefed his lieutenants.

'Stay clear of Kamakhel and get on to the Sur Pol–Kabul road. See that you stay well away from the road, there are regular security patrols on it,' Karamat warned. 'I want you to go to ground a few miles short of Kabul. You must be in position at least an hour before midnight the day after tomorrow.'

A longer discussion followed, which Iqbal was unable to overhear. Moments later, the raiding party split up, this time in two, and Iqbal found himself following Karamat with half the men.

The terrain soon turned difficult again as they

started up another mountain trail, as bad if not worse than the one they had navigated earlier.

By the time they broke for the day – it would be easier for the Americans to detect and interdict movement in daylight – Iqbal's body had ceased to feel anything. But his exhaustion returned with a vengeance the minute he threw off his rucksack and allowed himself to sink to the floor of the caves where they were taking shelter.

Iqbal woke up when the light in the cave had dimmed, as the sun prepared to drop below the ring of mountains. Despite the rest, he still felt exhausted. The others were surly and ill-tempered too, the light-hearted banter at the start of the mission was gone. The slightest remark seemed provocation enough for the men to pounce on each other.

The rest of the night was spent in another long trek. Every now and then, Iqbal could spot the lights of Kabul in the distance. Remembering what he had heard Karamat tell the others, he guessed the other team would approach Kabul from the other side.

They were about eight kilometres short of Kabul, coming down parallel to the Mir Bacheh Kowt–Kabul road which lay a few kilometres to their right, when Karamat brought them to a halt and made them go to ground. Gesturing silently, he selected six men, among them Iqbal and the young Chechen. Leaving the others behind, the seven men began to trek with Karamat leading the way. But this time they were moving very slowly, as though

Karamat was looking for something or someone. And because they were now close to Kabul, the possibility of being spotted by security patrols went up dramatically.

The reason for Karamat's cautious approach became clear when a man stepped out from behind a large rock and hailed them softly. Karamat motioned to the others to stop and went to meet the man. They hugged and exchanged greetings with the easy familiarity of men who know each other well. The stranger kept gesticulating over his shoulder as he briefed him. They spoke for a long time before Karamat returned. He took two of his men aside and briefed them at length before sending them back to the main party lying in wait, now almost a mile behind. Then he and the other four men followed the newcomer towards Kabul.

∾

Almost a dozen security posts had to be skirted before they finally reached a battered looking house deep inside the town. Most of the houses were in an acute state of damage and disrepair, silent spectators to the decades of strife that had torn the country apart. Considering the perpetual state of siege the city was in and the late hour – it was early morning by now – all the lights in the house were off, except for a low shaded lamp that lit up a room at the back. At this hour, anything more conspicuous would have drawn one of the patrols in for a closer look.

'Who will drive it?' the newcomer asked Karamat after they had all had a drink of water, some food, and settled down on the reedy carpet covering the uneven floor.

The newcomer was a tiny, heavily bearded man, dressed in a Pathani suit. There was a clean-cut, military air about him. It was especially prominent in the precise, collected way in which he spoke. He reminded Iqbal of the ISI agents who had often visited the LeT training camp in Muzaffarabad.

'He will.' Karamat beckoned to the Chechen. 'Come here. This is Pasha… he will help us complete the task.'

'Come on then, let's show him the vehicle and make sure he knows what he has to do.'

The agent provocateur named Pasha led them out to the courtyard in the back. The other men immediately lay down to relax but Iqbal casually got up and made his way to one of the windows.

He could see the Chechen sitting in the driver's seat of a Toyota Camry with Pasha next to him, while Karamat looked in from the window on the driver's side. The metallic-grey Camry seemed to be new. The rear springs of the car were sagging discernibly, as though the boot was heavily loaded.

Even as Iqbal watched, the three men began to walk back into the house. Iqbal hurriedly moved away from the window and lay down, pretending to be asleep.

'You are sure you have understood everything?' Pasha asked the Chechen as they re-entered.

'Yes, I am,' the Chechen murmured. 'Once I see the cars approaching, I have to head for the gates. I have to get as close as possible and then activate the switch you showed me.'

'Perfect. Now get some sleep. You must be well rested. Tomorrow is the day you make your mark.' Pasha gave the Chechen an encouraging pat on his shoulder. 'Remember, jannat awaits.'

'Inshallah,' the Chechen said softly, almost by rote.

The way Pasha smiled as the Chechen went to get his rucksack made Iqbal's hackles rise. How many times had he seen that smile? First, it was the maulavi who had recruited him, then it was the maulana who ran the Muzaffarabad camp, and not so long ago, it was that bastard Asif, who had recruited him for the Indian Mujahideen.

Jannat awaits!

The words sent a shiver down his spine as Iqbal realized that a suicide mission, a fidayeen attack, was in the offing. So that was why Karamat always kept the Chechen close to him. After all, even though the fidayeen training regimen was the toughest mental and physical training a man could be subjected to, there was always a chance that he would suffer a change of heart as the moment of death approached; after all, survival is the primordial instinct in all living things. So the fidayeen is always kept primed and pumped up by his controller, right until the point of no return, when death becomes the only available option. Till that moment, the controller shepherds him. And to deter the fidayeen from changing his mind, their families are often held hostage till the deed is done.

Iqbal lay awake long after the others had fallen asleep, his mind whirling as he tried to figure out the Chechen's target. *It must be something big. Why else would they go through all this trouble?* Iqbal tried hard but was unable to come up with anything meaningful, which was not surprising because his knowledge of Kabul was rudimentary at best, limited to what little he had read up in the Intelligence Summaries in Kasauli, and Ankita's briefing.

I wonder what the Chechen's name is. Does he know he is being conned by these bastards? Random thoughts began to gnaw at Iqbal's mind. *What difference does it make? Tomorrow he will die and take Allah knows how many more with him... and for what?*

Iqbal felt a sudden wave of anger. He remembered the intelligence reports he had read – the mean age of the suicide bomber in Pakistan was now down to sixteen and their families were paid barely a few hundred dollars in return.

Where will it end?

For the third night in succession, Tanaz's face was blurred when she entered his dreams, by now she seemed so remote that Iqbal could barely make out it was her. The battered face of the American soldier leapt out from behind her, beckoning wildly to Iqbal.

Iqbal was not aware of the tiny tortured moans he let out all night long. But he did not scream. *That* frontier had certainly been crossed.

∞

They were up early the next morning. The first person Iqbal saw when he opened his eyes was the Chechen. The young man was immersed in prayer, oblivious to everything around him. Iqbal noticed that from the other end of the room Karamat was watching him too.

The minute the Chechen finished praying, Karamat went across to him. They exchanged a few words in a low voice and sat down to eat. They ate in silence, Karamat's gaze still fixed on the Chechen.

It was a little over half past seven when Karamat, touched the Chechen's shoulder and gave a brief nod when the man looked up. They rose as one.

'I need two volunteers,' Karamat called out to the others.

Iqbal instantly raised his hand, grabbed his rifle and stepped forward. Altaf gave him a disgusted look as he followed suit.

So he is *my minder*, Iqbal noted with interest.

Karamat led the three men out to the Toyota Camry and motioned to Altaf and Iqbal to get into the back seat. 'Keep your weapons low, but be ready to bring them into action in case we have to fight our

way out. Of course, you will do so *only* when I tell
you to,' Karamat instructed as the Chechen started
the engine and carefully reversed into the street.

A strong smell of almonds pervaded the car. At
first Iqbal was puzzled, then he remembered that
plastic explosives like Semtex and C-4 emitted such
an odour. Iqbal wondered which one it was and
how much of it was in the boot of the car. More
importantly, where was it going to be used?

They drove through the streets of Kabul, sticking
to side roads, with Karamat constantly indicating the
route. Like the rest of the city, the streets bore the
scars of a hundred forgotten battles. Most buildings
had unmistakable pockmarks left by bullets and
yawning holes caused by rocket shells. Apart from
sporadic patchwork attempts, not much had been
done to restore them.

There were security checkposts on almost every
major road. Karamat guided them along empty,
dirty side lanes and back alleys. He had either been
here before or had been very thoroughly briefed
because they did not make a single wrong turn.

After half an hour of driving, the landscape began
to change. There was a distinct improvement in not
only the buildings, but also the type and condition
of the roads.

'Halt here,' Karamat commanded as they finally
came up to the mouth of an alley.

From the rear seat, Iqbal could see a large square
across the road. Further ahead, at the other end

of the square, was a long queue of people in front of a security barrier. The view was not entirely clear because of where the Camry was parked; obviously, they were not visible to the guards at the gate either.

'Switch off the engine,' Karamat said.

The Chechen complied wordlessly.

'Get out, you two,' Karamat told Iqbal and Altaf as he got out of the car, 'and leave those damn weapons in the car. Hide them under the floor mats.' He waited till they were out of the car before he motioned for them to follow him. The trio crossed the narrow alley and stopped outside a nondescript, three-storey building. We are going to get to the roof and take position.' He kept his voice low.

'What for?' Altaf interrupted.

'I will tell you when we get there,' Karamat snapped. He seemed very edgy, not like his usual even-tempered self. 'Wait here for a minute.' He returned to the Camry, leaned into the driver's window and spoke to the Chechen. Finally he reached in and patted the Chechen's shoulder. Then he made his way back to Iqbal and Altaf. 'Come on, let's go.'

'Stay low,' he cautioned as they came out on the roof. 'Most high buildings have snipers posted on them.' He slithered across to two large cement water tanks fitted on one side of the terrace, and Iqbal and Altaf followed suit.

An array of pipes led out from both tanks and ran

down the outer side of the building. Reaching past the pipes, Karamat pulled out a rocket launcher that had been hidden there. It was a Russian-made RPG 7V.

Evidently, a lot of planning, preparation and external support had gone into this operation. Whoever had masterminded it had taken care of every detail. Iqbal instinctively knew the operation had been set up by Pasha.

Karamat turned to the two men. 'I want you two to take position here with the launcher.' He gestured at the water tank closest to the terrace wall; it overlooked the square and shielded them from the road. 'If and when – and only when – I tell you to do so, you will fire at the Camry.'

'But…' Altaf started again.

'No buts, Altaf. Just shut up and do what I am telling you,' Karamat cut him off. 'And if I tell you to fire, aim for the Camry's boot.' He turned to Iqbal. 'You will act as his loader in case a second shot is required. Got it?' Both men nodded. He looked at his watch. 'Fine. Get ready.'

By the time they loaded the launcher, got the back-up rocket ready and took position, Karamat had moved to the other side of the terrace. Crouching behind the parapet wall, all three of them began to watch the road.

Iqbal surveyed the square below them. It took a minute for the flag on the building in front of which people had queued up to register.

He froze.

∽

Iqbal saw two cars drive up to the building. Almost at an equal distance, approaching the building from the other side, was the Toyota Camry. The sentries manning the gate had seen the two cars. One of the guards began to open the iron gates while the other pushed back the people lined up outside. Another pair of sentries shouldered their rifles and ran forward to drag away the spike strips that had been laid across the road to prevent any vehicle from forcing its way in.

No one noticed the Camry approach from the opposite direction.

The Camry weaved its way through the barrels placed on the road, meant to slow down a vehicle entering through the gate. It accelerated as soon as it had cleared the barrels. Even from the rooftop, Iqbal could see the Chechen sitting rigidly behind the wheel. He must have hit the accelerator hard just then because the powerful Camry lunged forward, the roar of its 2.5-litre engine filling the square.

This drew the attention of the security guards instantly. The men behind the sandbags grabbed their weapons, the one handling the gate tried to shut it, and the two who had pulled the road spikes out of the way tried to drag them back on the road, but that was about as far as any of them got – by then the Camry was almost upon them.

The first car had already entered the gate. The second car, a few metres behind, had slowed down due to the crowd in front of the gate. It braked when the gates begin to close and the road spikes were dragged forward again.

The Camry slammed into it with a loud crunch.

For a moment there was complete silence. Then a large black cloud erupted, engulfing both cars in a fireball. The sound of the explosion boomed across the square and slammed into Iqbal's ears a nanosecond later.

'Let's go.' Their ears were still ringing with the explosion so neither man heard Karamat's voice but they felt him tugging at their arms. Iqbal did not hesitate to obey. He knew that, very soon, security forces would cordon every building around, and there would be roadblocks at every exit out of the city; that was the standard security drill whenever an attack took place.

Pushing the rocket launcher behind the pipes, the three men raced down the narrow staircase. They were soon mingling with the crowd that had begun to gather.

Despite the compelling need to get away, curiosity got the better of Karamat. He stopped to watch the terror they had unleashed. Iqbal and Altaf, standing on the other side of Karamat, were also spellbound.

The Camry and the car it had rammed into had been totally obliterated. The car in front was in only marginally better condition. The sentries and the people who had been crowded near the gates had borne the brunt of the explosion. Not one of them remained standing. Barring a few shaken people at the end of the line who were trying to clamber back to their feet, bloodied, mangled bodies were strewn all around.

Some of the soldiers manning the inner cordon ran up to the gates. They fanned out and adopted a defensive posture, ready to ward off a secondary attack on the building. But there was none coming.

'Time to get out of here,' Karamat whispered in Iqbal's ear. Iqbal followed him as they made their way through the fast-gathering, nervously chattering crowd. A few people ran forward to help the survivors. But most hung back, afraid of another blast. The wail of emergency sirens began to build up as a host of ambulances and MRT vehicles converged outside the building. Iqbal's mind was reeling. He had just witnessed a meticulously executed fidayeen attack on the Indian Embassy in Kabul.

∾

When they got back to the safehouse, Pasha was sitting in front of the television, watching the news.

'Well done,' he greeted Karamat warmly. 'According to the news we got about sixty of them, including the Indian military attaché and another diplomat. Hopefully, some more of the 140-odd that have been injured will die soon. That will teach those Indian bastards to meddle with us.' They exchanged triumphant smiles. 'Well done,' Pasha repeated. 'Now just lie low for a couple of days.'

'Have you sent word to the others?'

'I will now. I will tell them to start the diversion day after tomorrow, sharp at midnight, okay?'

'That is fine with us... Oh, yes, the Ameer asked me to remind you about the money.'

'You need not remind me, miyan.' Pasha gave him a patronizing smile. 'It is on its way even as we speak.'

They parted at the door and a visibly cheerful Karamat went to share the news with the other men who had not gone with them in the morning. A current of jubilation ran through the room as he told them about the attack. Not one word was said about the Chechen who had been sacrificed.

Every few minutes, they heard a security vehicle thunder past. But that didn't worry them. As long as they did not roam about outside, bring any electronics into play or get betrayed, they would be safe. It was not possible for the security forces to search every single house in Kabul. Even the forensic evaluation of the attack would not reveal anything but the obvious. The car was a stolen one and the detonator and explosives used, whether C-4 or Semtex, were available in abundance all over the war-torn country.

As for the Chechen, even if they managed to piece together his body and identify him, the trail would lead nowhere. He was just another nameless, faceless pawn, one of several hundred illiterate youngsters who had been picked up for a handful of dollars and trained by Qari Hussain, the Ustad-e-Fidayeen, at the Spinkai Ragzai school in South Waziristan.

∽

Despite the euphoria of the successful strike on the Indian Embassy, the next two days took their toll on the patience and tempers of the men, who were confined to the house.

Karamat gathered them at eleven-thirty the following night. 'Get ready to leave in half an hour,' he said tersely. 'Weapons loaded and ready for action.'

'Do we fight our way out?' Altaf asked.

'If required, but I don't think we will need to,' Karamat said. 'Our teams will provide us with the diversion we need, and also give these bastards something to remember us by... a parting gift.' He laughed as he unfurled a map on the floor. 'Eight teams of two men each will attack these police stations.' He pointed them out on the map. The targets were scattered all over town and most were well away from the house where they had taken refuge. 'That will have all the MRTs hotfooting it to the stations under attack, because they will not be sure of what is happening. In the confusion, we can slip out of town.'

'What about the guys who are attacking?'

'Not a problem. They will fire a couple of rockets each and clear out. In any case, attacking like a swarm of bees always fucks the security forces and slows down their response. It keeps them guessing as to what our real intentions are and what the actual target is. The aim is to give us an open escape window and, of course, let these fools know that we can attack when and where we wish to.'

Weapon loads were rechecked, guns were cocked and fingers poised on triggers. Iqbal felt alive, aching to bludgeon forward into action. Iqbal knew the others were experiencing the same feeling.

The diversionary attacks began precisely at midnight. There was a scattered spate of explosions and a crackle of gunfire. The firing was far away and spread out: it sounded like fireworks in the distance. Almost on cue, the men surged forward.

'Hang on!' Karamat said sharply, holding up his hand, eyes glued to his wristwatch. 'Give the security guys time to respond.' The men held back but the tension was thick; though it was just five minutes, the wait seemed interminable.

Finally, Karamat told them, 'Let's go! One at a time and keep some distance from each other.'

By the time Iqbal ran out of the house, the man who had left before him was at the end of the road. Keeping his pace steady, his hand clutching the weapon under his shawl, Iqbal followed him, forcing his breathing to an even pace. His eyes darted about, taking in every stone and crack in the passing walls, ever alert to any threat.

The sound of firing, though intermittent, was now louder. The handful of people on the street at this hour scurried along, sticking to the shadows of the buildings on either side of the road. The fleeing men mingled with them. Every now and then, a security vehicle flashed past, going hell for leather for the closest point where the firing was going on. Each time one went past, Iqbal's grip on his weapon tightened, but not once during the half hour it took them to clear the town was he or any of the others stopped.

The team was waiting in a tight cluster when he ran up to them. They were now at the same spot where Pasha had met them three nights ago. Iqbal took up position in the defensive perimeter as they waited for the last man to join them. He knew they were out of danger now, though they all dreaded the night-vision capability of the drones and aircraft. But Allah seemed to be watching over them tonight.

∞

The return journey was another gruelling speed march as they moved by night and hid by day. Because of the intense aerial surveillance activity, it took them over twelve days to get back. Several times they were forced to go to ground as gunships swept overhead.

Twice, they came across signs of the revenge the ISAF had meted out to suspect villages along their route. Both times, Karamat gave a wide berth to the villages and kept going. Their task was over. The collateral damage that followed in the wake of such attacks and ambushes was not relevant. If anything, it contributed to their cause because disproportionate retaliation by the security forces only yielded more recruits for the jihad, more canon fodder for the security guns, and more retribution.

It was an exhausted but elated party that finally returned to the base. The Ameer himself was there to greet them when they stumbled into the village. He commandeered Karamat and the two men retired to the Ameer's hut.

∞

If Iqbal thought the action was over, he was mistaken. The men had been back barely a few hours when they were rounded up again.

Karamat looked furious when he came out of the Ameer's hut. 'The Pakistan government has reneged on its deal with us and sent in the army to drive us out of our homes,' he informed his team. 'While we were away, the Pakistani forces moved in and took Swat from our brothers there. We do not have too much time before those faithless pet dogs of the Americans reach here, so this is what we are going to do.' He turned to the team leaders who were standing to one side. 'I want everyone to be mobilized. We move out tonight with every single man capable of holding a weapon. I want you to take up defensive positions here, here and here.' He pointed at the map he had brought with him. 'Tell the men to be very careful. You should also expect trouble from some of the local lashkars. Any questions?'

There were several. Iqbal watched Karamat patiently answer each one before he proceeded to the final briefing.

'Now remember, we will not get into any pitched battles with the army. Hit! Run! Fall back! Hit, run and fall back! Keep them bleeding and slow them down as much as you can. They must not get past this line.' He pointed at the map again, tracing a line across it. 'No matter what happens. I will be with you at every step but we need to ensure the army does not cross this line, at least not until the Ameer and the other elders get to safety. Remember, our lives are not important, theirs are. Clear?'

Unflinching nods met his gaze. Most of the men were hardened fighters. The few that were prone to falter knew they would be gunned down at the first sign of flight.

'The army will try to evacuate everyone from this area,' Karamat continued. 'We have to prevent them from doing so, or at least make it difficult for them. Every man, woman and child that we manage to keep back here will give us the shield we need and slow down the army offensive because they will have to try and keep civilian casualties to a minimum. They will also be forced to cater to the population administratively. So we have to make sure the area is not evacuated.'

'How?' one of the team leaders asked.

'We will set up blocks here, here and here.' Karamat tapped out a series of positions on the map and designated the men who would defend each. 'Go for all patrols that come down these roads or any groups that try to evacuate the area.' Karamat pointed to another group. 'You lot, target the roadblocks and posts that the army sets up. No long engagements, okay? Just hit and get the hell out of there. Come back randomly from another direction and hit again. Use mines and IEDs wherever you can; those are the most cost-effective and will slow them down. Evoke as much uncertainty and fear as you can. Keep them guessing and on their toes; that will eventually wear them out.'

There were a few more questions. Iqbal was amazed at the way Karamat handled them. He could not help but admire the man's attention to detail. It did not strike Iqbal that they would be using women and children as a shield. The battle had sunk in too deep.

Finally, Karamat stood back and watched them break ranks and scurry away. There was a lot to be done: weapons had to be cleaned; ammunition, medicine and food supplies had to be drawn before they moved out for the assigned tasks. Iqbal was rushing along with the others when he was stopped by Karamat.

'You! Indian! The Ameer specifically asked about you.' He grinned. 'I told him you did well.'

'Thank you, janab.' Iqbal smiled. For some reason, he felt pleased.

'Go and grab your gear, then report back to me,' Karamat ordered. He saw the quizzical look on Iqbal's face and added, 'I want you by my side.'

∽

Seven days later, Iqbal realized that it was Karamat's sudden whim to take him along that saved his life. Iqbal never again met most of the men who had been there for the operational briefing.

The ones did not fall to the Pakistani military juggernaut vanished into the hills, some abandoning their weapons to merge with the flood of fleeing civilians, some returning wherever they had come from. Not many were captured; rather, the Pakistan Army did not take them alive. The few who were unlucky enough to be surrounded were gunned down in cold blood. The message was clear: the Pakistanis were not taking prisoners. Maybe they did not want the captured jihadis telling embarrassing tales of the support they received from the army and the ISI. Or maybe it was just too much effort for the army to hold prisoners. Perhaps the government needed to brag about the headcount to prove that it was doing everything possible to end terrorism.

Or maybe the line between the two sides had begun to blur, if it had ever been there. Whatever the reason, it soon became clear that capture meant certain death.

As Karamat, Iqbal and four other men flitted from one site of action to another, they saw an orgy of blood and death: the charred remains of policemen who had been burnt alive with their jeep; scattered bodies of innocent men, women and children who had been trying to flee the battle zone; and the rotting bodies of soldiers and mujahideen, some blown to bits by artillery guns, some torn apart by landmines, IEDs or grenades, some lined up and shot in the head.

Kotkai, Srarogha, Shrangrawari, Kunigram, Ladha and Makeen fell in quick succession as the three-pronged Pakistan Army offensive, backed by air force jets and choppers, forced the jihadis to withdraw. But they put up a credible resistance, egged on by commanders like Karamat.

The battle at Damadola, about 7 kilometres from the Afghan border, was excruciatingly intense. Located at a strategic junction, Damadola is a vital link to Afghanistan, Chitral, Swat and the main highway to China. It is certain that the complex of 156 caves would have fallen to the army within hours had it not been for Karamat. He was like a man possessed, moving his men from cave to cave, ensuring the line held firm. Eventually, the asymmetry of forces began to tell and it became

evident that the army would overrun resistance.
And then Karamat used his intimate knowledge of
the terrain to make himself scarce – jannat, after
all, is the privilege of the jihadi foot soldier, not the
leader. Iqbal and three of the original four were with
Karamat; they had lost Zia at Damadola.

With the bases in Swat already lost and South
Waziristan teetering on the brink, they now had
no option but to fall back to the smaller bases at
Bajaur, Mohmand, Khyber, Orakzai and Kurram
and try to break the forward momentum of the
security forces.

Simultaneously, Karamat unleashed a series of
suicide bombers in the more vulnerable rear areas of
the advancing army, striking at the vital supply lines
to impose delay and caution. In rapid succession,
the US consulate in Karachi, the Naval War College,
the headquarters of the Federal Investigation
Agency in Lahore, a police training centre, the anti-
terrorist police headquarters and ISI headquarters
in Islamabad and several supply columns were hit
by fidayeen squads. The attack on Karachi's Kemari
oil refinery failed, but by now enough damage had
been inflicted on the morale of the security forces
and on the confused Pakistani public.

∾

Perhaps it was the cumulative effect of these rear
area strikes, the rugged terrain and the dogged
resistance put up by the jihadis that finally turned

the tide. Despite the high-speed intensity of the army operations and the undeniable superiority of men and materials fielded by the security forces, by the seventh night it was clear that the army offensive had begun to grind to a halt.

During this time they did not spend more than a few hours in any one place. As they wove through the battlefield, Karamat's energy seemed limitless but Iqbal, though much younger than him, had begun to feel the strain. And overriding everything was the fear that he would die before he could take down the Ameer. Physically and mentally exhausted, Iqbal could not wait for night and those few hours when he could surrender to sleep, no matter how fitful.

SITUATION REVIEW

From: Director RAW
To: NIC
Security Classification: Director – Eyes Only
Priority: Urgent
Subject: Review of internal security situation in Pakistan

Pakistan has finally been compelled to act against the terrorist groups, because America and other donor countries have made this a precondition for monetary aid. Also, Taliban's breach of the Swat Valley deal, their advance towards Islamabad, a flood of 3 million displaced people, mounting pressure from a terrified population that is suffering a spate of bomb attacks, and a global media outcry has made it impossible for them to ignore the issue any longer.

Although the Pakistan Army operation Rah-e-Rast has made clear gains in the Swat area, it is clear that the war is far from won.

It is also clear that there is a definite divide in the minds of the government and the army regarding the terrorists. This dichotomy is evident from the fact that although bounties have been placed on some terrorist commanders and military action threatened in parts of Waziristan, there are other terror leaders and groups (like the Haq, Nasir and Gul networks) that have been excluded from these actions, despite the fact that they are providing physical, material and moral support to Al-Qaeda and the Taliban. These groups are still considered strategic assets which will enable Pakistan to exercise influence over Afghanistan as soon as the Americans pull out, reduce Indian influence in Afghanistan and also be used against India in the Kashmir Valley.

Some specific examples of the complicity between the jihadists and the Islamists in power are:

1. Rana Sanaullah, the law minister of Pakistani Punjab, openly travelled with Ahmed Ludhianvi, the leader of the banned Sipah-e-Sahaba (a Punjab-based radical Deobandi terror outfit and known Al-Qaeda consort), on a by-election tour and even visited its madrassa in Jhang. (It is pertinent to point out that both Hakimullah Mehsud, the Taliban commander who was killed in a drone strike, and Qari Hussain, the Ustad-e-Fidayeen, are ex-Sipah-e-Sahaba members.)

2. Hafiz Sayeed, chief of Lashkar-e-Toiba and known perpetrator of the 26/11 Mumbai ghazwa, is still openly addressing public rallies all over Pakistan.

3. Iliyas Kashmiri, the commander of the 313-Brigade, too has been openly addressing public rallies wherein he has threatened to attack the Commonwealth Games and the Indian Premier League matches being held in India.

4. The detention and subsequent release of five of the top Quetta Shura leaders.

Despite this, American military aid to Pakistan has crossed US$ 1.2 billion (up from the current US$ 700 million) in the previous year. Most of the military hardware being supplied (F-16s, drones and precision-guided munitions) is more relevant in a conventional war against India than against terrorists.

Reports also indicate that the ISI is quietly pulling out certain key, 'friendly' Pakistan Taliban leaders from Waziristan. Several HUMINT and SIGINT sources have confirmed this. It is a logical possibility, considering the current state of affairs and repeated public statements by various Pakistani commanders that Pakistan will not be able to rein in the terrorists unless its strategic interests are met; namely, the reduction of Indian influence over the Karzai regime in Afghanistan.

That is why it is unlikely that Operation Rah-e-Nijat (the Pak Army offensive in Waziristan) will go beyond the occasional air strike or cosmetic patrols. The operation has obviously been launched to show America that it means business, so that the dollars keep flowing in.

Given the presence of several senior terror leaders (of Al-Qaeda, the Afghan Taliban and Pakistan Taliban) in Waziristan, it is definite that any military operations will be met with a strong and determined resistance. The army has already faced several reverses in Waziristan during the period 2004 to 2008.

The terror groups are aware that any attempt by them to flee into Afghanistan will drive them into the anvil that ISAF has established along the Durand Line. Thus, to dissipate the pressure built up by the army in Waziristan, the terror groups are launching an average of two attacks per day on government installations and on soft targets like crowded markets. This urban jihad is designed to break the will of the Pakistani people and compel them to pressure the government into calling off the Waziristan offensive. Though publicly condemned, these attacks are secretly condoned by the powers-that-be in Pakistan, since they allow them to proclaim that they too are victims of terror and not the mother lode from where this problem originates.

The Taliban has also increased attacks in Tajikistan to disrupt American attempts to establish a new supply line into Afghanistan. Known as the Northern Distribution Network, the new supply line goes through Tajikistan and will reduce ISAF dependence on Pakistan.

The interrogation of several captured terrorists (by various foreign intelligence agencies) confirms that many key Al-Qaeda and Taliban leaders are presently sheltering in the Shawal Valley of North Waziristan, the Chitral district, further north in the Hindu Kush, and the Kurram tribal area which is barely 20 kilometres south of the Tora Bora caves.

In light of the escalated threat from drones, Al-Qaeda and Taliban have changed tactics; leaders have stopped using modern means of communication, which are easier to pinpoint and move around frequently, The large training camps of yore have been replaced by hut-based training and even the fighting cadres ordered to merge in urban areas in groups of ten or less men. These small groups are linked by human couriers carrying verbal messages, which are impossible to extract even if the courier is apprehended. Al-Qaeda Arabs have been instructed to speak in Pashto to help them blend in.

However, the fiscal strain on both Al-Qaeda and Taliban is apparent; their fund-raisers are working frantically and all western (European and American) recruits have to pay (US$ 1800 to US$ 2000 per person) for terror training, which had earlier been provided free.

Despite this, the strategic and operational capability of Al-Qaeda remains largely unimpaired and there are several unconfirmed reports of a major operation being planned against India, Australia, Britain and the American mainland.

Keeping in view the NIC directive to enhance HUMINT capability in this area, six penetration attempts have been launched, including the Force 22 mission to get an operative in place. The first four attempts were unsuccessful and resulted in the presumed loss of all four assets since there has been no further contact from them. Progress report on the other two follows.

Concerted efforts are underway to recruit a senior Pakistan Army officer, code-named Sukoon, currently posted in the Peshawar Corps HQ. Initial contact and his response appear to be favourable and now the financial arrangements are being worked out. If successfully acquired, Sukoon will prove to be a formidable source of real-time, actionable intelligence.

If you fear treachery from any of your allies you may fairly retaliate by breaking off your treaty with them.

Holy Quran

The five of them, Karamat, Iqbal, Imran, Mahroof and Niaz, left Bajaur when it became clear that the army offensive had stalled. On the first night, they halted at a small village well away from the battlefield. After weeks of bloodshed, this was the first time Iqbal came across anything close to normalcy. The sleepy little village felt like heaven. The others also seemed more relaxed.

Iqbal had just about fallen asleep when Karamat shook him awake.

'Where is Mahroof?' Karamat seemed tense.

'I have no idea. He was here before I went to sleep. I assumed he was getting ready to sleep.'

'That's what he told me too, but I can't find him anywhere. His rucksack isn't here either.' Karamat's mouth twitched suspiciously. 'I have looked for him everywhere. Something is not right.'

They stepped out of the hut, puzzling over the matter, when they heard a strange whistling sound. It coalesced into two sparks of light as a pair of missiles flashed out of the darkness. The missiles slammed into the hut Karamat and Iqbal had just vacated.

There was a harsh flare of light. Then a boom filled the air with deadly force. The hut disappeared. Debris was billowing out when a second set of missiles slammed into the village, one taking out the adjacent hut while the second churned up the open space beside it.

Iqbal felt a surge of fear, the nearness of death leaving a bitter taste in his mouth.

'That bastard!' Karamat hissed. 'Mahroof! The harami can't be too far.' Karamat swivelled around, trying to out-guess the man who had guided in the missiles. 'That way! That's the easiest place for him to hitch a ride out of here. Let's get him.'

He rushed off into the darkness, Iqbal hard at his heels.

They were soaked with sweat by the time they reached the path connecting the two villages. Up ahead they could hear the sound of a man running.

Mahroof must have heard them coming. He was reaching for the rifle on his shoulder when Karamat hit him on the head with his rifle butt. Mahroof went down at once.

'Indian, search his rucksack.' Karamat threw Mahroof's rifle away from him.

Iqbal overturned the contents of the rucksack on the ground. It took barely a minute to find the tiny electronic chip wrapped in foil. Iqbal knew it was a GPS transponder and, from the look and size of it, a very sophisticated one. Feigning ignorance, he held it out to Karamat.

'What is this?'

'It is a GPS transponder, meant to light up the target and guide in the American missiles. He will tell us who it was meant for,' Karamat said grimly.

'Bhai! Bhai! I am sorry.' Mahroof suddenly found his voice, the words dribbling out between terrified sobs. 'They made me do it. I was told that...'

'Who?'

'I don't know his name but I think he works for the agency. At least that is what he implied but I am not sure if he was ISI or CIA.' Mahroof went silent.

Karamat was too expert an interrogator not to recognize the power of silence. He knew that sometimes silence was the most effective question.

Mahroof began to blubber again. 'He told me that I just had to place one of these wherever you went to sleep. That's all. I didn't think...' His voice petered away. Once again Karamat's silence compelled him to speak. 'I didn't want to do it, bhai.'

'How much did they pay you?'

No response.

'How much, Mahroof?' His tone was sharper this time.

'Fifty thousand rupees, bhai,' came the strangled whisper. 'My family was starving. No one had eaten for days.'

'A lot of people are starving. Does that mean we sell our faith?'

'They said they would kill me if I didn't do it.'

'What do you think I will do?'

'Bhai, don't... please don't. I did not...'

'Don't worry, Mahroof, I am not going to kill you.'

Mahroof's face lit up. 'I promise you, bhai, I will...'

'By the time I finish, you will wish I *had* killed you.' Karamat laughed. He reached for his knife. The moonlight glinted coldly off the blade. He reached down and tore the clothes off the hapless man grovelling in the mud.

A continuous keening sound whistled out from between Mahroof's lips. The sound grated through Iqbal, setting his teeth on edge.

Karamat's knife slashed out. It did not penetrate Mahroof's body. Instead, it surgically split open the soft skin all along the lower half of the stomach, just below his belly button, in a thin red line. The line thickened as blood welled out, gaining strength with every passing moment, dividing Mahroof's body into two perfect halves.

As the knife ploughed deeper, Mahroof's high-pitched screams shuddered through the night. Iqbal watched in silence as Karamat systematically flayed the skin from the upper half of Mahroof's body. Every time Mahroof fainted, Karamat kicked him back into consciousness before he resumed the butchery.

With every slash of the knife, the stench of blood grew stronger. It mingled with the thick, pungent smell of excreta. Karamat's face was devoid of expression.

Iqbal found himself watching in fascination as the man writhed on the ground, his blood-soaked body absorbing the dust.

Karamat tired of the game suddenly. He drove the knife deep into Mahroof's chest. Still expressionless, he turned to Iqbal. 'We need to get out of here.'

They ran back to the village to collect Niaz and minutes later the four men had gathered their kit and melted into the night.

When they reached the next village, Karamat called for a halt. The minute Iqbal lay down and closed his eyes, the screams in his head began again. Mahroof's voice blended viciously with the American soldier's; the cacophony reverberated in his mind, jolting him awake, sweating and breathless.

Three long, painful nights elapsed before he finally managed to conquer his demons. The faces still called out to him in the silence of the night, but they did not excite any emotion in him any longer.

In his dreams he could now see himself stand by and watch the two men die.

On the fourth day, the Ameer's messenger found them.

'We have to go to Jandola. The Ameer wants us,' Karamat told them.

To Iqbal's surprise, the messenger led them to a station wagon.

'Is it safe to use a vehicle?' Imran asked.

'We have no choice,' Karamat replied. He too was not pleased with the transport; they all knew that cars were prime targets for the security forces, because the lashkars had commandeered all available vehicles.

∾

Just how dangerous it was became clear when a pair of helicopters rose from behind a knoll as they turned the corner a little short of Jandola. Karamat, who was driving, saw them at almost the same time as the choppers must have spotted the vehicle. Unfortunately, unlike the attack helicopters, the station wagon was neither armed with rockets nor machine guns.

With a warning shout, Karamat swerved to a halt, threw open the door and leapt out of the vehicle. On the other side, the Ameer's messenger did the same, as did the three men riding in the back. They all reacted quickly, but were not fast enough to beat the machine-gun fire that erupted from both choppers.

The heavy-calibre bullets riddled the vehicle like a sieve, blasting open the bonnet with a bang. Iqbal, Imran and Niaz were luckier: they had just managed to get past a curve in the road when the first rocket collided with it. The flaming blast and the debris fanned past Iqbal as he hit the ground. He crawled up to the rocks on the side of the road, behind which Niaz and Imran had taken shelter. Both were sobbing with relief.

Karamat and the messenger were not as fortunate. The latter lost the right half of his body as the bullets reached the fuel tanks and the vehicle exploded.

He died instantly.

Karamat was just marginally luckier – three bullets punctured his left side and the impact hurled him off the road, saving him from immediate death when the rocket hit the vehicle. He retained enough presence of mind to crawl to a depression off the road. He barely made it, as the choppers closed in and machine-gun fire churned the area around for several minutes.

Finally satisfied that they had thrashed the vehicle into oblivion, the Pakistani gunships pulled away, the clacking rotors slowly fading into the night.

Even as a plume of black smoke spiralled up from the charred vehicle, silence and peace returned. Only the smell of gunpowder, burnt fuel and burning rubber lingered.

Iqbal and the others stood up only when they were absolutely certain that the danger had passed.

Though he was bleeding heavily, Karamat was still conscious. 'We need to get away from here fast,' he told them. He dragged himself up with Imran's and Iqbal's support. 'Niaz.' His breath was heavy and each word came out with painful effort. 'Take us down to Jandola. Use the lower track.'

The next mile was testimony to Karamat's courage. Iqbal's admiration for the man increased with each step. Though he was obviously in agony, not a whimper escaped his lips as they hobbled along, stopping just once to bandage the wounds. The smell of blood and perspiration seeped into Iqbal's head as he half-carried the injured man with Imran holding him on the other side.

∽

Jandola was on high alert when they finally arrived. Two of the Ameer's bodyguards met them when they were still at the outer periphery. They urgently led the group away from the village.

Twenty minutes later, they were in the presence of the Ameer, safe in a cave above Jandola. He was pacing the floor of the gloomy cave when they entered.

'What took you so long, Karamat?' the Ameer bellowed. Then he saw the blood-soaked bandages and his expression changed. 'How bad is it?' he asked, his haste still evident, as also the lack of any real concern. Jihadis, even senior leaders, were acknowledged and appreciated only as long as they were fit enough to deliver. A seriously wounded man was no more than a liability.

'Bad enough, Ameer,' Karamat replied weakly.

'Don't worry, Karamat, you will be fine.' The Ameer patted him on the shoulder. 'You two,' he gestured to Imran and Niaz, 'take care of him. And you!' he addressed Iqbal, 'go and fetch a doctor to tend to him.'

'I do not know this area, Ameer,' Iqbal said hesitantly.

The Ameer recognized him. 'Ah, Indian! You again!' He nodded. 'Okay, you get a doctor,' he said to the bodyguard standing closest to him. The man left immediately.

'Karamat.' The Ameer turned to the wounded commander. 'I need to go. They have told me to move out now. These two will look after you.'

'Go, Ameer.' Karamat's voice was barely audible. 'Don't worry about me.'

'What about this guy?' one of the bodyguards asked as the Ameer was leaving the cave.

'What about him? Leave him here.'

'There are only three of us now. We may need more guns if things turn nasty. Should we not take him along?'

'Should we?' the Ameer asked aloud. 'Can we trust you, Indian?' He looked at Iqbal.

'You can trust him, Ameer,' Karamat called out weakly. 'He is a good man to have by your side.'

'All right. Come with us.'

A few minutes later, they were marching down the path that led to Jandola. When they were just short of it they turned off it and walked down a tiny foot track. An hour later, they were at the base of the mountain.

For they are all greedy for profit, from the smallest to the greatest, from prophet to priest. They all act falsely. They attempt to heal my people's wounds without efforts saying, 'peace, peace,' but there is no peace.

Book of Jeremiah

Even though he was used to surprises at every turn since he had left Faisalabad all those months ago, Iqbal was shocked when they hit the road. There were four army jeeps parked on the shoulder, twenty-odd soldiers deployed around them. Iqbal instinctively reached for the rifle slung on his shoulder when the hand of the bodyguard by his side reached out and stayed him.

'Calm down,' he cautioned Iqbal in a low voice. 'Stay still and keep your hands away from your weapon.'

A man stepped out of the first jeep. He was in plain clothes but his age, dress and demeanour suggested a rank far above what was ordinarily found in the Pakistani frontline. He stepped up to the Ameer.

'How are you, Colonel Imam?'

Iqbal sensed from the Ameer's tone that he did not like the man. They greeted each other with the cautious restraint of uncertain allies. Then the Ameer turned to his bodyguards.

'There are clothes in that vehicle.' He pointed at one of the jeeps. 'Get rid of whatever you are wearing and put those on.'

'The weapons too, Ameer,' Imam added.

'To hell with you,' the Ameer snarled. 'If you want our weapons you will have to take them from us.' His aggressive tone and stance dared the man to respond. Imam stared at the Ameer for a moment, shrugged and then stood back.

It took about five minutes for them to change out of the trademark black jihadi attire and get into the more anonymous shades of grey and white worn by the locals.

Then they were off with the army jeeps. Iqbal had no idea where they were going but he could hear the rumble of choppers overhead. Obviously, the army did not care to move about without adequate protection in this area.

∾

The road improved after some time. They crossed a number of small villages, then towns and cities. The convoy either raced through them or bypassed them wherever possible.

Several hours later, they entered a town and halted outside a pair of large black metallic gates. As they waited for the gates to be opened, Iqbal read the faded board above a shop across the road. They had reached Dera Ismail Khan.

Situated on the banks of the Indus, at the intersection of Punjab, Baluchistan and the NWFP, DIK, though only six hours by road from Islamabad, was the gateway to South Waziristan and the last major crossroad for terrorists and smugglers before the FATA. Like Quetta and Peshawar, it was also one of the hubs where the Pakistani state machinery and terror groups meshed into one.

The small convoy drove past the gates that had been pulled open by two armed men dressed in paramilitary fatigues. The gates clanged shut as the last vehicle entered.

'Is he here?' the Ameer asked Imam.

'Of course not.' The colonel gave an amused smile. 'This is where we spend the night. He is going to meet us in Lahore tomorrow.'

'I see. Are you also staying here for the night?' the Ameer asked suspiciously.

Imam nodded.

'Here, in the same house?'

'Yes, of course. The chopper will be here to pick us up at first light.'

They all trooped inside.

Iqbal's mind was in a whirl as he lay down to sleep. *Just what is going on here?* By now he had seen many facets of Pakistan's involvement with the jihad, but this one had blown him away.

∾

When the chopper landed in Lahore the next day, there was another set of vehicles with darkened windows waiting at the helipad. However, it was an assorted mix and none of the vehicles had any government markings. They swept the men out of the helipad and delivered them to the officers' mess of an army unit.

Apart from the sentries and a handful of mess staff there was no one around. It was obvious that the building had been vacated for them. Someone was going to great lengths to ensure that this meeting, whoever it was with, remained a closely guarded secret.

'Here?' the Ameer asked, as soon as they entered.

Imam nodded. 'He is already here. Let's go.' He began to lead the way and stopped abruptly when he saw the bodyguards gather around the Ameer. 'Not them, Ameer. They will stay here,' he said firmly.

'They will be in the very next room. Get that clear.' The Ameer strode forward in the direction Imam had been heading, swiftly overtaking him. The colonel watched as Iqbal and the others followed him, then he shrugged and picked up pace.

Imam stopped when they reached the mess anteroom. 'Your men can stay here. We are going into that room.' He gestured at another door in front of them.

The Ameer imperiously waved his bodyguards to a halt and continued towards the door, pushing it open without breaking his stride. As the door swung open, Iqbal saw a thin dark man with a sallow face sitting at the head of a long table. He had a cigarette in his hand. Flanking him on either side were two men in army uniform. Iqbal knew enough about Pakistan Army ranks and uniforms to note that both men were brigadiers.

'Welcome, Jalaluddin.' The man rose to greet him.

Then the door swung shut and they all vanished from view, as did all sound from within.

The bodyguards paced about anxiously.

∽

Iqbal would never have found out what was going on inside if not for the mess waiter who came in with a large silver tea tray. The waiter was about to set the tray down to open the door when Iqbal stepped forward and held it open for him. He waited for the waiter to enter before he allowed the door to swing shut, but he made sure he did not close it fully. It remained open just a crack, enough for a murmur of sound to filter through.

'How could you allow this to happen?' the Ameer was saying, his voice thick with anger.

'Grow up, Jalaluddin. You are not new to this game. You know there is too much at stake. If the world does not see us responding to what that foolish mullah friend of yours started in Swat, how long do you think the dollars will continue to flow?'

'That may be true but how could...'

'In any case, some of your people, like Barader, Yunis and Kabir have outlived their utility. They have drawn too much attention to themselves. That is not acceptable in the circumstances. We kept warning them but...'

'I am not talking about those fools,' the Ameer snapped. 'They got what they deserved.'

'I thought you would feel that way.' The other man laughed. 'After all, who does not love to get rid of the competition?'

'I don't care about that, general sahib. I can handle the competition without your help. What worries me is that many of my trained fighters have also paid the price for your damn dollars.'

'The fighters are easily replaceable, my friend. And do not forget who allowed you to recruit and train them. Right now we need the money far more than you need your fighters.'

'I wonder if you would feel the same way if we were talking about your life, general sahib.' The Ameer's tone had a nasty edge.

'Is that a threat?' Iqbal could imagine the general leaning forward. 'Do not get above yourself, Jalaluddin. Those blackguards of yours in the other room will not be able to save you...'

'Nor will the ones who run circles around you, general sahib.' The Ameer was not about to back away. 'Never forget that. No one can be protected all the time. Nothing that stands in our way will survive. So don't *you* dare threaten me either.'

A long pause followed. When the conversation resumed, tempers had simmered down.

'Anyway, let's not get worked up.' The general sounded at once angry and nervous. 'We want you to recall your suicide bombers and stop all attacks on the security forces.'

'Call back your dogs of war from the FATA and the NWFP and I will call back my fighters.'

'You know that's not going to happen. At least not right away. There is too much pressure on us. The new American president needs to show some results back home and even we...'

'Why is it so important to you what they need?'

'We need their money.'

'Give me a break, general sahib. You think the Americans do not know what you are doing with the money they give you? They *need* an enemy to fight, they need to give you the money as badly as you want it. How else would their weapon factories continue to make profits if they were not selling those damn things to Pakistan? The Harpoon missile and F-16 factories have *you* guys to thank.'

'Don't teach me politics, Jalaluddin. It's not just the Americans, there is too much international pressure on us right now. We have to show results. The army cannot sit back and give you guys a free reign any longer, not for some time at least… until the world gets bogged down with other issues and we go back to business as usual.'

'Then the suicide attacks will continue, general,' the Ameer said flatly.

'I don't care, but lay off the security forces. Those hurt us directly. That attack on the Qasim Market mosque in Rawalpindi cost me some very valuable officers.'

'Just as yours are costing me equally valuable people. We both have to do what we have to do.'

'Have it your way then. As far as you are concerned, you have to stay away from the tribal areas completely until this hue and cry dies down.'

'Why?'

'The Americans are baying for your blood, especially after the stunt your people pulled in Afghanistan. Hitting the Indian Embassy is one thing, but why did your guys have to hit the American convoy?'

'Who cares what the Americans feel? They have

never had the stomach to stand and fight. Despite their much-touted shock and awe since 2001, even today they barely control 30 per cent of Afghanistan. In any case, they will be gone from Afghanistan in a matter of months and we will be back in power.'

'But they are there right now and they are seriously pissed off about that ambush. They want their revenge.'

'Yes, that we can tell. Their drones are buzzing around like mosquitoes these days.'

'Well, we have no option but to comply, otherwise the money will stop. The economy is just too fragile... we cannot allow that to happen.'

'The economy or your bank balance?' the Ameer scoffed. 'Either way, that's your problem, general sahib.'

'It is yours too, you know.' There was a pause and the click of a lighter. 'Anyway, have you given any thought to what we spoke about... the peace talks?'

'What about them?'

'The new American president wants to talk with the good Taliban.'

'What the fuck is that? Does he mean the wimpy ones? Those who are ready to sue for peace and get paid for it?'

'Listen, Jalaluddin, I do not make the rules. I pass on their messages and take back your replies. I *can* give you some advice, though.'

'You are talking to the wrong man then. I suggest you speak to the mentor.'

'I already have.'

'And what did he say?'

'He said to keep giving them hope. If required, let some of you guys talk to them. It does no harm. They will be happy to start talks and when they are happy they pay us more. It will also take the heat off your people and give you time to marshal your forces again.'

'Fine, do that. I could do with the time right now, though I am certainly not going to be part of any talks.'

'Good! Meanwhile, before things get better, the FATA is going to see a lot more action in the near future. So don't go back. We will not be able to guarantee your safety there.'

'So where the hell am I supposed to go?'

'Don't worry about that. We will take care of you.' The general gave a self-assured laugh. 'You can stay here if you want, or you can even go and stay with the mentor in Quetta if you like.'

'No! Quetta is out.'

'It will be perfectly safe...'

'I know that, but Quetta is out.'

Perhaps he has been told not to go there by this mentor, Iqbal thought. *The mentor must be Mullah Omar. Everyone knows he is in Quetta. Who else could it be?*

'And you forget we are losing time,' the Ameer continued. 'There is a schedule to keep. The tanzeem has to meet.'

'The tanzeem?' There was a sudden interest in the general's voice. 'You have identified the ameers – the leaders? You have the group in place?'

'Of course. All six of them.' The Ameer chuckled. 'We now have one Ameer from every continent. They will take this battle forward, to its rightful conclusion.'

'When did that happen? Why did you not tell us?'

'I was going to, when the time was right.'

'You know how critical the tanzeem is to the jihad. They will be able to restore focus and give us the impetus we need to allow the will of Allah to prevail.' A brief lull followed and Iqbal could hear the tinkle of cup against saucer. 'Have you thought about tasking them the way I advised you?'

'I thought it over.'

'And?'

'And we see things differently.' The general started to say something but the Ameer interrupted him, 'I am not saying you are wrong but, for the moment, we have different priorities. The jihad must take priority.'

'Of course it must.' The general sounded frustrated. 'But can't you get one simple fact? Economic jihad is the way forward. Look at 9/11. Including airfares and training, it cost Al-Qaeda barely 500,000 dollars, approximately the cost of maintaining one American soldier in Afghanistan for one year, but the damage to the goras has been almost 500 billion dollars. The subsequent wars in Afghanistan and Iraq have already cost them close to 1 trillion dollars. And not just that, they have had over 35,000 wounded in Iraq and Afghanistan and another 300,000 psychological casualties suffering from post traumatic stress disorder. Do you know that is going to cost them another 600 billion dollars in healthcare costs? '

'Yes, yes, I know. America's national debt is now almost 15 trillion dollars... you have told me all this before.' It was hard to tell from the Ameer's tone whether he genuinely disagreed or was merely dissembling, just trying to be difficult as a bargaining ploy. 'I also know that every 9/11 or Glasgow makes them throw more millions into your kitty.'

'And thus into yours, my friend,' the general added drily. 'It also automatically weakens the western economies.'

'Yes, I know that.'

'Well then, why not take the more direct route that we are proposing? We can force them to spend billions with such little effort. The American economy has already been weakened and they have a lot of domestic opposition to the growing cost of their war. And you will agree that economic stability is a major component of political stability. Both of us need to get them out of Afghanistan and *this* is the right time…' The general suddenly broke off, perhaps realizing he was not making any headway. 'I would like to be there when the tanzeem meets,' he said instead.

'Not for the first meeting. That we do alone,' said the Ameer firmly. 'After that, we can come to Lahore or wherever you want and you can meet them.'

'Why not do it all at the same time? It is risky to have them here for too long.'

'I do not tell you how to run your army, general sahib. Let me handle my people my way.'

'Oh, well, let us go over it again when they come. And what has that got to do with your staying here or going back to the FATA? We can bring them here for your meeting.'

'No!' said the Ameer firmly. 'I will not allow them to see me hiding here like a stray dog. I have to meet them in *my* area. They must know that we command the area and have no fear of living in it. I know exactly where I am going to meet them.'

'That would be a huge risk,' the general protested. 'Do you know how many intelligence agencies are keeping an eye on the FATA?'

'I am aware of that, but the risk will have to be taken. It is a matter of face. If we expect the tanzeem to take us seriously we have to show them we are in control of our own area. In any case, all of them began their journey there. I want them to see that nothing has changed.'

Just then, Iqbal heard the waiter coming back and he hurriedly moved away from the door. The voices inside faded as the waiter shut the door.

I wonder what these bastards are planning, Iqbal wondered. *It is something really big... that much is clear from the interest the general is showing in the tanzeem.*

The door suddenly swung open and one of the brigadiers who had been flanking the general marched out of the room.

'Imam, get the map folder from the director's car,' he told the officer who had escorted them from Jandola, before returning inside.

There was a flurry of activity and the map folder, a large leather-bound case, arrived. Imam handed it inside and shut the door again.

Who are these six men the Ameer has selected and what is this tanzeem going to do?

The question plagued Iqbal as he fretted in silence with the other bodyguards.

∞

The Ameer strode out almost an hour later, the general beside him. The Ameer tossed the leather map towards Iqbal, who was standing closest to the door.

'Take it to my room,' he said.

'By the way, did you hear about the anti-jihad fatwa which that guy in London has issued?' the general was saying.

'Yes, I saw it on television,' the Ameer replied.

'We need one of your people there to take him down.'

'Don't worry, general sahib. I will speak to the ameer of that area when the tanzeem meets. That Qadri fucker will soon rot in hell.'

They parted ways at the mess reception. 'Allah hafiz, Jal... Ameer-ul-Momineem.' Realizing his minions were listening, the general corrected himself mid-sentence. 'Colonel Imam here will take care of you.'

'Allah hafiz, general sahib.'

Five minutes later, they were ensconced in three well-appointed guest rooms in the officers' mess. The Ameer was in the main suite while the four bodyguards took rooms on either side of him, two to a room.

Maqbool, the burly brute of a man who was sharing the room with Iqbal, hailed from the same village as the Ameer. Iqbal was sure he was a distant relative, as most of those chosen to protect the Ameer were. He knew that Rahim, the guard commander, and Sultan, the fourth bodyguard, were; they had mentioned it often enough.

'How long do you think we will be staying here?' Iqbal asked Maqbool as they settled in.

'Until the Ameer tells us to go,' Maqbool replied simply as he put down his weapon and took the bed near the window, plumping up the pillow before he lay down and stretched.

Iqbal shrugged and took the other bed, sinking into the soft, comfortable mattress.

Sleep, when it came, was deep and restful after a long time, without the threat of sudden death hanging over his head.

∾

The general lit a cigarette as he reached for the phone on his office table.

A cell-phone rang miles away to the south-west, in a bungalow on the outskirts of Quetta.

'Allah hafiz, Ameer,' the general said when the call was answered. 'It goes well.' He rapidly gave a gist of the meeting he had just concluded with Jalaluddin Haq.

'Excellent. Jalaluddin will deliver. Just allow him to get the tanzeem together and task them.'

'That we will,' the general concurred. 'There will be intense pressure on the Americans to negotiate if they want to get out of Afghanistan any time in the near future. We want you back then.'

'Inshallah,' Mullah Mohammed Omar murmured. 'Let us work at getting them out first.'

The call lasted only a minute more. As soon as it was over Omar took out another cell-phone from his pocket and dialled the single number stored on the SIM card's memory. The second call was much shorter.

'They have taken the bait,' he said simply when the call was answered. 'Go ahead with the plan while I take care of things at this end. We *must* have control of the nukes. Nothing will stand in our way then. They will give us the umbrella we need to ensure that Allah's will is supreme.'

'I will not let you down, mentor.'

'I know you won't. I trust you, Jalaluddin.'

'And that trust shall be honoured, Ameer.'

'Allah hu Akbar.'

When the call ended, both men removed the SIM cards from their cell-phones and cut them up, destroying them totally. They removed another SIM card from the tiny stack of eleven more that both had and inserted the ones that had number 2 written on the reverse with a red marker. The SIM cards had been procured some time ago from a little known sympathizer. Each one was sequentially paired and meant for one-time use-and-throw, making it virtually impossible for anyone to monitor their conversations. They knew the ISI kept track of every call made or received by them. And their agenda had nothing to do with that of the ISI, even though the short-term tactical goals might appear to be the same. One wanted Afghanistan and Kashmir. The other wanted both *and* Pakistan; after all, the jihad needed a firm base if it was to sweep the world. It also needed the nukes to keep the Caliphate secure and the Sharia supreme.

The wheels of treachery continued to spin. In this deadly game there were no friends. Each player had his own personal agenda. And each would do whatever was necessary to fulfil it.

∞

It was pitch dark when Iqbal woke up. His stomach was growling. He had not eaten in a long time. Maqbool was snoring contentedly by his side. Iqbal was about to get up when he noticed the map case lying by his pillow. He cursed softly, knowing that the Ameer would be livid if he realized it had not been put in his room. He was thinking of a suitable excuse when an idea struck him. He should have thought of it long ago.

After making sure Maqbool was still asleep, Iqbal silently got up and took the map case into the bathroom. He locked the door, opened the case and spread out the map. It was a military grade map of the FATA. There were numerous blue and red markings all over it, obviously the positions of the two sides engaged in the conflict. A thick black cross with a rough circle around it immediately grabbed his attention. The mark was shiny and, unlike the others, had been made with a black china graph pencil. Iqbal examined it closely. There were some pencil flakes still visible on the glossy talc cover of the map case. Iqbal could tell the mark had been made recently.

Iqbal mulled over the conversation he had overheard between the Ameer and the general. *This must be the place where the Ameer plans to meet them, the group of six men from different continents… the tanzeem.*

Iqbal quickly memorized the six-figure grid reference of the place marked by the cross. He repeated it several times, embedding it in his memory.

Closing the map case, Iqbal quietly returned to his bed and lay down, wondering how he could get word out to Colonel Anbu. Or whether he should try and take them down on his own.

∞

In the morning, the first thing Iqbal did was take the map to the Ameer's room. Luckily, the Ameer was on the phone when he entered and did not pay much heed to Iqbal.

'Tell the chief I said so,' he heard the Ameer say. 'These are the guys who are going to take the battle to the enemy, strike at their very hearts. They will hurt them so hard that not just their morale, even their economies will be devastated. At no cost do I want them to feel that we are scared, that we are not in control of our area. If all goes well, I want them to deliver the first hit just when the kafir are celebrating Christmas…' The Ameer's voice faded away as the door shut behind Iqbal.

He had barely reached his room when Rahim sauntered in.

'Get packed, guys. We are moving out in an hour.'

'Where to?' Iqbal asked. 'I thought we were…'

'You thought wrong,' Rahim cut him off. 'The Ameer is not going to stay at the same place for more than a night or two.'

'So where are we off to now?' Iqbal asked as he began to stuff his things back into his rucksack.

'You will know when we reach.'

Iqbal raised his eyebrows.

'I don't know for sure,' Rahim added sheepishly, 'but I am guessing we will head for another safehouse not too far away.'

'Well, let us hope it is closer to town than this crappy fauji mess,' Maqbool piped up from across the room.

'You are thinking of having some fun, aren't you?' Rahim leered at him.

'Why not? Who knows how long we have to live? Might as well enjoy life,' Maqbool said with a smile.

∽

They left in the usual mini-convoy that their numbers demanded, except that this time two sets of soldiers accompanied them. But no one was in uniform, the weapons they carried were well concealed, and they rode in civilian vehicles – there was nothing about them that would draw attention.

The drive through Lahore was surprisingly short. They raced down wide, well-maintained cantonment roads, then slowed to a crawl as they waded through a sea of cars, scooters and rickshaws that thronged the overcrowded commercial part of town. Sewage flowed through the streets. Tattered drapes hung over broken windows. Here and there one could see electricity siphoned out of ingeniously jury-rigged electricity poles and lines.

The incessant honking of horns and the cries of hawkers faded away as the convoy hit the outskirts of the city. They finally halted outside a large bungalow inside a posh residential colony. A couple of security guards manned the gates. Their weapons were safely tucked away in a fibre-glass guard hut just inside the gates.

They settled down, once again with Maqbool and Iqbal occupying the room to the right of the Ameer, and Rahim and Sultan in the room on the other side. The soldiers escorting them vanished into the surrounding grounds. Barring an old man who seemed to double as the cook and major domo, the house was bereft of life. It was exceedingly well appointed, obviously designed to cater to the top brass or special guests when they needed to lie low or be kept under wraps.

Iqbal was still unpacking when the door opened and Rahim strode in, grinning.

'The Ameer says we can take the evening off.' He surveyed them as though he had just delivered news of a great personal achievement. 'Two at a time, of course. So you guys hang around and keep your eyes open while Sultan and I go out.'

'When do we get to go?' Maqbool demanded irritably.

'You guys get tomorrow evening off.'

'We are here tomorrow too?' Iqbal enquired, anxious to know the plan. This could be the break he was looking for.

'Of course! Didn't I just say so?' Then Rahim was gone.

∞

The next day Maqbool was bathed and ready to go out an hour after lunch. He spent the next couple of hours fretting in the room, waiting impatiently for Rahim to give them permission to leave. His constant grumbling and festering excitement kept Iqbal distracted, which was a good thing because by now he was tired of all the questions whirling through his head.

They set off the moment Rahim gave them the go-ahead, Maqbool leading the way. It took them close to an hour to reach their destination.

∞

After striding through the crowded Urdu Bazaar with its countless musty bookshops, Iqbal and Maqbool finally entered Heera Mandi, the historical red-light area that Lahore had inherited from the days of the British Raj. It was a collection of narrow lanes, lined with grimy walls that bore little trace of paint. A colourful contrast were the women inside the houses, huddled on sofas that were visible from the street.

Mangy dogs dodged past people. An array of electricity and telephone wires crisscrossed the narrow lane. A medley of songs, most of them from Bollywood blockbusters, blasted out from the buildings. Hanging around near the open doors were muscular, betel-chewing pimps, keeping an eye open for customers and cops alike.

With the practised eye of a veteran, Maqbool walked down the lane, stopping at every door to check out the wares inside. At the fifth house, he spotted what he was looking for.

'You coming?' He looked vaguely over his shoulder at Iqbal, his attention on the girl who had caught his eye. Iqbal was still trying to find a suitable excuse to walk away when Maqbool caught his hand and dragged him in. 'Come on! You are behaving like a fucking virgin.'

They were halfway into the room when Iqbal's gaze fell upon one of the prostitutes. She was facing the other way, but there was something familiar about her. Then she turned and the familiarity faded. She caught Iqbal's stare and her mouth shaped itself into a professional pout. Iqbal felt something come alive within him. His fingers reached inside his pocket and drew out some money. He held it out to the pimp hovering beside him. It must have been more than the pimp expected because he nodded eagerly at the prostitute. With a broad smile at Iqbal and a suggestive twitch of her butt, she turned and headed up the narrow staircase. Iqbal followed. As he walked away, he could hear Maqbool haggling with the pimp.

With every step the beast that had been unlocked within him grew larger. By the time he entered the small dingy room, it was itching to break free. In the middle of the room was a queen-size bed. A green bedsheet with yellow stripes covered the thin cotton mattress on it. The stale stench of sex hung heavy in the air. Throwing the latch on the door, Iqbal walked up to the waiting woman. She was still smiling. Her smile faltered as his hands ripped apart her blouse.

'Araam naal, mere saand,' she said in rustic Punjabi. *Easy, my stud.* She made no attempt to cover her large, sagging breasts. Iqbal's thumbs began to caress her dark brown nipples. Her smile returned. And something inside Iqbal snapped.

The woman squirmed in pain as Iqbal squeezed both her nipples hard. Her hands instinctively came up to pull them free. Simultaneously, Iqbal's hands dropped and tore off her petticoat. He pushed her back, sending her staggering onto the bed. By now her pout had disappeared. Her mouth opened but her scream died in a whimper as Iqbal's hand clamped across her mouth. With his other hand he loosened his belt and pulled down his pants. Pushing her flat on the bed, he mounted her. She moaned. There was no pleasure in the moan, only fear and pain.

He came almost immediately. One massive surge and it was over. But he felt no satiation. He felt nothing but anger, though he was not sure at whom or what.

The anger kept a hold on him as he wiped himself with the hooker's blouse and left the room. He was still hard, but not with desire.

Maqbool was nowhere in sight when Iqbal went downstairs. Checking his watch, he quickly strode out of the whorehouse and made his way back to Urdu Bazaar. He had lost a lot of valuable time. Shaking off the lust that still throbbed inside, he began to refocus on the task ahead. He remembered the little cybercafé they had crossed on their way here.

He knew his options were to either get hold of a phone or find a computer and use the Indirocker site where Ankita had set up an account for him. Iqbal's instinct would not allow him to risk using a public phone. He knew that Colonel Imam wouldn't find it hard to home in on him if the call were tracked, and the odds were that any call to India would be.

By now the crowd had begun to build and it took Iqbal about fifteen minutes to reach the café. He heaved a sigh of relief when he saw that it was open. He was just sitting down behind the old, solitary computer when the lights failed and the room was plunged into darkness.

'What happened?' he asked irritably, his keyed-up nerves jangling out of control.

'Power is out, janab,' the owner's tired voice echoed out of the darkness. 'Happens here all the time.'

'Damn!' Iqbal checked the curses that threatened to flow out. 'How long before it comes back?'

'Who knows? It comes when it comes and goes when it goes,' the man said in a resigned manner. 'These days who knows about anything?'

He seemed to be in the mood to chat. The senseless banter kept Iqbal's mind occupied as he sat in the darkness, tapping idly at the keyboard. Every once in a while, he peered at his wristwatch. It had been almost an hour since he had left Maqbool. Just then, the lights flickered on, hesitantly at first and then gaining intensity till the room sparkled to life once more.

Iqbal switched on the computer and watched the ageing machine slowly boot up. When the main screen appeared, Iqbal clicked open the browser impatiently and keyed in the site address. The log-in process into the Indirocker website chewed up another minute. Thirty minutes left until his rendezvous with Maqbool. He figured he had ten minutes more before he got going.

Iqbal selected the 'Send sms' option and added Ankita Bhatnagar, Manoj Khare and Vikram Tiwathia's numbers to the recipient list.

'Tanzeem is a group of six men. One per continent. Identities not yet known to me. Handpicked by the Ameer-ul-Momineen to spread urban jihad across the globe. Tho'. He stopped as 'Message limit 160 characters' flashed on the screen.

Cursing, he deleted the last word he had typed and clicked on the 'Send message' icon. The message swirled slowly on the screen for a moment before the 'Message sent' confirmation flashed. With a sigh of relief, Iqbal began to compose the second message.

He had just begun to add the recipients to the list when the computer screen signalled a 'Message received' alert. His fingers were shaking as he discarded the message he was typing and clicked open the incoming message. It was from Captain Tiwathia.

Tiwathia's return message was brief. 'Glad to hear from you. We have been very worried. Hope you are well. Send whatever details you have.'

Iqbal was suddenly overwhelmed to be back in contact with Force 22. The fact that they were worried touched him more than he had expected. It felt incredibly good that someone out there was actually thinking of him. He pushed aside the emotions clouding his mind and began to reply, aware of the message limit this time.

'Am well. Ameer is Jalaluddin Haq. Don't have details about tanzeem but they are coming to meet Ameer. Will try to get word to you when that happens.'

Yet again, the reply was instantaneous. 'Use codeword Majnu to indicate when they are meeting and Laila to give the grid reference of location.'

Despite the situation, Iqbal couldn't help chuckling at Tiwathia's choice of codewords. He suddenly remembered that he already had the grid reference and began to write another message. He was about to send it when there was a sudden spurt of light and the room plunged into darkness again.

He cursed out loud.

'I told you, janab, the power supply here is a real pain,' the café owner's voice piped up. 'We hardly get any work done these days.'

Iqbal looked at his watch. Four minutes left. He threw an uncertain glance at the public phone near the door. He was reluctant to pass on the grid reference on the phone. There was also the fact that he was not entirely sure that it really was the venue, he was simply assuming it was, based on the conversation he had heard and the fact that the mark on the map had been made during the Ameer's meeting with the general. And if it was the venue and the Pakistanis came to know that it had been blown, they would simply shift the meeting to another place and Iqbal might not be able to find out this information again. He decided it would be better to wait till he was sure.

His despair mounted as he waited for the electricity to return. Two more minutes ticked by. He knew it would not bode well for him if Maqbool saw him coming to the rendezvous point from the direction of Urdu Bazaar. Everyone was suspicious and there would be questions. He had not been able to erase the log-in history; if anyone came to check it would give him away at once.

With a frustrated thump on the keyboard, Iqbal got up, paid the owner and quickly walked back to the rendezvous point. It was a good thing he left when he did because Maqbool sauntered up moments after Iqbal reached.

'How was it, miyan?' Maqbool asked. He had the contented smile of someone who had been laid after a long time.

'Good, good!' Iqbal aped the grin.

'*Just* good. Man, you should have come with me. What a woman that was!' He grinned again, scratching his crotch. 'I really needed that.'

They began the long walk back through Urdu Bazaar. Iqbal was hoping the lights would not come on until they had crossed the cybercafé. He heaved a sigh of relief as they walked past it. But at that moment, the lights returned with a vengeance. Once again, the market was lit up by a multitude of yellow and white lights. Iqbal fought the urge to step up his pace as they navigated through the crowded lane. They had barely walked a few more steps when the café owner's voice reached him over the din of the market.

'Arre, bhaijaan, you can use the computer now.'

Ignoring the man, who was a few feet behind them, Iqbal kept walking. However, the man was not to be thwarted easily, business was obviously not good these days.

'Come, miyan. We are back online,' he called out again. Iqbal continued walking, but Maqbool turned and looked back. The owner waved at him. 'Tell your friend he can use the computer now.'

Maqbool was perplexed. 'Is he talking to you?' He nudged Iqbal.

'I have no idea who he is talking to,' Iqbal mumbled, cursing under his breath, not breaking his stride.

Maqbool looked back at the café owner and then at Iqbal. Suspicion was writ large all over his face. He started walking again but he was pensive and did not exchange another word with Iqbal as they headed back to the safehouse.

Iqbal took note of the taut expression on Maqbool's face and knew he would not fail to report this incident to Rahim. *That will blow the game away for sure. Rahim will come back to check the facts with the cybercafé owner. Or he will ask Colonel Imam to do so.*

That was a risk Iqbal knew he could not afford to take. With a mental shrug he made up his mind. There was no choice left, not if he wanted to stay alive.

They had left the busy part of town and were passing through a deserted, tree-lined street. Soon the residential area would begin. Iqbal knew he had to act now.

Looking around to make sure they were alone, Iqbal checked his stride and allowed Maqbool to get a step ahead. In one swift motion, he drew the knife from his waistband and drove it into Maqbool's back, angling it upwards at the heart. The blow fell woefully short. Maqbool grunted in surprise and his mouth fell open. Iqbal lunged forward and cut off his scream. At the same time he pulled out the knife from Maqbool's back and slashed it across his throat. This time the wound was fatal. Iqbal held him fast as life drained out of him. Then he dragged the body towards the edge of the tree-lined street, taking care to stay clear of the blood streaming out from the long gash in Maqbool's throat.

Dumping the body in the thick hedge running along the pavement, Iqbal cleaned his knife on Maqbool's clothes. He wiped the flecks of blood that had splattered on his sleeves and hands. Then he quickly walked away. He knew the body would be found before long.

∞

By the time he reached the safehouse, his story was ready. He headed straight for Rahim's room.

'I am not sure if Maqbool is coming back.'

'What do you mean?' Rahim looked confused.

'I saw him leave with some men.'

'What men?'

'I have no idea. He dropped me off at this whorehouse, saying he would check out another one. I went in but came out a few minutes later because the pimp was asking for too much. That's when I saw Maqbool talking to some men. I was about to call out to him when they walked away.'

'Why didn't you try to stop him? Where the fuck has he gone? Who were they?'

'I have no idea, but it all looked very suspicious to me. I came back at once to let you know.'

'Who do you think they were?'

'I have no clue, miyan, but it certainly does not bode well for us.'

'Do you think I should tell the Ameer?' Rahim said doubtfully. 'Maqbool has been with us for a long time. I would never have guessed...'

'I would tell the Ameer right away if I were you,' Iqbal interrupted. 'We need to get clear from here just in case...' Iqbal let his voice fade away as he saw the seed of doubt thrown by him grow in Rahim's mind, especially after what Mahroof had done just a few days ago.

Rahim nodded and headed for the Ameer's room.

The Ameer did not waste a single moment. The fear of treachery loomed large in everyone's minds. A flurry of frantic phone calls followed.

Fifteen minutes later, they were off again. This time the journey was much longer because the Ameer had decided that he did not want to stay on in Lahore any more. The six vehicles sped through the night and they were in Rawalpindi before dawn.

❧

The safehouse that the ubiquitous Colonel Imam arranged for them in Rawalpindi was another army officers' mess. Like the others, it was vacant, barring a two-man staff.

News of Maqbool's death reached them the next morning, through Colonel Imam.

'They must have killed him when they did not find us at the safehouse,' Rahim chipped in when Imam finished giving the details to the Ameer. 'They must have thought he had lied to them when they did not find you there.'

'Serves the bastard right!' the Ameer said furiously. 'I would have fed him to the dogs had I laid my hands on him. How could he have done this! He was related to me by blood.'

No one in the room dared to respond. The Ameer's unpredictability and anger were legendary. The expression in his eyes left no doubt in anyone's mind that Maqbool was better off dead.

❧

The direct consequence of the Maqbool episode was that they now moved houses every second day and no one was allowed to go out for anything. This effectively put paid to any chance Iqbal had of contacting Force 22 again. He knew it was vital he do so, even though he was still not sure of the venue for the tanzeem's meeting, or when it would take place.

The next five weeks were a blur of activity as they moved from house to house. Rawalpindi, Islamabad, Nowshera, Mardan, Abbottabad, Haripur... they flitted from one city to the other. Although no one spoke about it, each one kept a closer eye on the others.

Imam started to show signs of exasperation at the Ameer's almost paranoid suspicions, but obviously he had been given orders to keep him in good humour. Not that it made any difference to the Ameer. With each passing day he got increasingly agitated. News of the renewed Pakistan Army offensive in the FATA and NWFP made matters worse. He would fret in front of the television and over newspapers for hours every day and Iqbal and the others would hear him raging and ranting on the phone, his deep voice booming through the walls. All three of them, Iqbal, Rahim and Sultan, bore the brunt of his frustration and anger.

The situation worsened as the offensive lost steam and dropped off the front pages, replaced by the now predictable rash of suicide bombers that had begun to systematically decimate the major towns in Pakistan. The death toll mounted rapidly. But that was not what bothered the Ameer.

'Why can't we head back now?' Iqbal heard him ask Imam. The two of them were sitting in the verandah outside the Ameer's room. Their voices trickled into the adjacent room, which was occupied by the three bodyguards. 'Things seem to be normal now.'

'Not yet,' Imam replied. 'I need to check with the director first.'

'Then do that. I can't keep staying this way. I need to get back and organize things for the tanzeem.'

'I will, I will. You know he will not agree as long as the American secretary of state and Pentagon staff are here.'

This unleashed a tirade from the Ameer. But Imam kept his cool.

Another three weeks and several more safehouses went past before Imam came back with the news that they could return. The Ameer was thrilled. He had them packed and ready to move before Imam had even finished speaking.

Despite the fact that they were heading back to the area where the uncertainty of death always hovered overhead, even Iqbal was eager to break out of the futile monotony of the past ten weeks.

The Ameer spent the last two days before their departure on the phone. They would not have free access to secure phones much longer. Later, as they headed towards the waiting vehicles, Iqbal heard him tell Imam, 'It's all done.'

'Excellent. When do they reach?'

Iqbal missed the reply as Imam and the Ameer got into the car and the doors were slammed shut.

∾

The return journey was almost an exact replay of the way they had moved out from Jandola. An uncomfortable ride in the Pakistan Air Force helicopter and a few dusty hours of driving later, they were back in the rugged heights of the frontier region.

There were three station wagons waiting below Jandola, where they had first met Colonel Imam.

Iqbal felt a familiar knot of stress begin to coil in the pit of his stomach as the vehicles nosed their way down the narrow dirt track and drove into Jandola.

Twenty minutes later, they were back in the caves where they had left the wounded Karamat. There was no sign, however, that he had ever been there, and Iqbal knew that Karamat had not made it. He also noticed that the Ameer did not once ask about the man who had stood in the line of fire for him all these years.

I wonder who will remember me if I do not get back alive. My son? He does not even know me... Perhaps Colonel Anbu will tell him about me. But do I want him to? Some day, perhaps, when he is old enough to understand... Will he ever understand?

Iqbal pushed the thought away, forcing himself to focus on other issues. He wondered what was going on at Force 22, whether they had given up on him; weeks had passed since he had been in touch with them. And he still hadn't managed to get across the grid reference of the meeting place to them. He knew that, no matter the cost, he had to let them know in time when and where the tanzeem was meeting. It was now no longer just a matter of killing the Ameer to avenge Tanaz. Iqbal was keenly aware of the impending disaster and massive loss of lives if the tanzeem executed its plan.

Iqbal's mind turned to his son yet again. Those fleeting memories of the infant he had handed over to Anbu clung to him as he lay in the dark solitude of the night. He did not know when sleep came, but finally it did. And with it came the terrible dream.

∽

Iqbal was holding his son in his arms, a warm, tiny bundle of life. In the next moment, the infant had grown up. Now he was a little boy, chuckling as he tottered along on unsteady feet, trying to get away from his father as they played catch. Iqbal was laughing with the same gay abandon.

Then the father's face changed. It was now Anbu. Or was it the Ameer? The little boy's face changed too, to that of the American soldier they had bayoneted.

Iqbal began to run, like a sprinter closing in on the finish line.

Suddenly he was a young man dressed in athletic shorts and a vest. There was a number printed on his vest. Six. The number was written in bright red on a white square cloth. It was stuck to his body, glued in place by the sweat. Iqbal knew that number. It was the number he had worn when he had broken the school record for the 100-metre sprint. As he ran, he saw his family standing among the crowd of spectators, cheering him on.

He could see Tanaz too, standing beside his mother. But he could not see their son. Where had she left him? He was too young to be left by himself.

Troubled, Iqbal almost stopped running.

I have to win.

He looked at the finish line ahead. The glossy red tape strung between the two white poles fluttered in the breeze, teasing him.

When he looked down at himself again, he was dressed in the black attire of the Lashkar-al-Zil.

The poles holding the bright red finishing tape vanished. They were replaced by the dead American soldier on one side and Mahroof on the other. The red ribbon of the finishing tape was a thick stream of blood. Standing just across the bloody line was Maqbool. With his slit throat and arms wide open, he was urgently beckoning Iqbal on.

Iqbal knew he needed to win, otherwise his family, especially his father, would be disappointed. He glanced at the stands. They were still there but no one was cheering him now. Instead, they were looking at him sadly. His mother, sister and Tanaz had tears in their eyes.

Suddenly, his mother's head exploded. Blood,

brains and tiny shattered pieces of bones confettied over the people in the stand.

The soundless explosion jolted Iqbal awake.

∞

The dull sunlight of an overcast dawn entered the room. Despite the bitter cold, Iqbal's body was soaked in sweat. And the Ameer's voice was calling his name. It snapped him back to reality.

'Where is Rahim?' the Ameer asked from the doorway. 'Call him quickly.' For a change, he was smiling. There was a piece of paper in his hand. 'We have work to do.'

Iqbal did not know it yet but the end game had just begun. In a few days, the six leaders chosen by the Ameer to constitute the tanzeem would be on their way.

SITUATION REVIEW

From: Director RAW
To: NIC
Security Classification: Director – Eyes Only
Priority: Urgent
Subject: Review of internal security situation in Pakistan

As expected, the Pakistan Army offensive against terror groups along the Durand Line has ground to a halt. This has as much to do with the resistance put up by the jihadi fighters in the area as with the terror bombings across the Pakistani heartland which have eroded public support for this operation. There is also significant evidence that several Islamist, right-wing political and politico-religious leaders have been exerting pressure on the Pakistan government to call it off. Large-scale desertions from Pakistan Army units engaged in this offensive have not only thrown morale in disarray but enhanced the mental divide that exists amongst senior army and ISI commanders, with a number of them openly in favour of jihadi groups.

Two of the remaining three intelligence operations (of the six that we had originally launched) to identify the Ameer-ul-Momineem and penetrate his organization have also not made any headway; both operatives have failed to make contact for several weeks now. Fresh efforts are being launched, but no noteworthy results can be planned for in the immediate term.

However, the Force 22-assigned operative seems to have successfully infiltrated the Ameer's organization. There is still no reliable, continuous line of communication established with this operative, but during his last contact the operative confirmed that the Ameer-ul-Momineem is Jalaluddin Haq. A detailed dossier on Haq is attached.

Haq has been maintaining a low profile and has only recently started getting into action. He seems to be operating with the blessings of the Quetta Shura and the ISI.

American intelligence has confirmed that the Pakistanis have stonewalled all efforts to eliminate Haq or provide any information about him.

It has been established that Haq is one of the key terror leaders who moved out from the FATA during the recent Pakistan Army offensive.

The Force 22 operative has also confirmed that Haq has constituted a new group of leaders, one from each continent, simply called Tanzeem, meaning 'group'. While nothing further about this group is presently known, the operative has reported that Haq plans to use the tanzeem to spread urban jihad across the globe. He has also reported that the tanzeem is soon likely to assemble somewhere in Pakistan to meet Haq.

It is also pertinent to mention that there has been no contact with the Force 22 operative since then. We do not know if he is still effective or has been neutralized.

The intel provided by this operative confirms reports of a major jihadi operation currently underway to strike at various targets across the globe.

Although time does not seem to favour more operations to verify these facts by getting HUMINT sources in place, all possible ELINT and SATINT sources have been deployed over the target area.

Also, intelligence-sharing efforts with known friendly agencies operating in the FATA and NWFP areas have been strengthened to ascertain the intent and time plan of this operation, as well as to confirm the identity of the six tanzeem leaders.

Finally, efforts to cultivate SUKOON, the senior Pakistan Army officer posted in Peshawar Corps HQ, have made headway. The asset has agreed to the remuneration offered by us, but a secure line of communication with him is yet to be established. This task has been assigned due priority and we expect to have it in place very shortly.

Full details of SUKOON are being forwarded under sealed cover.

And I will strike down with great vengeance and furious anger those who attempt to poison and destroy my brothers.

Book of Ezekiel

G.K. Rao, the Indian National Intelligence Advisor, had just finished reading the latest Int Sum. Despite the progress it reported, he was in a grey mood when he finally put it down. Something about it bothered him. He sat back and began to go over the report in his head.

He gave up after several minutes. The nagging feeling wouldn't go away but he knew they still did not have enough actionable intelligence to put together the bigger picture. He started to reach for the phone, and stopped. Calling up the director of RAW and pushing him to set up the communication link with Sukoon would not help. Rao knew that undue haste could easily blow the lid off an asset's cover or scare him off.

His gut told him that contacting the Force 22 operative was a safer option. He reached for the phone and began to dial Colonel Anbu's number. Maybe he could come up with a way to get hold of the operative.

≈

Miles away, seated in the rear of a station wagon, the man Rao was thinking about watched the rugged frontier terrain flee past. Excitement gripped the occupants of the vehicle, primarily due to the Ameer's infectious energy. They all knew the next few days would be momentous.

As soon as the vehicles jolted to a halt, the Ameer got out. There was a spring in his step and he was beaming as he surveyed the compound. The others followed suit. Iqbal was the last one out. He stretched his limbs as he looked around.

So this is where the tanzeem will meet.

Iqbal watched as the Ameer walked up to the men waiting to greet him. It was not long before he was shooting out orders. After all, there was much to be done, with only two days to go.

≈

Unlike most other compounds in Waziristan, this one was huge. It was almost like a series of heavily fortified compounds strung together in a tight defensive perimeter. Lying in neat, circular lines was a well-planned, triple-layer defence that posed a formidable barrier of lead and steel to any attack.

The innermost defensive ring, which lay 100 metres from the outer edge of the compound, was manned by the fiercest, most trusted mujahideen, all of them related by blood to the Ameer-ul-Momineem, a man they all revered. This was the ultimate Praetorian Guard. Any head of state or religious leader in the world would have been proud to call them his. Each of these warriors had proved his unflinching loyalty to the cause and to the Ameer. Each one had been bloodied in battlefields all over the world, wherever the call for jihad had taken them. And each one would die a thousand deaths before he allowed a hair on the Ameer's head to be harmed.

The second layer, of almost equally formidable fighters, comprised the others who walked under the Ameer's banner. It was a mix of foreign fighters and Pashtun warriors. Strung approximately a kilometre outside the innermost ring, this was the densest layer and would provide enough resistance and tactical depth to the compound in case of a ground assault.

Iqbal, now a trusted warrior of the Ameer's camp, held the northern flank of this defensive layer. Probably due to Maqbool's alleged betrayal, all three bodyguards who had travelled with the Ameer had been dropped from personal protection duties and relegated to the second layer.

If he swivelled it around, the machine gun Iqbal

manned commanded a clear field of fire of the entire compound. But in many ways, his was also the most redundant position, because the rugged mountain peaks towering over him posed an invincible barrier to man and beast alike, making it unlikely that anyone would attempt a ground assault from this direction. Iqbal's companion an inscrutable, surly man they all called Uzbek, was lounging next to the machine gun.

The third and final layer, about 500 metres deep, was another kilometre away from the second line of defence. This was manned by a battalion of Pakistan Army. The troops were out in full force, the Eleventh Corps Commander ensuring that every able man, including the battalion commander of his most trusted battalion, was present in the trenches. A full regiment of artillery guns and a complement of attack helicopters were on stand by. Circling high in the sky, like tiny specks of lightning, a flight of F-16s ran a protective CAP over the sector. They were there to see that no harm came to the compound from the air. Their presence did not stand out, in light of the current offensive against jihadi leaders by the Pakistan government, or rather the Army-ISI combine which yielded power in the country.

'You have to make sure that even if the Americans get wind of this meeting and decide to get trigger-happy, you are there to give them a bloody nose. We will worry about reprisals and the diplomatic fallout later, but nothing must get through. No attack helicopters, no drones, no Special Forces, no air strikes. *Nothing!* Do whatever you have to, but make sure the compound is not disturbed in any way for the duration of the meeting.' That was the mandate the corps commander had given him and that is what the battalion commander would ensure, or die trying to.

'And there must be no large-scale troop activity during daylight hours,' the general had said. 'I do not want anything to alert the Americans. I have told the muj to see that none of their people mucks around in daylight. One never knows who is watching.' The corps commander pointed his finger skywards, referring to the shoal of spy satellites that circled unseen above them. 'Don't worry, the muj will ensure their fighters move into position immediately after last light and spend the night laying out the camouflage.'

By morning, all activity on the three defensive lines came to a halt. As the sun strengthened, under the uneven shade of scores of camouflage nets, men hunkered down with their guns and got ready to tide through the day. Nothing moved, barring the occasional man stepping out to use the shithouse, which was deemed permissible since some activity is normal around every place humans inhabit. In fact, the total absence of activity might have drawn unwanted attention to the compound.

Unseen and unheard, high in the sky, the spy satellites did take note of the trenches in and around the compound but they raised no flags in the minds of the intelligence analysts examining the satellite feed; with the current Pakistani offensive to secure this area, it was only logical that they be there. This time the Pakistanis had been vehement about American drone attacks in this area on the grounds that their operations would get jeopardized. Keeping in view the sensitive stage at which relations between the two countries were currently poised, the Americans had decided to oblige.

∽

Curled up beside the machine gun, Iqbal's companion was fast asleep. While the Uzbek was undoubtedly a ferocious fighter, he did not have the temperament to sit patiently through an entire day of watching and waiting.

Iqbal was grateful that the man was asleep. He needed to think and he needed to do so in peace.

His eyes restlessly scanned the area in front of him, using the binoculars that had been provided to all those who were manning machine guns. The binoculars were standard Russian Army ones, as most military hardware in this part of the world tends to be, a lasting legacy of their misadventure into Afghanistan. The ones cupped in Iqbal's hands had seen extensive use, but were in surprisingly good shape. He could see the compound with acute clarity. All the while his mind was churning in fervent overdrive.

How the hell can I get word out to Colonel Anbu about this meeting?

For the umpteenth time he looked at the battered watch on his wrist. It was 0700 hours. He had almost the entire day to get word out.

But how?

He scrutinized the area again. He knew the machine gun was useless. Apart from punching a few holes in the walls and killing some of the guards, he knew it would be unable to get at any of the tanzeem.

And how long will I last if I open fire?

He visualized the wave of fighters who would instantly converge on him. Discarding the option, Iqbal widened his scrutiny and noticed the ZU.

Though he was barely able to see it due to the camouflage nets, he knew about the ZU-23-2 anti-aircraft gun that had been deployed 400 metres to the right of his trench. It covered the break in the mountains to the north since that was a likely ingress point for aircraft wanting to attack the compound. Iqbal knew it was a weapon that could wreak serious havoc.

But will it be enough?

Iqbal thought back to the time he had seen the ZU in action, during the ambush they had sprung on the ISAF convoy in Afghanistan. He remembered the thunderous roar of the twin auto-canons as the ZU tore up the convoy. The vehicles had been shredded to bits.

Iqbal tried to work out how he could use it to destroy the dangerous group of men who would arrive at the compound very soon. He glanced at his watch again. It was forty minutes past noon.

Bloody hell! Where did the morning go?

In the distance, about 500 metres to the north, Iqbal could see one of the Pakistani soldiers from the outer cordon head towards the rocky outcrop that had been designated as the shithouse. It was not on the windward side of the defensive positions, nor were there any men deployed in the immediate vicinity.

Iqbal checked his watch again. He realized he had barely four hours left to decide what he was going to do and execute it. The thought sent a fresh wave of anxiety through him. He could not fail after having come so far; he couldn't allow the tanzeem to leave this place alive.

Iqbal shuddered at the thought of the death and destruction these men would unleash all over the world if they managed to get away. He turned his mind to the task at hand.

The ZU was one option. It might not get all the bastards but it would certainly cause considerable damage. He ran through the possible sequence of events in his head. He would first have to get rid of the Uzbek, then get to the ZU and take out the crew.

How many will there be? Three? Four at best! It would be difficult to take on four men at once, but it was his best possible option. He would have to launch a sudden assault with a knife. Gunfire was too risky.

He had to take the chance. If he managed to take out the crew of the ZU, he would have to wait for the tanzeem to reach the compound and then open fire on the house they entered.

Using his binoculars, Iqbal eyed the house in question. He had never been inside, so he had no idea of the layout or strength of the walls. It seemed to be a sturdy structure.

Should I cut loose with the ZU when they start walking inside? If I can catch all of them in the open, I may be able to get all six of them, and the Ameer too. But will they all wait to go in together or will they go in one by one as they arrive? He reflected on this for a moment before he realized that there was no way he could come to a logical conclusion. *And how long will I get before the men in the other trenches decimate the ZU – and me?*

Iqbal concluded that it was not at all a sound plan. There was too much scope for error and for chance to dictate the outcome, but it was the best he had.

He threw another glance at his watch. 1405 hours. Shocked at the speed with which the hours were bleeding away, Iqbal returned to his planning, his mind assailed by a renewed sense of urgency. With each passing moment, his spirits sank as no other solution presented itself.

1550 hours.

They would start arriving in another hour. Last light was approaching rapidly.

Iqbal made up his mind with a snap. *The ZU is my only shot. I will just have to take my chances.*

With the decision made, he closed his eyes for a moment and tried to focus on the crucial moments ahead. His breathing picked up pace and a coil of steel began to grip his heart. He knew there were no more decisions to be made, no more dilemmas to be resolved. This was the time for action… to kill or to be killed. *No! Just to kill.* Iqbal knew he could not fail. The price of his failure would be paid by thousands of innocent men, women and children… like his mother, sister and wife.

Reaching for the knife in his belt, Iqbal crawled across the trench silently. His hand came up and the knife slammed into the Uzbek's throat, with all the force Iqbal could muster. The Uzbek died instantly.

Iqbal began to lift the camouflage net to get out of the machine-gun pit. His hand had just caught hold of the net when he froze. Coming up along the horizon of his vision was a Pakistani soldier. He was bent forward as he made his way to the shithouse, the way most radio operators do when they are on the move, hunching to compensate for the extra weight on their back.

Iqbal got out of the trench and began to saunter towards the shithouse, keeping his pace casual. By the time he had wandered into the rocky outcrop, the radio operator was squatting near a rock, his ass facing Iqbal. Along with his rifle, his radio set rested against a nearby rock, hissing softly with static.

The soldier turned his head slightly to see who was intruding on his happy commune with nature. By then Iqbal was almost onto him. He caught the top of the man's head with his left hand while the blade in his right sliced open the extended throat. Air escaped from the gaping cut with a hiss. The man toppled backwards, collapsing into his own pile of shit.

Iqbal returned the knife to his belt, caught hold of the man's arms and began to drag the body towards the narrow crevice between two large rocks a few metres to the right. Grimacing at the smell of fresh shit smeared all over the man, he shoved the body into the crevice. He pushed it in as far as possible and threw some dirt and leaves over it, camouflaging the body as best as he could. By now he was breathing hard, as much from the fear of getting caught as from the exertion. He picked up the Paki's rifle, grabbed the radio set and began to scout for a suitable hiding place.

He spotted a ledge on one of the larger rocks in the outcrop just 30 metres away. It would offer only partial cover but Iqbal had no choice; time was running out.

Lugging the radio set and the rifle, Iqbal made his way up to the ledge, careful to stay low. Crawling to the farthest corner of the ledge, he sat down and surveyed the radio set. It looked pretty much like the sets they had practised with in Kasauli.

Iqbal turned the dial, setting the frequency that Ankita had drilled into him, and pressed the transmit button.

'Babur for Fox Base!'

That was the code name they had given him when Iqbal had gone into Pakistan with Sami and Tiwathia to hunt down Salim. He had taken to using it during the practice sessions at Kasauli.

'Babur for Fox Base!' Iqbal transmitted again, unable to keep a note of desperation out of his voice.

≈

They say that when evil walks the face of the earth, the gods return to combat it. Someone at the Force 22 Base *was* listening.

Flight Lieutenant Ankita Bhatnagar had just stepped out to get a cup of coffee and was standing at the ops room door when she heard Iqbal's transmission. The words were not very clear, but she recognized his voice immediately. The coffee cup hit the floor as she ran across the room and snatched up the handset.

'Babur, this is Fox Base.'

Ankita's crisp voice crackled out of the set with startling clarity, shocking Iqbal. For a moment he just stared at the radio set in amazement; he could not believe he was actually listening to Ankita.

Shaking away an unexpected surge of emotion, Iqbal pressed the transmit button again.

'Fox Base, this is Babur. Majnu.' He tried but was unable to keep the excitement out of his voice. 'I repeat, Majnu. Laila 997428.' Iqbal felt a huge burden lift off him as he rattled out the grid reference coordinates of the compound. 'Fox Base, do you copy?'

'Say again, Babur. You are strength one.'

'Shit!' At the other end Iqbal cursed. Strength one meant that Ankita was barely able to make out what he was saying. Clicking his tongue in exasperation, he dragged the radio set to the other end of the ledge; maybe changing the position would improve the transmission. However, he was now almost fully exposed to anyone passing by.

'Fox Base, I say again, Majnu.' Iqbal spoke slowly, hoping to break through the static and make sure that Ankita picked up the codeword, which Tiwathia had told him to use whenever he located the tanzeem.

'Babur, I copy Majnu,' Ankita replied after a brief pause. 'Give me Laila at alt three.' The ever alert Ankita had just invoked the first, most basic security rule: when in doubt, always assume the enemy is listening.

'Alt three means you have to step up the transmitting frequency by five,' he remembered Ankita telling them during the training, before the YPS operation.

'Five, but you are saying three?'

'You must always add two to the figure we give you the first time, and then subtract three the next time, and so on… Keep alternating. We will use this procedure whenever we are transmitting from insecure sets or if our transmissions are in the clear. The process is a little tedious and certainly not foolproof but it makes it harder for the enemy to get the whole conversation since he has to work at finding the frequency we are moving to next.'

Switching frequency rapidly, Iqbal resumed transmission. 'Laila 997428.' He was acutely aware that he was running out of time; sooner or later someone would come.

'I copy, Babur. I repeat, Laila 997428. Alt two now.' Iqbal heaved a sigh of relief as Ankita correctly repeated the grid reference.

∽

Ankita's professional tone betrayed none of the shock she was experiencing. Hearing Iqbal's voice so suddenly had pulverized not just her but also Captain Sami who had been walking past and saw Ankita drop the coffee cup and rush into the room. He had run behind her and was at the door when Iqbal transmitted the second time. They could hardly believe that the man they had given up for dead, that too for the second time in as many years, was back. Sami had reached for the telephone while Ankita snatched up the radio handset.

Sami's call brought an equally surprised Colonel Anbu to the ops room just as Ankita was repeating the grid reference coordinates.

Iqbal's mission was complete. Force 22 would now do whatever was necessary to put an end to the madness.

'Pull up that grid reference on the map,' Anbu said to Sami as he took the handset from Ankita.

∞

Meanwhile, at the other end of the tenuous radio link holding them together, a column of dust just beyond the compound caught Iqbal's eye. Scoping it out with his binoculars, he saw two SUVs drive up to the compound. As the vehicles came closer, there was a flurry of activity in the compound. Several people emerged from the houses. Standing among them was the unmistakable figure of the Ameer.

The SUVs came to a halt in front of the waiting men. Most of the men who stepped out of the vehicles carried weapons. But the one who strode up to the Ameer walked with his hands free. Like the Ameer, he had an aura of command and authority. Iqbal saw the two leaders embrace. From a distance they looked like friends meeting after a very long time; one would never have guessed that they were meeting to plot murder, to deliver death to thousands of people across the world.

The first of the tanzeem had arrived.

The two men were turning towards the house when one of the men in the entourage pointed. In the distance Iqbal saw another cloud of dust and another pair of vehicles. They would reach the compound in twenty minutes.

Iqbal hit the transmit button again. 'One has arrived. Second coming in now. Majnu window closes in five or six hours.'

'Say again, Babur. This is Fox. Alt four,' Anbu replied.

The colonel's voice brought back the memory of Tanaz and his baby boy. He forced himself to focus on the radio set and changed the frequency.

'I repeat. Majnu closes very soon.'

'Babur, I copy Majnu closes very soon. Alt five now.'

Iqbal automatically switched to the desired frequency.

'Babur, is Majnu intact?' Anbu was asking if all the tanzeem members were together. 'Alt six now.'

'Negative, Fox.' Iqbal switched frequency yet again. 'Majnu has just begun. Only two are in so far. It should be intact by last light.' Checking the time on his watch, Iqbal estimated that last light was not more than an hour away. He could see the second set of vehicles clearly now; they were almost at the compound.

'Not good enough, Babur. You need to tell me...'

Iqbal suddenly heard the sound of approaching footsteps. Clicking off the radio set, he hauled it back to the far end of the ledge, and crouched into the shadows.

∽

Back in the Force 22 ops room, all three officers were staring at the radio set, waiting for Iqbal to respond. As the silence grew longer, their unease deepened.

'Maybe he got interrupted and had to go silent,' Ankita murmured hopefully.

'Let us hope that is what happened,' Sami muttered.

'Guys, this isn't the time for mind games,' Anbu said, taking charge. 'Show me the location.' He watched as Sami highlighted the area on the map on the huge LCD screen at the far end of the room.

Anbu gave it a moment's thought. 'That is way out of the range of any assets we have in the area, or can hope to get there in the time available.'

'It *is* way out, sir,' Sami conceded.

'I need to take this up the ladder, MS.' He turned to Ankita. 'While I do that, show me what's happening there.'

Striding across to the secure phone on the table, Anbu called G.K. Rao and quickly apprised him of the situation.

'Are you sure of the intel?'

'Positive. I have a man on the ground watching them right now.'

'Who?'

'That is not important at the moment. What's important is that he is a solid asset and I trust him. You can meet him when he gets back. Right now, let's worry about what we have to do. We have very little time to take action; just a couple of hours, as a matter of fact.'

'Okay, I understand. We may not be able to do much from here, but the Americans can. They have all the firepower they need in Afghanistan.'

'I know, that's why I called you,' Anbu replied. 'I need you to get the big man's approval. Tell him to request the Americans to cooperate. After all, they have as much to lose as we do.'

'I agree,' said Rao. 'This is our chance to take out the entire leadership team. We can't blow it. Okay, hold on while I get the prime minister on a concall.'

There was a burst of music as Rao put Anbu on hold. After several minutes, his voice came back on.

'Colonel, I have briefed the PM. He agrees.'

'I must say you are right on top of things once again, Anbu,' the PM cut in, sounding pleased. 'Excellent work!'

'Thank you, sir, but it is far from over. We need to act fast.'

'Rest assured we will,' the PM said firmly. 'I want

you to stay by your phone. You will be contacted very soon.'

The prime minister put down the phone and activated the hotline.

∾

Far away in Washington, a phone in the basement of the White House began to ring. It was one among several phones that lay in neat rows along one side of the room. The computer screen in front of the duty operator told him the name of the country that had activated the hotline. Startled, he leapt up and took the call. Within minutes, there were phones ringing all over the place.

∾

The phone lines were also starting to burn in the Pakistani Corps HQ in Peshawar. The corps duty officer who took the first call was shocked when he heard what the SIGINT man at the other end reported.

'What are you saying?' he asked several times. 'Are you sure it's coming from that area?'

'Of course we are, sir.'

'You triangulated the location?'

'I am sorry, sir. It was not on air long enough for us to triangulate the precise location, but the set seems to be somewhere in the compound.'

'Tell me more.' The duty officer turned to the battle board, trying to focus on the map and gather the data he knew the corps commander would ask for.

'It is definitely one of ours.'

'What are you saying?'

'We have a positive ID.'

'Right!' the duty officer said, quite confused by now. 'Shoot me the transcript.'

'We don't have one, sir,' the SIGINT officer said in an apologetic voice.

'What do you mean? If it was one of ours, how could you *not* get a recording?'

'Whoever was transmitting switched frequencies manually at every transmission. So we just managed to get a couple of garbled words.'

'Give me what you have, you idiot!' the duty officer snapped.

'Well, the word Majnu was mentioned a couple of times, and then there was something about a Laila.'

'Laila? Majnu? Are you trying to make a fool of me?'

'No, sir, I can assure you that is what we caught.'

'What are you saying? What on earth could it mean?'

'I think, sir...'

'Don't think, you fucking idiot! You can't record a transmission from our own radio sets and you want to start thinking. Bloody fool!' He slammed down the phone, wondering what he would tell the corps commander. Normally, a dozen senior staff officers would have insulated him, as he was just the corps HQ duty officer. But this morning he had been ordered to pass on all inputs related to the meeting directly to the GOC.

He knew the general was going to blow a gasket. As it was, he had been behaving strangely the last few weeks, prying into all kinds of details he usually never concerned himself with.

Dreading the call but realizing the urgency, he reached for the phone and dialled the corps commander's office.

The duty officer's dread was not unfounded. General Tariq Khan, the GOC 11 Corps, blew several gaskets. Even under normal circumstances, the general was known to have a temper that ran on a very short leash. By the time he finished shouting, the duty officer was starting to rue the day he had been posted to the Corps HQ, a prized, relaxed posting under normal circumstances.

'Tell those idiots to keep their ears peeled. Monitor all likely frequencies and keep me posted.'

'Should I tell them to activate the jammer, sir? That way we can make sure whoever is using the radio will not be able to get anything else out.'

'No, you frigging idiot!' Tariq Khan grated. 'That will knock all our troops out of communication. Just put the SIGINT morons on listening watch and tell the battalion commander to send out patrols. I want every inch of the area swept clean. Got that?'

'Yes, sir,' the duty officer replied in a suitably chastened tone.

'And tell the CO I want each and every radio set of ours accounted for. I want that fucker caught and brought here – alive – whoever he is.'

'I will get on to it right away, sir.'

∽

General Tariq Khan paced the room as he pondered the situation.

He wondered if he should alert the muj, or if he should tell the Ameer to abort the meet. But the general knew the Ameer would be as pissed as hell, as would the chief. The whole thing had taken months of coordination and planning. If they aborted now, they would not be able to organize this meeting again soon. A third alternative suddenly occurred to him. *Who would find out?* Greed and fear skirmished in his head. Fear won, at least for the moment. He knew that no matter what he did, he needed to cover his ass.

He walked to the end of the room, turned and began to make his way back to the other end.

He ran through the likely threats and the precautions they had taken. Even if the Yanks came to know, would they dare to strike when there was a battalion of Pakistani troops around the compound? Not likely. They would not be sure if the Pakistanis were conducting an operation themselves, and surely they wouldn't attack without a warning. After all, they were allies. And even if they did attack, they had enough men to beat off anything the Americans could put together in the little time available. Khan knew the battalion could handle anything short of a full-fledged, brigade-size offensive, and that was not likely to happen in the short time available. *What else? Air strike? Drones?* Khan decided to get another flight of fighters up as an additional precaution.

He reached for the phone. Miles away, another flight of F-16 fighters hit afterburners and screamed up in the air, heading for the compound they had to protect. Khan, meanwhile, continued to patrol his office.

∞

The man who had delivered this unexpected headache to the Pakistani corps commander was still crouching in the darkest corner of the narrow ledge. The rapidly approaching darkness seemed to have unleashed a desire in a number of people to shoot off their load before night fell. Iqbal sighed wearily as he settled down to sit out another shitter. He dared not transmit again, not until he was alone.

From where he was sitting, Iqbal couldn't see the Pakistani patrols that were combing the outer perimeter. The hunt for the elusive man transmitting from the area had begun. Luckily, they had started the sweep from the western side. It would still take them some time to reach the northern centre, which was roughly where Iqbal lay.

From his vantage point, Iqbal could see the road leading up to the compound. As he looked up he saw the third convoy thundering down the road.

∞

Like General Tariq Khan, the normally placid Anbu was also pacing the Force 22 ops room. When the secure phone rang again, he ran across the room and caught it on the first ring.

'Colonel Anbu?' For a split second the American accent caught Anbu by surprise.

'Yes!' he replied, recovering quickly.

'Hi! I'm Colonel Powell,' the man at the other end continued. 'I'm with Force HQ Afghanistan. We just got orders to coordinate a mission with you. The orders came from the high end of the foodchain. They told us this had to be done day before yesterday. Do you wanna put us to speed on it?'

'That's right, colonel. This is what is going on…' Anbu spelt out what needed to be done.

'Hang on a sec, let's take a closer look at the target area.' There was a pause. Anbu could hear muted commands being given in the background. 'I have the satellite feed of the area coming in now, colonel. There certainly is a lot of activity taking place there. In fact, right now I can see a couple of suburban-type vehicles heading towards the compound. You want to tell me who these dudes are?'

Anbu told him about the Ameer-ul-Momineem and the tanzeem.

There was a much longer silence at the other end, as though the man was deliberating how much he should share of what he knew.

'Right! We have also been getting intel on this guy but haven't been able to pin him down yet, though we almost got him once…' Powell paused. 'So we can't let these dumbasses walk out of this place. Right?'

So much for intel sharing, Anbu thought with a wry smile. 'That's right, colonel. If we allow them to get away this time, it will set all counter-terrorism efforts back by decades. If these leaders take charge of the jihad you can bet the world will see many more deadly attacks. We need to get a strike in there and we need to do it really fast.'

'I get your point, Colonel Anbu, but I dunno if you can see the stuff they have down there… it's a bugger's muddle. There's even a heavy-duty CAP, and I can see more F-16s coming in to join them. Say, do you have eyes on the target?'

There was a slight pause as Anbu considered the question. He did. In fact the real-time video feed from the Indian Cartosat 2 series satellite overhead was beaming in loud and clear on the screen in front of Anbu. That was what Ankita had been doing while he had been on the phone with Rao and the PM.

But he saw no point in telling Powell this.

Powell took Anbu's silence to mean no. 'Right!' he answered his own question. 'Tell you what, colonel, just gimme the parameters and let me hook you to our feed.'

That ate up a few more valuable minutes as Powell used the parameters provided by Ankita to hook Anbu to the satellite feed from the American spy satellite.

In the Force 22 ops room, Anbu watched the gigantic screen in front of him split into two. Soon the American satellite feed filled up one half of the screen and the Cartosat feed occupied the remainder. Barring some difference in aspect and angle, there was not much to choose from between the two in terms of resolution or quality.

'Right, colonel,' Powell resumed, 'if you look closely you will see that we need a full-scale brigade offensive to break through the defensive perimeters, and that's no use. It will take too long to put together that kind of force level. And even if we are able to get it there, by the time we break through the outer cordons the tanzeem will be long gone.'

'I agree, Colonel Powell. I was thinking in terms of a precision air strike. We have no assets in that area and little chance of reaching in time.'

'We have the assets, colonel, but the boss says it's too risky,' Powell explained. 'The compound is in a really lousy location for an airstrike. To complicate matters, the Pakis are running a heavy duty CAP over that area... F-16s... Any air strike that goes in will definitely take heavy losses, so my boss has ruled that we execute a standoff strike. That way we put no men or machines at risk.'

'What do you guys have in mind?'

'The locals have two SMERCH regiments not too far away from the target. In fact, even as we speak, both units are on the move and should be within striking range very soon. Are you familiar with the SMERCH, colonel?'

'Yes, I am!' Anbu ran through the tech specs of the weapon system in his mind as he replied.

Designated BM-30 or 9K58, the SMERCH (Tornado) 300 mm Soviet multiple rocket launcher comprises a battery of twelve rocket launcher tubes mounted on an 8×8 MAZ-543M chassis. All twelve barrels can be fired singly or simultaneously in as little as 38 seconds and are capable of hitting a target 20 to 70 kilometres away. Designed to defeat manpower, armour, artillery, missile systems and soft-skinned vehicles in a concentration area, a SMERCH regiment comprises twelve launchers which, when fired simultaneously, saturate an area of over 1 square kilometre with a veritable blanket of death. Depending on the target being engaged, the SMERCH can fire High Explosive Fragmentation, Cluster or Anti-Armour sub-munitions.

'Then you will understand what I am talking about, Colonel Anbu. We will unleash both regiments at one go.'

'That is all very well, Colonel Powell, but there are three problems with this plan.'

'Shoot!'

'The first is that it is possible to live out a SMERCH attack if one is in a well-fortified bunker. We really have no clue about the strength of the building those guys are in. They may have fortified it. So we will not know if all of them have been neutralized.'

'You're bang on, colonel. That is why – oh, didn't I mention – we will give them a couple more salvos of SMERCH as soon as they reload, and send in a few cruise missiles. The missiles will be launched by B-52H bombers operating Beyond Visual Range and targeted precisely on the house, so pretty much everything in and around it is going to be toast. Thereafter, just to be on the safer side, we will have our gunners deliver a series of well-timed Fuel Air Explosive strikes a bit later, just when the survivors down there, if any, are starting to feel a little secure. We have a HIMARS battalion already moving to get within striking range. I am sure you will agree that is going to be more than enough.'

'Damn right it is,' Anbu muttered. The HIMARS is a highly mobile artillery rocket system that offers MLRS firepower on a 6×6 all-wheel drive, 5-ton wheeled medium tactical vehicle. HIMARS has the capability to fire any rocket or missile in the MLRS family of munitions; but because it has only one pod per vehicle, it has a much faster deployment time and can deliver either six MLRS rockets or one ATM to a target 35 kilometres away. It can also deliver the longer range ATACMS guided missile, which comprises 950 anti-personnel, anti-material baseball-size M74 sub-munitions to ranges exceeding 165 kilometres. Anbu guessed that in the given scenario they would be using the latter option with FAE sub-munitions.

Anbu shuddered as he tried to visualize the devastation this kind of firepower would wreak on the target. Hardened though he was by years of combat, the mere thought of the diabolical FAE bombs made him cringe.

The FAE bomb is designed to disperse an aerosol cloud filled with fuel over the target area. This aerosol is ignited with an embedded detonator, causing a massive widespread explosion, which in turn causes a rapidly expanding wave front. Due to the massive overpressure, the explosive shockwave flattens everything in proximity of the epicentre and causes extensive damage even over the surrounding areas.

'The FAE will ensure nothing remains alive in that area,' said Powell, reading Anbu's thoughts. 'Neither man nor beast, not even an insect; anything that breathes will die. And just to make doubly sure, we are going to have some Reaper drones standing by to hunt down any survivors.'

'Sounds good to me.' Anbu was impressed. The American had thought it through in detail. It was an excellent plan, especially considering the minimal reaction time that had been available to him.

'It's as good as it can get in the time and with the resources available in that area, colonel.' Powell sounded pleased with himself. 'In any case, when we have got the chance, why settle only for the leaders? Let's get a bunch of the other shitheads too.' Anbu could not fault the logic. 'Now, what did you say the other two problems are?'

'How do you plan to get all that artillery within range of the target without the Pakis coming to know?' Anbu paused momentarily, reluctant to offend, but then decided this was no time to be coy. 'I know they are your allies, but you can see for yourself that they are playing both sides of the fence.'

'Yeah, I see that and I have been thinking about this issue,' Powell replied earnestly. The picture on the screen in front of both of them showed how deep the complicity lay. 'The aircraft, Cruise missiles and HIMARS are cool since they are all going to be beyond detection range throughout the op. But for the SMERCH there is no obvious solution. The Pakis will pick them up sooner or later. We can only hope they waste some time checking with us about the movement and that their chain of command does not permit them to engage targets across the border without clearance from Islamabad.'

'You are willing to chance that, colonel? Those launchers will be sitting ducks for the F-16s they have up there.'

'Yeah, right!' Powell sniggered. 'If they decide to fuck with us across the border, we will blow their asses away. Have no doubt about that. I'm gonna have some of our own fighters standing by.'

'Well, they don't really need to tangle with you guys,' Anbu pointed out. 'They just have to warn the Ameer's people to get the hell out of there if they spot the SMERCH regiments moving up to the border and realize there is a possible threat.'

'That's a possibility. Which is why they are just moving parallel to the border right now, not actually heading for it. Just before the SMERCH regiments get within range, we will unleash a barrage of radio chatter instructing the regiments to stop for a refit and reorg. We will make no attempt to camouflage their move. That should keep the Pakis from getting antsy.'

'You hope.' Anbu sounded doubtful.

'Do you have a better idea?'

'No, not really. Guess we will just have to chance it. Of course, if we do see the tanzeem start to scatter we can always send in the Cruise missiles, the HIMARS and the Reapers, and hope they finish the job.'

'That's the plan, Colonel Anbu.'

Both men knew it was not foolproof, but then most combat operations do need some luck to succeed, much as the military mind may find that abhorrent.

'So, what is the last problem?'

'I have an asset in the area, colonel, a very valuable asset. He has already given a lot to this war.'

'Then I suggest you get him out before the ordnance goes in.'

'I wish I could, but I have no way to contact him.'

'Isn't he the one who guided us to the target?'

'He is, but I cannot call him; he has to call in, if he can.'

'When did he last check in?'

'We were talking a while ago when he suddenly went off the air.'

'I see. What if he is unable to call in… or if he has already been neutralized?'

'Well, in that case we wait for the remaining targets to clock in and then go for the strike,' Anbu answered unhesitatingly.

'So there's the answer. You have fixed the problem yourself, colonel. I suggest we cross each bridge when we come to it. In any case, you will appreciate that it is the life of one man versus the lives of thousands who will certainly die if the tanzeem is allowed to get away. As you yourself said, we may never get this opportunity again. God knows when and where they will all come together again – if at all – and even if they do, will we be lucky enough to have an asset on ground to inform us?'

'I understand and I agree with you, colonel,' Anbu replied. The soldier in him did, but the heart beating within did not.

'Let's hope your man checks in soon, colonel,' said Powell sympathetically, 'before they all get in.'

'Let's hope so,' Anbu murmured, anxiety starting to build in his head as he saw the fourth set of SUVs enter the compound. On both sides of the screen in front of him, the image was startlingly clear. He could, if he wanted, zoom in and read the number plates of the vehicles. 'I can see the next one coming in right now.'

'That's right, Colonel Anbu. I see it too. Let me get this thing going. I will be in touch soon.'

The call ended as Powell returned to execute the plan.

Miles away from both officers, men and machinery raced into position, getting ready to deliver death to the assigned target.

The next mini-convoy of vehicles was visible on the extreme corner of the screen. It was still some distance from the jihadi compound but it was closing in rapidly. Anbu estimated they would be there in about thirty minutes.

They were moving too fast for Anbu's liking. He scoured the satellite feeds on the screen before him, trying to spot the man whose call he awaited so desperately. With the high-resolution feed coming in, it was possible to identify anyone. In fact, all this while Ankita and Khare had been zooming in and recording the details of each man they could spot, especially those who were arriving with the tanzeem members.

They knew that every little input was invaluable. After all, even after the tanzeem had been neutralized, it would still be important to know who they all were. That would allow security forces and intelligence agencies to home in on their allies, supporters and sympathizers. This closure was extremely important if the tanzeem had to be wrapped up fully and sustainable damage done to the terror networks.

'Anything?' he asked his two int officers.

Khare and Ankita reluctantly shook their heads without taking their eyes off the screen.

'Where are you, Iqbal?' The question echoed in the eyes and minds of each person in the Force 22 ops room.

∞

The same question plagued the Pakistani corps commander. He had just finished another restless circuit of his office when the phone rang.

'Have they got him?' General Khan snapped as he recognized his duty officer's voice.

'No, sir, they are still looking for him,' the youngster admitted reluctantly. 'But this is about something else, sir.'

'Now what?'

'We have reports of a couple of Afghan artillery regiments moving along the border.'

'Damn! You sure? Are they moving to the border or along the border?'

'They are moving along the border.'

'Where are they now and what route are they following?' Khan asked, walking across to the map on his office wall.

The duty officer told him.

The general identified the position. 'Damnit! That will put them in range of the meeting place very soon. Any idea what this is all about?'

'I'm not sure, sir, but there is a lot of chatter between them and the ISAF HQ. It seems to be an admin move.'

'How likely is that?'

'Possible, but not very likely. It seems too much of a coincidence, though we can also see a supply convoy heading towards them from the opposite direction. So maybe...' The duty officer offered his opinion reluctantly, knowing he would be in trouble if he got it wrong. After all, generals never take the fall.

'Right.' The general was no fool either, but he needed the meeting to take place successfully. 'If they stop and begin to deploy, let me know.' He banged down the phone.

He did not realize his preoccupation with the earlier report of an illegal radio transmission had screwed up his judgement, otherwise he would have asked his duty officer what type of artillery was coming up to the Af-Pak border. Any staff officer worth his salt would have done so. That, in fact, is why all HQs have staff officers, to make sure the commander receives a comprehensive intelligence picture at all times. By short-circuiting the chain of command, the general had actually made things even more difficult for himself.

The duty officer *had* been told they were SMERCH units, but had been so flustered from the bollocking he had received a while ago that he forgot to communicate this vital fact to the GOC. Had he done so, it is certain that Khan would have aborted the tanzeem meeting immediately. After all, SMERCH units were capable of deploying and firing almost instantly. That, coupled with someone transmitting from inside the protected area, did not leave any room for doubt that the meeting had been compromised. However, the corps commander, due to retire soon and eyeing the governor's slot, was under immense pressure to see that the meeting concluded successfully.

General Tariq Khan continued pacing his office. 'Why the fuck do these things have to happen on my watch?' he cursed out loud. 'The chief will not be pleased. He told me a million times that we need to get this meeting over and done with.' A bout of indecision wavered through him. 'Well, as long as they do not stop and deploy, we should be able to get the meeting finished and get the frigging muj out of there.' His head was beginning to hurt, he could feel another migraine coming. 'This could also be the ideal opportunity to... should I?' He looked at the phone on his table. He knew it was a secure line and the chances that anyone would ever find out about the call were remote, but there was still a chance. *Was the money worth it?* The dilemma deepened, worsening his headache. 'I wonder who that bastard with the radio set is. He must have brass balls.'

∽

While the Pakistani corps commander and his duty officer had been talking, the man with the brass balls, still trapped on the far end of the tiny ledge, was watching the fifth tanzeem member arrive. By now, huddled motionless in one tight corner, Iqbal's body had begun to cramp and he yearned to stretch.

Meanwhile, the Pakistani patrols finished sweeping the western quadrant and moved on to the southern part of the defensive perimeter. Although they were moving slowly and cautiously, since they had to scan every corner of the rugged terrain, it would not be long before they reached the shithouse. Slowly, inexorably, the noose was tightening on the man who was making life difficult for Pakistan.

∽

For the next twenty minutes, the boredom of an extended watch returned. It ended when Iqbal spotted more movement on the horizon.

It was the final member of the tanzeem. He would reach the compound soon. As the minutes ticked by,

Iqbal felt excitement and anxiety begin to pace the corridors of his mind restlessly.

After marching along the southern part of the compound, the Pakistani patrols had now entered the eastern quadrant. The ragged line of soldiers advanced slowly, poking and prodding through every bush and rock that could conceal a man. They were now barely 800 metres away from the ledge on which Iqbal lay hidden. Luckily for him, they were following the lay of the land and it would be a little longer before they got to him.

Iqbal saw the sixth cavalcade race up the final stretch of the road leading into the compound. The Ameer stepped forward to greet his comrade-in-terror. He watched the two men embrace before they trooped across to the house where the meeting was being held.

That's it! One more call to the colonel and I am done here.

Iqbal had no idea that Anbu had a clearer view of the target than he did. At that moment, Anbu's team was recording every movement and every face in the crowd of men in the compound.

Iqbal suddenly realized he was alone. There wasn't a single sound in the rocky outcrop around him. Cocking his ears, he began to scan the area to make sure there really was no one there.

He realized that the crucial moment was finally at hand. Everything that he had gone through in the past year was now about to bear fruit.

Gripping the radio set in one hand, Iqbal began to crawl across to the other end of the ledge, where the signal strength was better, to send one last message to Colonel Anbu.

∽

The Pakistani patrols finished sweeping through the eastern quadrant and now focused their attention on the northern and central parts of the compound, the only two areas that remained. By now it was obvious to the company commander who had been entrusted with the task of sweeping the compound that the man he sought must be here. Luckily neither of these areas was as large as the other parts of the compound. It was with a keen sense of anticipation that he turned to focus his men on them, ordering one platoon to take on the northern sector while he himself headed for the centre with another platoon.

∽

By the time Iqbal spotted the first soldier and then the rest of the leading section, they were barely 400 metres away. The section was advancing in an extended line with their rifles ready. The bayonets affixed on the rifles gleamed wickedly in the red rays of the setting sun.

Iqbal instinctively knew they were hunting for him. Either the radio operator had been reported missing or they had picked up his transmission. He knew the game was up. He began to evaluate the options available to him; there did not seem to be too many. He could possibly abandon the radio set and head back to his machine-gun post.

Iqbal was still struggling to make up his mind when the first Pakistani patrol turned its attention on the shithouse. Much as the section commander was against the idea of rooting through a shit-strewn area in the fading light, he knew it had to be done.

∞

The Pakistani corps commander snatched up the phone even as it began to ring.

'Sir, the Afghan SMERCH units have stopped.' The duty officer's tone was now strident with panic. 'The first one has already stopped and the second one is coming up now. They seem to be deploying.'

'Fuck! Why the hell didn't you tell me they were SMERCH units?' For a moment the general almost lost it, then his training reasserted itself rapidly. His decision was instantaneous. 'Abort the meeting. Get those muj fuckers out of there. Now!'

Ending the call with trembling hands, the duty officer began to make another, then realized it was not possible, the muj were only available on radio. Some fool had not felt the need to lay a phone line to the mujahideen. Or perhaps it had been sheer overconfidence that such an eventuality would not arise.

Dropping the handset, he charged out of the room.

General Khan glanced at his watch; he knew the SMERCH had an emplacement time of about three minutes. At the most five or six, if the Afghan gunners were not as well-trained. That was a reasonable assumption, given the current level of training and recruitment in the Afghan army. Even then it was close. Too close. The Ameer's group *might* just make it out if they moved right away.

Should I have the F-16s go for the SMERCHs? They could neutralize them in the time available, hopefully. He ran through the options. *Should I play safe and speak to the chief first?* It was a fair bet; even if they did not get all of them, the F-16s could degrade the SMERCH strike.

The general knew that this time he had to make the right choice, and he had to make it fast. There was too much at stake. For himself, most of all.

Making up his mind, Khan reached out for the phone and began to dial another number. One that he had not used for a very long time.

≈

Anbu scooped up the handset as the phone rang.

'Colonel.' Powell's voice was crisp and curt. The time for talking was over; the operation had moved into the action phase now. 'That's it then! The last man is in. We have the tanzeem where we want it.'

'That's right, colonel,' said Anbu reluctantly, his eyes still desperately seeking Iqbal on the screen.

'The SMERCH units and HIMARS have almost finished deploying, the B-52s are in place, the missiles are hot, and a flight of Reapers are in position. Is there anyone or anything else we need to wait for? I need your confirmation on that, colonel.'

'No. As per the intel we have on this, the tanzeem has assembled.'

'Then we are a go!'

'It's a go!' Anbu replied.

'Any news of your man, colonel?' Powell asked gently.

'No, not yet.'

'Get him out now if you can. We have a couple of minutes before the guns go live. Another couple of minutes flying time and then it will be over.'

'Please go ahead, colonel. What has to be done has to be done!' Anbu said in a flat voice. 'We have no way to reach our man.'

Powell knew what Anbu was going through and he empathized with the man. It always hurt to see one of your own go down. But the show must go on, both knew that. 'Good luck, colonel.'

Powell turned to give the command to fire. 'Tango Charlie for all units. Thunderstorm.' He enunciated each word loudly and clearly. 'I repeat, Thunderstorm.'

A series of Ten-Fours acknowledged his crisp command.

Within seconds, rows of artillerymen, strung all along the Afghan-Pak border, Americans and Afghans alike, reached for their weapons. Miles away, high up in the sky, two American B-52H bombers snarled through the air, moving into strike position; both were capable of unleashing six AGM-86B cruise missiles from each of the two externally mounted pylons and an additional eight from the modified bomb bay rotary launchers. Vertically separated by a few thousand feet, the killer Reaper drones began their wait, their electronic eyes scanning the target area, their missiles waiting to destroy. They would ensure no one in the compound got away, *if* anyone survived what was going to be lobbed at them. Each man checked his watch. The strike had to be perfectly synchronized.

The countdown to Thunderstorm had begun.

∾

Even as Anbu picked up the phone to talk to Powell, the duty officer at the Pakistani Corps HQ in Peshawar ended the call with the GOC and ran to the radio room at the end of the corridor.

A minute later, the radio set in the hut about 100 metres away from where the tanzeem was meeting chirruped to life. It took another minute for the import of the message to get through.

There was immediate panic. Tossing down the handset, the mujahideen radio operator raced out of the communications hut and towards the meeting place.

There was a stunned silence in the hut when he burst in without warning.

'What the hell are you doing here?' the Ameer growled. Then he saw the look on the man's face and realized something was amiss.

∞

Around the same time, the corps commander finished talking to the CO of the unit that had been defending the compound. The battalion commander, who himself was in the trenches with his unit, was understandably upset at what he heard.

'How long do we have, sir?'

'Not long,' the general replied tautly, 'get your men out now.'

Throwing down the handset without bothering to sign off, the battalion commander rushed out of the command bunker, shouting orders. Deciding to lead by example, he turned and headed away from the compound at a rapid pace. He knew enough about SMERCH rockets to know that he did not want to be here when they arrived. Had he known about the Cruise missiles, HIMARS and FAE bombs also coming in, he would have run even faster.

The sight of him rushing off communicated the urgency of his orders far more efficiently than anything he could have said. The rifle company around him also began to move swiftly. The other sub-units saw them and followed suit.

∾

The Pakistani section had reached the fringes of the shithouse when the section commander heard his platoon commander shouting. The man was still far away, so the section commander had to shout back and query him. Finally, he understood the message as well as the urgency with which it was relayed. Immediately, the section turned and began to jog away, following the rest of the battalion.

By now, several of the mujahideen in the area were tuning into what the Pakistani soldiers were doing. They were still not clear as to what was going on but they realized it was something serious, and more and more of them emerged from their weapon pits and trenches.

Still huddled just 60 metres away from the section commander, Iqbal too heard the shouted exchange. He saw the section peel away and realized he was alone again. Iqbal immediately reached for the handset and pressed the transmit button.

And you will know that I am the Lord when I lay my vengeance upon thee.

Book of Ezekiel

Powell had put down the handset after activating Thunderstorm. The Pakistani duty officer had passed orders to abort the meeting. The mujahideen radio operator had conveyed the orders to the Ameer. The tanzeem had begun to move out. And the Pakistani battalion commander was now almost 100 metres from his command post and going strong.

Just then, the radio set in the Force 22 ops room suddenly crackled to life. For a moment everyone in the room froze as Iqbal's voice filled the room.

'Fox Base, this is Babur. Majnu is intact.'

'Babur, this is Fox,' Anbu replied sharply. 'We have eyes on you. Confirm your location.'

Iqbal was perplexed. This was the last thing he had expected to be asked to disclose on an unsecured radio link. But he did not doubt Anbu even for a second. 'The large rocky outcrop about 1200 metres north of the main compound. The largest one, just below the cliff face.'

Back in the ops room, eager eyes swivelled to the screen.

Ankita located it and frantically tapped some keys, zooming into the rocky outcrop.

It was not far enough.

'We have you, Babur. I want you to drop everything right now and head for the cliff. Get to the other side and lie low.'

'What is the problem, Fox?'

'The heavies are about to fire, Babur. You have barely a couple of minutes. Drop it and move. *Now!*' The last word jolted Iqbal into action.

Artillery guns? Aren't artillery guns area weapons? I thought they would go in for a precision strike!

Tossing aside the radio set and the rifle, Iqbal leapt off the ledge and began to run like a man possessed. He had no idea of the lethal firepower that was being unleashed on the target, but he knew that Anbu was not a man to panic without reason.

∾

At the other end of the compound, there was a flurry of activity as the tanzeem members stormed out of the hut. Orders were shouted and men exploded into action. Drivers raced towards the vehicles which had been scattered around and parked under camouflage nets all over the compound to avoid aerial or satellite detection. Escorts and bodyguards grabbed their weapons and ran towards their respective protectees to hustle them into the vehicles.

No one, not even the Ameer himself, was really sure of the magnitude of the threat coming at them but they all knew they had to get clear of the compound. Or die. The duty officer had made that much abundantly clear.

∞

In the ops room, on the large screen showing the Cartosat feed, Anbu and the other Force 22 officers suddenly saw a man emerge from the shadows of the rocky outcrop and begin to race towards the cliff. He was going flat out, like a 100-metre sprinter, except that he had a lot more distance to cover.

Go! Go! *Go!* they began to urge him on silently.

∞

Several miles away, the Thunderstorm clock hit home stretch with shocking speed.

Two regiments of SMERCH roared into action, the thunderous boom splitting the countryside for miles around. An Armageddon worth of rockets soared into the sky, making their way to the target. Both regiments immediately began to reload.

The Cruise missiles were already en route, they

had been launched seconds earlier to compensate for the longer distance they had to traverse. Clinging to the terrain to evade radar detection, the salvo of lethal missiles raced forward in NOE mode, carrying their message of death and destruction. The HIMARS let fly a few moments later.

Thunderstorm had been unleashed.

∞

On the wider screen that was now being projected by the American spy satellite, Anbu saw blinding flares of light as the SMERCH launchers roared into action. Further away, he saw the HIMARS flame to life. On the more focused screen of the Cartosat satellite feed, he noticed the first of the jihadi vehicles reach the hut where the tanzeem had been meeting. Several other SUVs were driving up.

Damn! Are they going to make it out of the kill zone?

On the other side of the silent screen, he saw Iqbal run towards the cliff. Would *he* make it out in time?

Every eye in the ops room was fixed on the screen.

To one side they could see two of the tanzeem vehicles converge on the hut, pick up their charges and race away. Each man in the ops room wanted the rockets to swoop in before any of them could get clear of the compound.

On the other side of the compound, they could

see Iqbal running to safety and they wished the rockets would fly slowly so he would have enough time to get away.

The terrain-hugging Cruise missiles were not visible on the screen but Anbu saw the rockets flame through the sky, moving with great speed. They reached the zenith of their trajectory and began to arc down on the target, gathering speed with every passing second.

Anbu saw the first two tanzeem vehicles rocketing away, now hitting the edge of the compound and making for the exit. The Ameer's SUV was leading the way. The second was barely 20 metres behind. The other five vehicles were torn apart, two had started driving away from the hut, there were men trying to scramble inside the next two, and the last one was now pulling up outside the hut. The final set of bodyguards could be seen hustling their protectee into his car.

At the other edge of the screen, Anbu could see Iqbal running, regardless of the attention he was drawing from the men in the other trenches; several of them were gawking at him, thoroughly puzzled. A few of them were reaching for their weapons, still trying to figure out what was happening. They could see the pandemonium and hear the vehicle engines being gunned mercilessly as panicked drivers tried to steer clear of each other and get out of the compound. They could also see the Pakistani soldiers clearing out. But no one had given them any orders. They did not know that the ones who could have given them orders were burning rubber to get clear of the area. Despite that, the panic spread contagiously and some of the men began to hightail it out of the compound. Confusion held the others for a moment before they followed suit. By now the entire compound was in an uproar.

∞

None of the men on ground could see them, but the rockets and Cruise missiles were closing in with incredible speed. Another few seconds and the piercing screech of inbound rockets would be audible to the men below. Of course, by then it would be too late for them to react.

And in the thick of it all, Iqbal kept running. He was still 100 metres away from the safety of the cliff.

Safety was almost thrice as far away for the tanzeem vehicles, but they had far more powerful engines gunning them away in the opposite direction.

Iqbal had covered most of the remaining distance when the rockets arrived over the target, beating the inbound Cruise missiles by a fraction of a second.

He heard the screech of the incoming rockets. It drove shards of fear through him. *Shit! Shit! I'm not going to make it!*

Iqbal sprinted full tilt, throwing himself forward.

*If not the cliff, then at least that little fold in the
ground just short of it. At least it offers some cover,
maybe enough…*

With a final, superhuman spurt of speed, Iqbal
launched himself into the air.

∾

On the other side, the Ameer's vehicle had cut
across the compound and was almost clear. In a few
seconds, it would be out of the danger zone. The
second vehicle was still following closely. However,
the other five vehicles were still navigating their way
through the compound. They too must have heard
the rockets coming in since all of them drove faster,
the drivers coaxing every ounce of speed out of the
madly revving engines.

∾

Though unleashed from guns and aircraft miles
apart from each other, an almost incalculable
tonnage of precision-guided ordnance arrived on the
target almost at the same time. The SMERCH salvo
hit first, beating the Cruise missiles by a few seconds.
Already en route was the second SMERCH salvo.
Following hard behind was the first of the FAE
bombs. And within effective range was a complete
array of Reaper drones, watching to see if anything
left the area alive.

∾

A stunned silence held the ops room. They were all hardened soldiers and not one of them doubted the supremacy of the mission, but inside they were only human. And at that moment, to each one, the life of their comrade who had delivered the tanzeem to their guns was as important as the destruction of the tanzeem.

They all saw the tanzeem vehicles flying towards safety with alarming rapidity. On the other hand, the distance between Iqbal and the cliff receded with terrifying slowness.

Just as the rockets covered the final remaining mile to the target, they all noted the sudden and final burst of speed as the tanzeem vehicles and Iqbal accelerated, both moving with the same aim in mind but in opposite directions.

They saw Iqbal launch himself into the air. They knew he must have heard the rockets coming in.

Iqbal was flying through the air, his body inches short of fold in the ground.

By now the Ameer's vehicle had hit the edge of the compound. In seconds it would be out of danger zone. The other vehicles were also making good time, as people tend to do when death is on the rampage.

Anbu, Sami, Tiwathia and Ankita... they all saw the rocket salvo descend with a harsh blaze of light. Both windows of the screen in the ops room lit up in a huge seething, churning cauldron of flame and fury, the effect ominous due to the absence of any sound. The crescendo of the Cruise missiles slammed in almost simultaneously, adding to the devastation.

With bated breath, they watched the target explode as the rockets and missiles pounded and decimated it into nothingness. Then the lethal load lobbed by the HIMARS arrived and the FAE burst over the target area like a broiling sea of fire, obliterating it from view.

The devastation continued. They all knew that by the time the flames settled down and finally died so would every living thing in the area.

The tanzeem was, undoubtedly, as dead as it is possible to be. No one in those vehicles that had been speeding away or in any of the huts or trenches in the compound could have survived the massive onslaught. Not by a long chalk.

∞

Mission accomplished!

For once, these much-anticipated words did not bring with them the satisfaction they usually did.

Every person in the Force 22 ops room stayed glued to the screen long after the explosions had died down.

They all watched with unblinking eyes but nothing stirred on the screen. They focused on the small patch where they had last seen Iqbal begin his desperate dive for life. Barring the smouldering fury of the fires that raged over the target area, nothing moved.

Yet, not a single eye looked away from the screen. And every eye was glistening wet.

It is true that the mind is restless and difficult to control, but it can be conquered, Arjun, through regular practice and detachment.

Bhagavad Gita

Long after the others had left the ops room, Colonel Anbu remained standing. His eyes were still fixed on the point on the screen where he had last seen Iqbal.

The devastating effects of Thunderstorm had subsided and the stillness of death shrouded the target area. The vehicles that had been carting the tanzeem barely existed any more. Here and there, one could spot parts of human bodies or broken bits of a building, vehicle or weapon. Other than that, death and destruction hung heavy over the area.

Eventually, everything faded away and the huge screen receded into darkness as both satellite feeds shut down one by one. But Anbu did not register any of this.

Anbu's mind saw the life of the tormented but infinitely brave young man whom he had taken under his wing, who had unflinchingly stepped in harm's way whenever the occasion had risen.

Anbu saw the beautiful young woman who had loved and believed in Iqbal, walked bravely beside him, and paid the price. The memory of her tortured body seared through Anbu to this day. That was a failure the colonel would carry on his conscience all his life.

And he saw the baby boy they had left in his arms, one when she went to her death, the other when his karma beckoned to him.

Anbu suddenly remembered consoling his sister when Arjun, her husband, his comrade, had fallen on the battlefield. Despite the passage of years, his words rang out loud and clear in his mind as though it had happened yesterday. 'Just remember that he was a soldier… soldiers die.'

Anbu remembered the first time he had lost one of his men in battle. And he remembered Lord Krishna's words to the warrior Arjun. 'You grieve over those who should not be grieved for… Arise, O son of Kunti, determined to fight. Treating alike pleasure and pain, gain and loss, victory and defeat…'

And just as they have done down the ages, these words delivered some peace to the colonel from Chennai, the warrior who had to kill so that the rest of India could sleep in peace. And eventually, some of the calm that had always held him in good stead all his life returned.

Finally, Anbu turned and headed out of the room. There was still a task to be done. There would always be. For a country like India, with the kind of neighbours it had, there would always be a job for the soldier who stood sentinel on its borders.

As Anbu walked out of the ops room, his spine became straighter, his chin was held high and the resolve of the soldier returned to his eyes.

The end of birth is death; the end of death is birth; this is ordained! And mournest thou, chief of the stalwart arm! For what befalls which could not otherwise befall?

Bhagavad Gita

The little boy was playing in the sprawling garden of a colonial bungalow located in the heart of the army cantonment in Delhi when a black Ambassador with darkened windows came to a halt at the gate. A small red flag fluttered from the flagstaff fixed to the side of the bonnet. A red plate sporting a solitary brass star shone above the car's number plate.

The child was so engrossed in trying to snatch the ball back from the golden retriever he was playing with that he did not notice the car. The dog was almost twice his size and bounded around him with ease, letting out playful growls as he kept the ball away from the boy's tiny hands.

A man got off the car and walked towards the gates. He was clad in the olive-green uniform of an Indian Army officer. He sported the stars and crossed swords of a brigadier on his shoulder boards. He was carrying a well-worn, black leather briefcase.

The minute the man's hand touched the gate and slid open the bolt, the dog cocked its head. It turned and looked up, dropped the ball and, barking loudly, streaked across the garden like a furry bolt of golden lightning. The man quickly closed the gate behind him and put down the briefcase, bracing himself against the assault.

Barking madly with joy, the dog launched himself in the air at his master. Hard in his wake, the tiny tot ran up with shaky, excited steps, shrieking in delight.

The woman inside the house drew back the curtains of the living-room window. By now they had him down on his knees; one was licking him lavishly while the other tried to fight past the dog and get to the man he knew as his father. There was a glow of contentment in the woman's eyes as she watched the excited trio.

Brigadier Rajan Anbu's eyes were moist as he finally got past the dog and swept up the toddler in his arms.

'Down, Sandman!' He tried to calm the dog. 'Down, boy!'

'Daddy! Daddy! Daddy!' the boy screamed as he clung to him.

'Yes, my son! I am right here!' He picked up the boy and held him close to his heart. And for that one brief moment they were as one, father and son.

'Daddy will not go to office now?' the boy asked, his unformed speech further slurred by excitement.

'No, son, daddy will not go to office till next Monday.'

'Yay! Gimme five!' the little boy shouted, aping the two elder siblings he was growing up with, as he held up his tiny palm. 'Daddy play now?'

'Yes, daddy will play now,' Anbu replied with a laugh, giving him a high-five and holding the boy close, Sandman still running in circles around them. Together, they went to retrieve the abandoned ball.

One day, my son, Anbu thought, I will tell you about your real mother and father. I will tell you about the man and woman who sacrificed everything they had for the sake of our country. They died unsung and unacknowledged, but they died true heroes in every sense of the word and this nation owes them a huge debt of gratitude.

Deep within, Anbu mourned for the couple he had grown to love and missed ever so much... for the man he somehow felt he had let down. And for his son, this innocent boy in his arms, who had never known his mother or his father.

But I swear to you, my child, you will never feel the absence of either, not as long as I am alive. I promise you that.

Anbu held the laughing boy closer to his heart.

Yes, my son! One day I will tell you about the man named Iqbal...

Acknowledgements

Before all else, I must thank Goddess Saraswati, for enabling me to finish this four-book series as planned. I couldn't have done it without the unflinching support I received from all those people who have shared my life during these years. To each one of you, I offer my humble and most heartfelt thanks.

To my wonderful family, for giving me the time and space to indulge in the (almost) solitary love of my life: writing.

To my comrades-in-arms in the Indian Armed Forces who were kind enough to ensure that I did not make any major blunders while writing about tactics, weapons and weapon systems.

To my publisher and now dear friend, Karthika V.K., and to my wonderful editor, Neelini Sarkar, for believing in me, keeping me on track and giving final shape to this book and this series. Without them watching over me, I do not think I could have achieved my goal of bringing out a book every year for the past four years.

And to P.M. Sukumar, Philip Jojy, Amit Sharma, Shuka Jain, Lipika Bhushan, Ratna Joshi, Ayushi Srivastava and the others at HarperCollins India who have helped to make this book and this series possible.

To the National Arts Council, Singapore, for providing me the wonderful opportunity and mindspace I needed to finish this book in double-quick time. Their faith and support have been unquestioning and unfailing. It freed me from routine worries and enabled me to focus single-mindedly on this book.

And, last but not the least, to each of you readers who has egged me on with praise and criticism, by writing to me, by blogging about these books and, of course, by buying them.

Abbreviations

ATGM	Anti-Tank Guided Missile
CAP	Combat Air Patrol
CIA	Central Intelligence Agency
DGFI	Directorate General Forces Intelligence
ELINT	Electronic Intelligence
FANA	Federally Administered Northern Areas
FATA	Federally Administered Tribal Areas
HUMINT	Human Intelligence
ICV	Infantry Carrier Vehicle
IED	Improvised Explosive Device
IM	Indian Mujahideen
ISAF	International Security Assistance Force
ISI	Inter Services Intelligence
MRT	Mobile Response Team

NIA	National Intelligence Adviser
NIC	National Intelligence Command
NOE	Nape of the Earth
NWFP	North West Frontier Province
QRT	Quick Response Team
RAW	Research and Analysis Wing
RPG	Rocket Propelled Grenade
SATINT	Satellite Intelligence
SIGINT	Signal Intelligence
SOF	Special Operations Force
UAV	Unmanned Aerial Vehicle

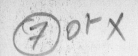